There was a taste of the world she knew, just beyond the walls. "Let's go," Aurora said. "Now."

He laughed. "Are you crazy? Even I don't have that much of a death wish."

"Why?" she asked, the word rushing out of her. "Why is it crazy?"

"Because we have no way to get out, and no way to get back. Not without being seen. Not without breaking our necks. And of course," he added, when she didn't reply, "there are the ghosts to think about."

"Ghosts?"

"Ghosts," he said. "And monsters. Werewolves. Trees that come alive and grab at you as you try to sneak past."

"Liar," she said. "There aren't any monsters."

"Oh really?"

"There are only bears. And wolves. And the occasional lion. But no monsters. Don't tell me you're afraid of them?"

"You're mad. Completely, utterly mad. And yes, to answer your question. I don't fancy becoming supper for some ravenous beast."

She pressed her chin down into the palms of her hands and closed her eyes. "I'm not mad," she said. "It's just . . . it's somewhere I'd like to go. It reminds me of home."

"Do you miss it?"

"All the time. But . . ." She opened her eyes. Even in the darkness, she could see the outline of his face, the slight frown that curved his mouth. She shrugged. "There's no going back now."

A WICKED THING

RHIANNON THOMAS

An Imprint of HarperCollinsPublishers

HarperTeen is an imprint of HarperCollins Publishers.

Library of Congress Cataloging-in-Publication Data
Thomas, Rhiannon.
A wicked thing / Rhiannon Thomas. — First edition.
    pages cm
Summary: One hundred years after falling asleep, Aurora wakes to
the kiss of a handsome prince and a kingdom that has dreamed of her
return, but her happily-ever-after seems unlikely as she faces grief over
the loss of everything she knew and a cruel new king.
ISBN 978-0-06-230354-7
[1. Fairy tales. 2. Princesses—Fiction. 3. Princes—Fiction. 4. Kings,
queens, rulers, etc.—Fiction. 5. Magic—Fiction. 6. Courts and
courtiers—Fiction. 7. Revolutions—Fiction.] I. Title.
PZ8.T3653Wic 2015   2014001897
[Fic]—dc23   CIP
                                                                  AC

Typography by Torborg Davern
15 16 17 18 19 PC/RRDH 10 9 8 7 6 5 4 3 2 1

First paperback edition, 2015

For Phoebe
who shares every story
and read this one first.

A WICKED THING

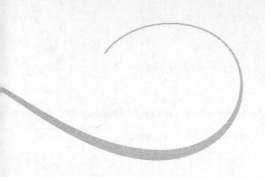

ONE

SHE WOKE UP WITH A KISS.

Not a birds-singing, heart-stopping, world-ending sort of kiss. A light spot of pressure on her lips.

Aurora opened her eyes.

A stranger loomed above her. A boy. He stared at her. "I did it," he said. "I actually did it."

Aurora screamed.

The intruder jerked backward, and Aurora kicked out, scrambling to the other side of the bed. Her feet hit the floor, and her knees buckled. Her left hand slammed onto the stone. Sunlight poured through the windows, stinging her eyes.

"I'm sorry." The boy's words rushed together. "Are you all right?"

There was a stranger. A strange boy. In her bedroom. Kissing her while she slept. And then . . . apologizing?

"Princess?"

She stared down at her hand. Her elbow shook. What did you do when apologetic strangers broke into your room and kissed you? It seemed important, somehow, to pick the right response, to behave the way her mother would expect, but her mind was a haze, and the ground seemed to vibrate under her fingertips. Or maybe that was her.

"I'm Prince Rodric," the stranger said, when she did not reply. "Son of King John the Third, and future king of—" He broke off. "I mean—Rodric. You can call me Rodric. If you like."

She would not face an intruder from the floor. Aurora grabbed the edge of the bed and pulled herself to her feet. The world shuddered and lurched. "I don't care who you are," she said. "What are you doing in my room?"

He stood completely still, like a child struggling not to startle a baby deer—or afraid that the deer might be a bear after all, and bite off his hand before he could blink. "Well, I'm—I'm here to save you."

"To save me?"

The boy continued to stare. He did not look particularly threatening, with his gangling limbs, gaping expression, and

light brown hair that stuck out of the top of his head, but despite his endearing appearance, he was clearly insane. Aurora took a shaky step backward. This time she kept her footing. "I'm calling my guards."

"Wait." The boy—Rodric—moved toward her, arm outstretched. His knees thudded against the side of the bed. "I mean—do you not remember?"

"Remember what?" She took another step backward, but her legs swayed underneath her, and she stumbled. Her dress weighed her down—not a nightgown, she realized, but a heavy, silken thing, as though she were dressed for a ball and had drifted off to sleep along the way. Numbness prickled across her skin.

"Please be careful," he said. "You must be weak."

"Oh, must I?" she asked, stepping backward again, her hand pressed against the wall to hold herself steady. "And why would that be?"

"Because—because of the spell."

She stopped. "You cast a spell on me?" Panic rose in her throat, freezing her in place, but she forced it back. Raised her chin slightly in defiance. She hoped he would not notice how it shook. "You work for the witch Celestine?"

"No!" He scrambled around to her side of the bed. In response, she slid sideways, close to the wall, trying to keep the distance between them. "No, nothing like that! I came—I was trying to break the spell. I was—I was helping."

Nothing could break the spell, except waiting. Certainly not awkward strangers who said they were princes and did not realize that you were only meant to kiss princesses when they were awake. She stepped closer to the door, but her foot caught on the hem of her skirt, and she slammed into the wall again. It was the ball gown, she realized, that her mother had ordered specially for the night of her eighteenth birthday, for the celebration that would mark her freedom. Freedom from magic, freedom from the curse. But if it was daylight outside . . .

"The ball . . ." she said. "It was last night. Does that mean—" She had reached her eighteenth birthday, she had escaped, she was free.

"You pricked your finger," Rodric said, and he sounded hopeful, like he thought she finally understood him. "You fell asleep."

She could not remember. She had been preparing for the ball, so happy that the curse was finally broken, and then . . . something was tugging at the corners of her memory. Singing. She remembered singing, and a light, moving upward from a tower that had no up left to go. A woman, her features blurred. And the slightest point of pressure on her fingertip.

She looked down at her hand. A bubble of blood rested on the pad of her index finger. She brushed it with her thumb. Red smeared across her skin. "Why did you kiss me?"

"The—the story," he said, as though that meant anything at all. She stared at him, shaking her head slowly back and forth.

"The kiss of true love," he added, when she didn't reply. "Whoever wakes the princess with a kiss—they're destined to get married and live happily ever after."

True love? Destiny? Perhaps he was a madman after all. "I do not even know you," she said.

"But the story—"

"What story?" she asked. "What are you talking about?"

"The story of you, Princess," he said. "The sleeping beauty."

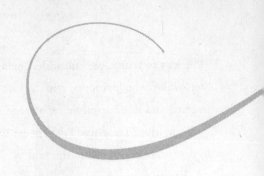

TWO

HER FINGER ACHED. SHE PRESSED THE TIP INTO her palm, squeezing the pain away, but that boy, that prince, was still standing there, still watching her like he could never have believed she would be here, and had no idea what to do now that she was.

"There is no story of me."

"Oh, but there is, Princess." Rodric took another step forward. Eagerness radiated from him, as though this was the moment, this was when everything would become clear. "Everyone loves you. You can't imagine how wonderful things will be now that you're awake."

"Awake?" She pressed her hand against the wall to steady herself.

"We tried to awaken you before, of course," Rodric said quickly. "Lots of people tried over the years. But it didn't work. Before today." His cheeks were pink. "I didn't think it would be me. I mean, I'm glad it is, but . . . I'm not usually big on the whole heroics thing."

Over the years?

"How long was I asleep?" she asked in a careful, measured sort of voice, like it wasn't really an important question at all, like she already knew the answer and merely wanted to check.

"We tried," he said again. "But it's—it's been a while." He stuttered over the words, dragging them out of some cautious, uncertain place. "Longer than we hoped. Not forever, but . . . a while."

Not forever. A while. He said the words the way her father did, when he first locked the door to her tower and told her she could not wander around the rest of the castle any longer. It wasn't safe. She needed to stay inside, for her own protection. *For a little while,* he said with a slight frown and an evasively comforting smile. *Just a little while.*

That had been eight years ago. And then she had fallen asleep.

"Tell me," she said. She stepped toward him. "Tell me how long it has been."

He looked away. The silence stretched between them. "One hundred years."

"One hundred years?" She repeated the words in her head, trying to make them stick, but they didn't seem to mean anything at all.

"Well—one hundred and two."

But everything looked the same. Her book was still propped open on the table. Her candle stood half-burnt, wax frozen in a drip down the side. Every ornament was in the same place as yesterday, every detail identical to the day before her eighteenth birthday, when she had brushed out her hair and tried on her new dress and celebrated the fact that soon she would be able to go out into the world. Yesterday.

"No," she said. She shook her head. Her hair brushed against her neck. "You're lying."

"Princess—" He reached for her again, and she jerked away.

"You're mad," she said, but she did not believe it. The air tasted heavy and old. She stumbled to the door and tugged it open.

The landing beyond looked like an abandoned ruin. Dust coated everything in the small circular space, from the little table opposite to the staircase that spiraled down out of sight. Rodric's footprints led to her door, and thicker patches trailed beside them, as though other people at other times had made the same trek. Spiderwebs hung from the corners, and her favorite tapestry, the one of a rearing unicorn in a forest of light, was moth-eaten beyond saving.

"Princess . . ."

She let go of the door. It swung closed with a creak. Impossible. It was impossible. A trick. She stepped back again, and again, then turned and hurried toward the window, desperate for a breath of fresh air, for the reassuring sight of the forest.

It was gone. A city sprawled into the distance, as far as she could see. The sun bounced off red roofs, houses all jumbled together between weaving stone roads. The air hummed with the sound of chatting and laughter.

An entire world, sprung up in an instant.

"Princess?" Rodric said. "Are you all right?"

She did not reply. Her fingertip throbbed. Everything was gone. Everyone . . .

"Where is my family?" she said, forming each word carefully, like they might explode if disturbed. "Did they sleep as well?"

Silence, unbroken except for the hum of the city. She continued to stare at the view, watching people scurrying along the road below. She did not want to touch the question again, did not want to ask, but the silence dragged on, each second heavy, and the truth hardened in her stomach.

"Rodric." She dug her fingers into the window ledge, pressing until her knuckles turned white. Forcing the pressure down, away, out of her body and into the stifling stone. "Where is my family?"

"I'm sorry, Princess," he said. "They're—they died. A long time ago."

"They died," she repeated. Meaningless words, really. How could your family, your whole world, vanish while you slept? It wasn't death, with aging and sickness and pain and grief, when they were simply gone. Lost decades ago, while she remained young and unchanged. She slid her hands off the windowsill and stared at her pale skin.

Was it the sleep, or the shock, or just her own weakness that made her feel numb, like she was in a dream still? She did not scream. She did not cry. A small part of her curled up in her chest, and when she looked up, the light burned her eyes.

"I'm sorry," Rodric said again.

She did not reply.

"Should we go downstairs?" he asked. "Everyone is waiting."

"Everyone?"

"Some of the court. My family. Not as many as you might hope, but . . ."

She turned, her hair trailing across her neck. He had a gentle face. He seemed to mean well. "Your family?" she said. *My family is dead.*

He smiled, a hopeful little smile. "They can be your family now too."

She stared at him.

He blushed. "Shall we go?" He held out his arm.

"Yes," she said slowly, carefully, clinging to the word. Her legs shook, so she placed her hand on the crook of his elbow, as lightly as she could. His doublet was soft under her fingertips.

"Are you all right?"

"Yes." It was all she could say.

Rodric ducked his head. "This way." As if she needed prompting.

Dust settled on her lips and between her eyelashes as they walked. It coated everything, rising up in a cloud every time Aurora took a step or brushed her hand against the banister. It scratched her throat, the lines behind her teeth, and she coughed.

They walked down the stairs, around and around, until Aurora's head spun. The staircase became neater with every turn. The dust thinned. New tapestries hung from the walls. In one, a golden-haired girl kissed a prince under a wedding arch. A few steps farther down, the same girl slept in a huge bed, lit only by the glow of a thousand fairies. Then she was sitting before a rickety spinning wheel, a single finger raised. Aurora stopped and brushed the same finger down the cloth. Her nail caught on the rough thread. "These are of me?"

"Yes," Rodric said. "They were gifts. In honor of you. I don't—I don't know from whom."

Aurora looked back up the spiraling staircase, straining to make out the wedding picture. Her promised future, captured on the wall for all to see.

They walked on, until the decay began to seem almost artistic. Cobwebs hung from some corners, but they did not block the stairs, and there were no spiders in sight. The stones only had a light coating of dust, and a few torches lit the way. "Someone has cleaned here," she said.

"No one's used the tower in years," Rodric replied. "But people visited sometimes." He spoke quickly and a little too loudly, his voice reaching out to fill the silence. "Not to—not to try to wake you, of course. That—that was only princes and—and people like that. There is a bit of a superstition, actually," he added. "About entering the tower. Only the boy who goes to awaken you in his eighteenth year can climb the stairs. Everyone else must wait below. If he is accompanied, or if anyone else disturbs you, you will never wake up. But some people still got a glance. At the tapestries. And the stairs."

Aurora stared at her feet. A thousand tiny needles prickled inside her head. She could think of no reply.

A heavy wooden door waited at the end of the staircase, blocking out all sound from beyond. Aurora stared at it. She had not walked through it in years, not since her father decided that even the rest of the castle was unsafe for her. It was longer than years now. Lifetimes. The door had marked the way out, the way to freedom, for her whole quiet little life. What was it now?

Rodric's hand hovered over the brass knocker. The moment lingered, and then he nodded, once, and pushed. The door slid open, just an inch, wobbling as though uncertain whether to swing forward or slam shut.

"Well?" A sharp voice cut through the gap. "Is she awake?"

"Yes," Rodric said. His voice cracked on the word. "Yes," he repeated with more conviction. "She's awake."

The door was torn open. Aurora blinked, raising one shaking hand to cover her face.

A woman stood before them. She had a long bony face, brown skin, and sleek black hair tied in an elaborate knot at the back of her head. She stared at Aurora, mouth open, cold eyes scanning her, as though searching for some flaw, some sign she wasn't real. "It's true," she said, as though she did not quite believe it. "The princess is awake."

A pause. Then chatter, growing louder and louder, the voices running over one another and rattling in Aurora's head. A crowd stood beyond the door.

Aurora had not been around more than ten people at a time in her whole life. Her parents, her guards, her maid, plus the occasional foreign visitor when she was younger, before her father grew too afraid. They were all dead now.

The woman grabbed Aurora's hands and pulled her forward, over the threshold of the tower, into the corridor. Aurora tugged back, trying to slip her hands out of the woman's grip, but she did not let go.

A tall and portly man stood beside the door. He had a thick brown beard, and his smile seemed to cover half of his face. Men and women filled the corridor behind him. They huddled in small groups, whispering behind hands and golden-feathered fans. They all wore brightly colored silks and rich velvets, and the women were dressed in sweeping sleeves and high-waisted dresses. Jewels glinted around their necks and between the twists in their hair. The whispering stopped as soon as she appeared. Every one of them stared at her.

"Presenting the Princess Aurora," the woman said with an imperious trill. Her hand tightened on Aurora's wrist, and when she spoke again, it was so quiet that Aurora could barely make out the word. "Curtsy."

Aurora grabbed her skirts and bent her shuddering knees, bowing her head and letting her hair fall across her face. She could feel every eye boring into her, judging every inch of flesh they saw. Aurora kept her head low. So many strangers, all staring, all evaluating her like she was some exotic, impossible creature. She squeezed her hands into fists around the cloth.

"Oh, don't waste time on formalities," the jovial man said. He had a booming voice, more that of an actor than of a ruler, but his golden crown declared that he must be the king. "You will soon be family, my dear!" Before Aurora could stand up again, he pulled her into a bone-crunching hug that stole the air from her lungs. She stood limp in his arms, her face flat against his chest. He smelled of sweat and heavy perfume. "We are so happy to have you here!" When he released her, she swayed backward, and her hand slammed into the wall to steady herself.

Perhaps if she could sit, if she could close her eyes, this would all fade away like a bad dream, and she would be home again.

"Now, now, John," the woman said, her voice light but as

thin as a needle's point. "Let's not smother the girl." She rested a hand on his arm.

The king chuckled. "Of course, of course. I am just excited to meet our future daughter-in-law in person."

"Pardon me," Aurora said. Her voice sounded far off. Even those two polite, meaningless little words exhausted her. "But I don't know who you are."

The woman started, a slight frown forming between her eyebrows, as though surprised that Aurora had spoken. She stretched her lips into a thin smile, but the king beamed. "I am King John the Third, ruler of Alyssinia for the past ten years, and this is my wife." He gestured vaguely at the woman, who bobbed her head.

"You may call me Iris."

Aurora nodded. Her hair tickled her cheek.

"My daughter, Isabelle, is the young thing hiding over there," the king continued. "Isabelle?"

"Don't be shy, dear," a woman said. "Greet the princess." She pushed a small brown-haired girl forward. The girl blushed. She looked eight or nine years old. When she curtsied, her whole body shook. "And of course you've met our son, Rodric."

Rodric bowed, his hair flopping about his face.

"Well," the king said. "Now that we're all acquainted, I think we had better make the announcement, don't you?"

The queen looked Aurora up and down, taking in her dust-covered feet and the blood spotted across her hand. "I am sure the people will forgive you, my dear, if you are a little less than pristine. Just this once. You have come rather a long way to join us."

"Oh, I think she looks lovely," the king said with a grin. "Quite quaint. Come along then, come along. Sir Stefan," he said to a man beside him. "Please send out the heralds. A little extra pomp and circumstance, if you please. It is hardly a normal day."

The man bowed stiffly and set off down the corridor. The king followed him, and then the queen, snatching Aurora's hand again as she passed. Aurora stumbled forward, trying to keep up with the woman's hurried pace. The courtiers fell into step behind, and the whispering began again, a surging rush that pressed against the inside of Aurora's skull and shoved her thoughts aside. The queen held her hand so tightly that it throbbed.

"Say nothing," the queen said in her ear as they turned onto another corridor and headed down some sweeping stairs. "You only need to smile. We will take care of the rest."

The rest of what? Aurora wondered, but she could not challenge this severe, elegant stranger. Each footstep echoed in her head, driving in the thought that her parents were dead, dead, and a century had passed.

They reached a large set of doors with standing bears carved into the wood. The hallway felt familiar, an echo of the last time she had seen it before her tower door had been locked, but every difference jumped out, breaking up the picture into a hundred jarring fragments. The bright red of the banners, like blood running down the walls. The guards, dressed in red too, staring at her with disbelieving eyes. The sharp trill of trumpets, muffled and distorted by the door.

The queen pressed Aurora's hand against Rodric's arm, squeezing until the fabric bunched beneath her fingers. Then she nodded, once, her eyes shifting to her son. "Well done," she said softly. "You will make us proud." She paused, as though she wished to say something else, but then she simply nodded again and followed her husband through the doors.

Aurora and Rodric waited on the threshold. Through the gap between the doors, Aurora could see flashes of color, hundreds of people, all surging together.

"They have been waiting since morning," Rodric said quietly. "The optimistic ones. I was certain I would have to go out and disappoint them. . . ."

Instead, he was bringing the prize. Aurora wanted to release his arm, to step away, but her hand would not move.

A herald's voice rose over the crowd, so loud and clear that even Aurora could make out the words. "Presenting, for the first time, the Princess Aurora!"

Hands pushed open the doors. Rodric stepped forward, and Aurora stumbled with him, her feet still tangling in her impractical skirts. All dressed up for a celebration, a century ago.

The roar of the crowd hit her, knocking the breath from her lungs.

They stepped onto a dais, with stone steps leading down to a square below. Everything else was hidden behind the mass of people, filling every space, crammed together into spots of jostling, bustling color, blurring before Aurora's eyes. And the noise they made . . . the screaming, cheering delight, chanting her name, chanting for Rodric, celebrating like their savior had just stepped out of the mist.

She still had blood on her finger. *How improper*, she thought vaguely. She burrowed it deeper into Rodric's sleeve, clutching the material so tightly that her hand ached.

The queen stood to the side, staring at Aurora expectantly. Slowly, carefully, Aurora sank into another curtsy. The roar grew. Hidden behind a wall of blonde hair, Aurora screwed up her eyes, fighting back the panic that clutched her chest, the scream that scratched the back of her throat. *Everyone I know is dead*, she thought. *And yet these strangers act as though they love me.*

She held the curtsy for a long moment, her knees shuddering under the skirts. One. Two. Three. Then she released her grimace and stood up straight, pulling her face back into something neutral, if not a smile.

The king was speaking now, his voice booming over the crowd. Words about hope. A new era. How proud he was of his son. Aurora could barely listen. It was important, she knew, to understand what was going on, but she could only stare at the sea of faces, the hundreds and thousands of strangers watching her, like she was something from their dreams.

And then Rodric was bowing, and the crowd was cheering, and the guards were steering them back into the castle. Aurora concentrated on each step, on keeping her knees steady, on avoiding the treacherous, ill-chosen hem.

The door thudded behind them. The queen hurried to Aurora's side. "I think that went well," she said.

"And that's just the beginning!" the king said, half to Aurora, and half to the courtiers who still milled around them. "We will prepare a big celebration for you. An engagement presentation, a ball of some kind, and the wedding, of course . . ."

"I don't—" The words were no louder than a breath. Every muscle inside her ached in protest, but the feeling was dull, faraway. The pain of another girl, in another time. She could not drag it into a coherent thought, so she let the protest melt on the air, unspoken.

"In the meantime," he continued, as though he had not heard, "I'll organize a dinner for our two young lovebirds. Food. Candles. Conversation. Would you like that, Rodric?"

"Yes," Rodric said. "Thank you."

"Excellent, excellent." The king clapped his hands together. "Come along then, son. We have many things to speak about."

Rodric kissed Aurora's hand. Foreign lips among speckles of blood. Their eyes met. His cheeks were pink. Aurora curtsied without a word.

The prince bowed. His footsteps clattered down the corridor as he and the king walked away.

"Ruth, please find a room for the princess," the queen said. "In the east wing, if you would. Third floor. And find her a maid—someone we can trust. Or at least, someone no one else will."

The maid curtsied.

"I have a room," Aurora said. Even that tiny protest took enormous effort, and as she spoke the words, she wondered why, out of all things, that was what she chose to say. She had spent her whole life in that tower, dreaming of the day she would be allowed to leave. But her spotless, ageless bedroom was her only remaining connection to the past. It was the only thing left that was hers.

The queen would not allow her even that small concession. "Oh, you don't want to stay in that dusty old tower," she said, and she turned and looked at Aurora. Really looked at her, into her eyes. Her smile was so thin that her lips vanished into her cheeks. "Allow us to take care of you. We are so happy to have you here."

Aurora looked at her feet. Heavy silks ballooned around her, so she took up three times as much space as the other women of court. The small group of nobles watched her expectantly. Waiting for her to speak. The silence pressed in. "Thank you," she said. She could think of nothing else to say.

The nobles continued to watch her. Two women, with matching purple feathers skewered into the knots of their hair, leaned together, covering their mouths with their hands.

"She does not seem quite bright," one of the women murmured. The other giggled and smacked her with her fan.

The queen smiled. "Carina, Alexandra," she said. The woman who had whispered stood up straighter, her gloved hand falling to smooth her skirts. "You are no longer needed. I am sure the princess will call upon you if she requires any of your ample wisdom."

The women flushed. They curtsied to the queen, and then hurried away. Nobody spoke after that.

When the maid returned, she was followed by a girl with huge eyes and bushy brown hair. She looked about fourteen.

"This is Betsy," the first maid said. "Her mother has worked in the castle for years. She is young, but hardworking. I think she will be a good fit for the princess." Betsy kept her eyes on the floor, her knees half-bent in a perpetual curtsy, but even her skin seemed to glow with pride at the praise.

"Very well," the queen said. "And you have a room prepared?"

"Yes, Your Majesty."

"Then we will go now." She turned to the nobles who lingered around them, some still watching Aurora with fascination, others plucking at their sleeves and staring absentmindedly at the walls, as though they had tired of the proceedings. "Thank you for joining us for this occasion," the queen said. "If the women return to our suite, I believe the maids will have laid out lunch. I will join you as soon as I can."

The watching women curtsied, almost as one, and the queen swept Aurora away.

"Insufferable," the queen murmured. "But we do what must be done."

Once again, Aurora was led through the winding corridors of the castle, past paintings in gilt frames, of forests and queens and conquering heroes. Small tables covered in flowers waited around every corner, filling the hallways with a dying sweetness. Guards and maids bowed and curtsied as they passed, but the queen did not pause.

Eventually, they emerged from a staircase onto a corridor that was empty except for a few paintings and a single door, midway between the stairs and the point where the corridor turned. An ornate silver lock rested below the handle. The door was slightly ajar.

"Here we are," the older maid said. "All ready for the princess."

The room was large and square, with all the clinical tidiness of a space kept ready for any temporary guest. A four-poster bed filled one corner, and a couple of soft chairs sat around a low table in the center. Logs had been placed in the small fireplace, but the tongs and shovel and extra wood were missing. A few lonely books slumped on an otherwise empty shelf, and a plain-faced clock ticked out the seconds on the wall. The windows had been thrown open, but the fresh air did little to mask the musty smell of disuse.

"It will do," the queen said. No one asked Aurora's opinion. "Betsy, make sure that Aurora is refreshed before her dinner with my son. Ruth and I will find something suitable for her to wear."

Aurora gripped the sides of her skirt. She had been wearing the same dress for over a hundred years. Part of her itched to tear it off, to throw the heavy skirts away, but the fabric was familiar against her skin, her legs protected by layers upon layers of silk.

"Your dresses will be too old-fashioned for comfort now," the queen added, "even if the moths have left them. And you will not want to linger in the past." She rested a hand on Aurora's shoulder. "The best way to deal with change," she said in a lower voice, "is to embrace it. Forget what you knew before. Your place is with us, Aurora."

Ruth and the queen left, Betsy filled an iron bathtub with hot water, and Aurora sank into it, letting it scald her skin red. Betsy washed the dust from Aurora's hair, her fingers gentle against the tangles, and began to chatter, quietly at first, but then louder and with more confidence, about Aurora, about how honored she was to work for her. Aurora did not take in a word. She stared at the unburned wood in the fireplace, not really seeing it at all.

"Would you please leave me?" she said softly, once her hair had been towel-dried and she sat in a robe. "I want a moment to myself."

Betsy bit her lip, but she curtsied without protest. "Of course, Princess."

With the maid gone, Aurora waited for the hollowness inside her chest to turn into tears. The pressure grew, bursting against her ribs, and Aurora sank into one of the chairs, but she did not cry. None of it felt real enough for her to cry.

I am here, she told herself. *I am here, and I cannot go back.*

The fireplace stared blankly back at her. The clock ticked on the wall. But Aurora did not cry.

THREE

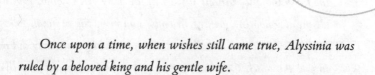

Once upon a time, when wishes still came true, Alyssinia was ruled by a beloved king and his gentle wife.

Aurora's parents stared up from the page. In the picture, her father's beard was too thick, her mother too tall, but there they stood, the idea of them, carefully painted and within her reach. She ran her finger down the image, tracing the bumps and flow of the paint.

Aurora had found the book on the otherwise sparse bookshelf. *The Tale of Sleeping Beauty*. Its corners were battered, the leaf somewhat worn, as though it had been read again and again by the castle's visitors through the years. Each page was accompanied by an illustration, painted copies of the tapestries she had seen on her tower walls only a few hours before. And the words . . . Aurora swallowed them with feverish speed, running her eyes back and forth over the sentences as though they would fade if left unseen.

The kingdom flourished, but the king and queen suffered a great sorrow. They desperately longed for a child. They hoped, and they wished, and they dreamed, but they grew older, and they remained alone. Then, one day, when they had almost ceased to hope, they had a beautiful baby girl. They named her Aurora.

All in the kingdom rejoiced for three days and three nights, and the king and queen threw a feast in the baby girl's honor, inviting all the neighboring princes, friends, and even the common folk to celebrate with them. However, there was one creature they did not invite: the witch Celestine, a cold and powerful woman who lived in a tower deep in the forest, and the only being that the people of Alyssinia had to fear.

Aurora's history books spoke of several powerful witches through the centuries, but none had ever been as terrible as Celestine. When she thought she had been slighted, when she believed that someone had cheated her, or simply when she thought the kingdom's joy had grown too great, she would attack. She destroyed crops and sent plagues that killed people with no apparent cause or cure. She bewitched men into committing horrific deeds and tricked foreign allies into claiming some insult that had never occurred. Some even said she had drained Alyssinia's magic away, so that no one could enjoy power but she. But the naïve and the desperate would still go to her tower, begging for solutions to their problems. She would offer them all their hearts desired, for unthinkable costs, and then laugh as she twisted their dreams into living horrors—exactly what they asked for, but broken in ways they had never thought to forbid.

Celestine saw herself as a queen in her own right. Her exclusion from the celebration of Aurora's birth had been the worst kind of slight.

Filled with rage at being ignored, the witch appeared suddenly in the middle of the banquet and, before anyone could stop her, gathered baby Aurora in her arms. With a needle, she stabbed Aurora's tiny fingertip and placed a curse upon her. Sometime before the princess's eighteenth birthday, she would prick her finger on a spinning wheel and fall into a terrible sleep.

"But I am not heartless," Celestine said, "and it would be a wicked thing to allow such beauty to go to waste. My gift to this child is true love. She will sleep only until she tastes the kiss of her beloved, and then she shall awaken, as fresh and as beautiful as before."

In all the years that the curse had chased her, Aurora had never heard anyone speak of "true love" as its cure. It sounded like a wild fantasy, a romantic little detail thrown in over the decades, when the reality of the curse had faded away.

Surely people did not really believe it.

The king and queen burned every spinning wheel they found in the kingdom and launched a desperate search for Celestine, but the witch was nowhere to be found. And so Princess Aurora grew up, spending her days in a tower in the castle, hiding from the world, locked away from those who would harm her. But curses cannot be broken so easily. On the night before her eighteenth birthday, Aurora was enchanted by Celestine. She pricked her finger on a forgotten spinning wheel and slipped into the deepest sleep.

The king and queen tried everything to awaken their daughter. Every spell in the land was cast upon her. Every man was sent to hunt for the witch. Every prince from every kingdom came to try to awaken her with a kiss, but the Sleeping Beauty slumbered on.

Aurora tried to picture them, countless strangers, coming into her tower and kissing her while she slept. Princes and nobles, people she had never spoken to, men now old or dead, all bowing before her, pressing their lips to hers, expecting her to gasp in delight and open her eyes again.

An itch crawled under her skin, like something foreign, something unwanted, had nestled inside her.

As the years trickled past, the kingdom of Alyssinia fell into

ruin. When the good king and queen died, the line leading back to the great King Edward himself ended. Lords and kingdoms fought over the throne. War came to the land for the first time in centuries. The people suffered, and all the magic in the kingdom melted away, except in that one room, where that one girl slept peacefully on.

And one day, not too long from now, a handsome prince, the chosen future leader of our people, will kiss the princess and awaken her and all the magic that the world forgot. He and the princess will marry and return peace and prosperity to the land.

And we will all live happily ever after.

Aurora stared down at the painting of herself, beautiful, untouchable, lost in the joy of her wedding to the handsome prince. The walls felt too close. She couldn't quite fill her lungs.

But it was only a story.

She had spent years locked in a tower, unable to see anything of the world but the scrap of forest beyond her window, but stories had provided her escape. New books, old books, dramas and histories and fantastical adventures, stories of ordinary lives, stories of dragons and demons, murders and mysteries and myths from long ago. A hundred possible worlds, more true to her than her own, more compelling than a life of staring at the same walls and same trees, waiting for the day when the lock would click and she would finally be allowed to be free.

A story could not hurt her.

"Princess? Are you all right?"

Betsy slipped into the room. A couple of dresses hung over her arm.

Aurora closed the book, snapping its prophecies out of sight. "Yes," she said. She pushed herself to her feet, ignoring the way her legs ached.

"I brought you some clothes," Betsy said. "They might not be perfect, but I think—I hope—they'll do nicely. A little old-fashioned, but . . . the queen said that would be all right for now." She held up a glossy green thing, with bubbled sleeves to the elbow and skirts that swished to the floor. It was unlike any dress Aurora had ever seen. Nothing like the dress she had worn before, but similarly unlike the elegant gowns worn by the current ladies of court. A dress to mark her as different. "Prince Rodric will love you in this. The green will bring out your eyes. Or I have something pink—"

"The green is fine." The color reminded her of the forest after rain, light reflecting off the leaves. "I mean—it's lovely. Thank you."

Betsy helped her into it, chatting all the while. Aurora let the words wash over her. The skirts moved around her like water, but the waist was a touch too tight, stealing the little breath she had, while the neckline gaped slightly at the back. "I'll just fix this," Betsy said with a quick curtsy, and then she was reaching and pinning and stitching and talking, always talking, about the exciting, amazing, wonderful, dreamlike miracle that had happened today.

"I was so honored, Princess, when they asked me to assist

you. I never expected it! But then, I never expected you'd be standing here, if you don't mind me saying. Not that I didn't think Rodric could be your true love, because of course he's wonderful, but it always seemed too much like a dream to ever happen while I was here. Things will be amazing, now, you'll see. Everyone loves you already. How could they not?"

Aurora thought of the words at the end of the story, the promise to the reader: *we will all live happily ever after.* Her true love would kiss her, she would awaken, and the curse would be over. But nothing Celestine did could ever be good. Her curse could not lead to happiness for anybody, least of all for her. "What happened to Celestine?" she asked. "The witch who did this to me?" The words were heavy in her mouth, and even heavier in the air, but Betsy barely paused.

"Nobody knows," she said through a mouthful of pins. "She enchanted you and disappeared. They searched all over the kingdom for her, and beyond, but she was never found. I think," she added, in a conspiratorial whisper, as she ran a needle up and down, "that she used up the magic when she cursed you. Poof! Gone. And she was too ashamed of her new weak self, so she fled."

"Oh." Aurora stared at her reflection. Celestine was dead, she told herself. A hundred years had passed, and even Celestine was dead. Yet she could not shake the creeping sensation that someone was watching her unseen.

Rodric waited for her in the banquet hall. A long table

stretched down the middle of the room, surrounded by paintings and hanging tapestries. Some of them were familiar, but most of them were entirely new, bearing foreign crests and scenes from stories she had never heard. She had attended a few small parties in this room when she was young, when her father trusted those attending enough to allow her presence, and it had seemed lively, fun, full of possibility. It had been one of the few places where she could meet strangers, hear music and laughter, live like she wasn't cursed. With only the prince waiting inside, the room felt abandoned and cold, too large and too austere.

Rodric stood when he saw her enter. "Princess Aurora," he said, and he hurried toward her, stumbling slightly over his feet. "You look—you look beautiful." He smiled shyly. "I mean, you always look beautiful. But you look especially beautiful tonight. Is what I mean."

Aurora stretched her lips into a smile. "Thank you," she said.

"Shall—shall we eat?" Rodric rubbed the back of his neck. A light blush colored his nose. She stepped toward him, and the ground seemed to twist away under her feet, making her head throb. It was hardly a storybook sensation. She took his arm anyway and let him lead her to the end of the large table.

A servant, dressed in extravagant red clothing, brought them each a bowl of soup. Aurora did not speak. Rodric did not speak. Spoons scraped against bowls, echoing in the otherwise empty hall.

"You missed the snow," Rodric said eventually. "We had several inches a couple of weeks ago, but not again, I don't think. It will be spring soon."

Aurora nodded, staring at her bowl.

"My sister, Isabelle—she was excited to meet you," Rodric continued. "She is so quiet, but—she is excited. She's just not good at meeting strangers."

Well, that makes three of us, Aurora thought. She nodded again.

"Is it true," Rodric said as he finished his soup, "that before—" He stopped and blushed again. "I'm sorry. You might not want to talk about it. About before."

Aurora tightened her fingers around her spoon. They must talk about something. "What were you going to ask me?"

"Some of the books mention that you had magic to entertain you at feasts." He smiled, sounding lively for the first time. "Not tricksters and magicians. Real magic."

"No," Aurora said. The thought made her shiver. "No, that isn't true."

"Oh." Rodric was staring at his plate, but Aurora got the feeling he was actually watching her closely, out of the corner of his eye. "People hoped—I hoped—" He trailed off. "Magic as common as that, brought back with you . . . it might be useful."

"Hoped?" Aurora closed her eyes. How could he be so naïve? "You're better off without it."

"So your family never—"

"No," she said sharply. "Why would my family use magic? They were not fools." *But they did use magic*, she thought. If the book could be believed. They poured it into her to try to break the curse, to save her from this place.

Rodric frowned down at his empty soup bowl. "I am sorry, Princess, I do not mean to contradict you, but—magic cannot be foolish. It brought you here."

"A curse brought me here."

"But still—we have been without magic for a long time, Princess, and nothing has been quite right since you fell asleep. Now things will be better. That has to be good, right?"

She shook her head. "I can't imagine magic creating anything good. Once, perhaps, it could, but not since I was born. Only a few sorcerers were left, even then." Men who charged riches for their talents, women who offered cures and fed poison instead. And Celestine. The witch who cursed her. "They were not good people."

Her father had tolerated a few who used magic, before she was born. There was always the hope that one would be able to cure disease or protect the kingdom from threat. But after Celestine's curse, he had accepted that the magic itself was twisted, and that anyone who controlled it was a threat to them all. The use of magic became punishable by banishment. The use of curses became punishable by death.

"My father—" Rodric paused, as though unsure whether he should speak. "My father says that some people still have magic now. Only a little. He says that they stole it for themselves, and if we fight them, it will come back."

"You can't steal magic."

"Why not?"

She opened her mouth, ready for a firm reply, but no words came. Magic came from outside you, that she knew. It was drawn from the air. Some said that you had to be wicked to tap into it, that all the good magic had been used up and all that was left was resentment and ill will. But what it actually involved, Aurora did not know. She had read many books, but the truth of magic had always been kept from her, as though even the idea itself could snatch her away.

Rodric plowed on over the silence. "It will come back," he said firmly. "Now that you're here. And it will do all the good things I said. I mean . . . why else—why else would you be here?"

Her hands shook. The spoon rattled against the side of the bowl like a drum roll, and the loss rushed up inside her, squeezing her chest until she could barely breathe. No home. No family. Just empty promises of true love and the idea that she would restore something that should never have existed at all.

She stood up. Her chair fell back with a scrape and a thump. "I have to go," she said. "I'm not hungry."

Every step jolted her knees, and suddenly she was running to the end of the banquet hall, her feet pounding the floor. Outside the room, a window hung open, and she pressed her hands against the stone frame, letting the cool breeze brush her face. She gulped down the fresh air, eyes closed tight.

"Princess?"

Rodric. She kept her eyes closed, her face lost in the breeze. He seemed nice. A bit hapless, a bit unsure, but nice. Yet he was a stranger, a strange, ungainly boy who claimed her as his own, and she did not know what to do. She had nothing else, no one else, and the threat of loneliness tore at her stomach until she almost swayed from sickness at the thought. She could not leave. But she could not stay here, with his presence so near, his awkward eyes seeking out salvation in her own. "I'm sorry," she said. "I would like to be alone."

"Princess, I am sorry I upset you."

"I am not upset." She forced herself to take another breath and opened her eyes. "This place—it is foreign to me. I don't belong here."

"I know. But—here we are, Princess. Fate."

She flinched. Fate. "Why do you keep calling me Princess? That is not my name."

"I know, but—it's what everyone's called you for so long. The Princess. That or Sleeping Beauty." He smiled shyly. "And it really was true. You are beautiful."

"My name is Aurora."

Silence. He nodded, head slightly bowed, pink burning his nose and cheeks.

"I really would like to be alone."

"Please," he said, offering the crook of his elbow, "let me escort you back to your room."

She smiled, a tight, shivering, broken smile. "Don't worry," she said. "I know the way."

She did not sleep that night.

When she tried to close her eyes, her breath caught in her throat, leaving her lungs gasping and empty. Her heart raced, and her limbs itched. A mishmash of a person, forced into a space where she did not belong.

She paced back and forth, her feet beating a steady rhythm against the smooth stone floor. She sped up with each lap of the room, walls pressing in closer and closer with every breath. If she stopped moving, even for a moment, she might melt away, vanish like everything else in her life. So she walked around the room, staring at the foreign walls and her familiar hands, her mind running over everything that had happened.

Every now and again, it would strike her, like a punch to the stomach, that this was real. That her family, her whole life, was gone. She would pause in her pacing, knees bending, stomach caving, her breath stolen away. But the certainty slipped away within moments, too impossibly huge to grasp for long. It would slip back into the realm of fiction and dreams, and she would continue to pace, until she thought, so casually, of whether her father would visit tomorrow, and it would strike her all over again.

And so she spent the night.

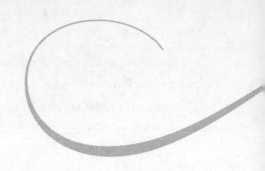

FOUR

MIST TRAILED IN THROUGH THE OPEN WINDOW at dawn, wrapping around Aurora's clammy, feverish skin as she leaned against the sill. She ached all over, in the insides of her elbows and the backs of her knees.

The city below was gradually coming to life. The buildings seemed to climb on top of one another, far into the distance, until they met a large wall, as tall as the castle at least, dotted with towers and flags. Women hurried along the cobbled street below Aurora's window, baskets balanced on their arms. A couple of carts passed too, slow things hauled by donkeys, half-full of grain or bursting with cloths.

The door creaked open. "Aurora, dear. I'm glad to see you're awake."

The queen stood in the doorway. Even at this early hour, she looked the picture of royalty, her eyes clear and bright, her black hair braided around the crown of her head. Aurora caught a glimpse of her own reflection in the glass on the wall: beyond pale, with lips like bruises amid a tangle of golden hair. Sleeping Beauty indeed.

"I do hope I haven't disturbed you," the queen said as she swept into the room. "I thought we might have breakfast together."

Aurora fought the urge to step back against the window. "But I am not dressed, Your Majesty."

"That is no matter," she said as she beckoned in a servant with a wave of her wrist. "We are all women here, aren't we? Besides," she added as the servant set a tray of fruit and tea on the table, "I wished to speak with you before the day grew too late." The queen was smiling, all politeness and ease, but something sharp nestled in her eyes and in the points of her cheekbones. "Shall we sit?"

Aurora nodded. She got the feeling the queen wasn't someone you refused. The queen sat, carefully, sweeping her skirts out of the way with one smooth motion. Aurora balanced on the edge of the other chair, her stomach tight.

The queen poured herself a cup of breakfast tea. "I am sure you must be excited," she said. "About the wedding. I am afraid

I must disappoint you. I know you will want to be married as soon as possible, but my advisors have informed me that the best time will not be until three weeks from today."

"Three weeks?" They planned to marry her in three weeks. Twenty-one days.

"I know," the queen said. "I was quite upset as well. But our best dressmakers are away in Fellbridge, the stewards tell me that we do not have enough food for an adequate feast, and we must declare it a holiday, of course. . . . I am afraid to say that you have caught us quite unawares." She sighed and sipped her tea. "However, we shall have an engagement ceremony in eight days, which is what I wanted to discuss with you. The people already love you, but it never hurts to be prepared—"

"Your Majesty." The queen paused, her cup of tea suspended halfway to her lips. *I have to stop this*, Aurora thought. Her lungs were squeezed in a fist, her heartbeat little more than a tremor in her chest. *I have to speak.* "It's so soon," she said. "I don't—I mean . . . I hardly know him."

The queen frowned. "The wedding has been prophesized for a hundred years," she said. "Surely you know him enough."

"But . . ." She stared at her hands. *Say it*, she thought. *You have to say it.* "What if I don't want to marry him?"

The queen placed the teacup on the table. The clatter of porcelain sliced through the air. "This is why I wanted to talk to you now, dear. It would not do for others to hear you speaking this way. Prewedding jitters are perfectly natural, but in the end, we cannot let these silly fancies take control of us. You know it is for the best."

"No," she said. "I don't know. I don't mean to hurt Rodric's feelings—"

"Oh, I do not mean Rodric, my dear. Everyone is going to be talking about you, and if you do not marry him as soon as possible . . . do you not see how dangerous that would be? You spent your whole life in the castle, is that right? You have never seen the outside world. So tell me, Aurora. Do you know what happens to valuable resources when they remain unclaimed?" Aurora forced herself to look the queen in the eyes. She could think of no reply. "You mean so much to so many people. Everyone will fight to control you, to lock you up and use you for their own ends."

"Everyone?" Aurora said. "Who is everyone?"

"It is enough to say that many people, ruthless people, want to gain control of this kingdom, and many will see you as the key to doing so. If you do not take your rightful place here . . . well, I dread to think what will happen." The queen raised her two perfectly arched eyebrows into a look teetering between admonition and concern. "Do you want to be the cause of war in the kingdom? Do you want innocent people to die because of you?"

Aurora dug her fingers into the arms of the chair. Once, when she was very young, she had broken into her father's library and stolen a book of stories. In one of the tales, a girl had wished for beauty that would enchant everyone who set eyes on her. So many men fell in love with her that they began to fight, chopping off one another's heads and running children through with swords. When the men surrounded the girl, they all grabbed a limb, a piece of clothing, a scrap of hair, and pulled, until she was torn into enough pieces for everyone to share. Aurora had had nightmares for weeks, of hands grasping her out of the darkness, pulling her left and right, snatching every second of her life away. And that was just for beauty. *They will hurt me*, she thought, *if I do not do as they say.*

"Well?" the queen asked. "Do you?"

"No," she said softly. "No, I don't."

"No," the queen said. "And we cannot protect you until the marriage takes place. Do you see?"

Aurora saw. The king and queen would not help her until she confirmed that she was theirs. "Yes," she said. "I see."

"I knew you would understand. I know I was terrified before my marriage to John, but we are women, Aurora. We can be strong." The queen still watched Aurora, her forehead dented by the smallest of frowns. "The wedding will be in twenty-one days. You should not concern yourself over it. Smile. Curtsy. Be quiet and predictable. We can practice, if these things are beyond you."

"No," she said tightly. "I can manage."

"Come along, then." The queen clasped Aurora's chin and

tilted it upward. "Give me your best smile."

Aurora attempted a sickly whisper of a smile. The muscles in her face shook. Her eyes stung.

"It will do." The queen released her chin and stood up. "I must go and speak to Rodric, set the preparations underway. But this was a good talk, Aurora. It is important that we see eye to eye on these matters."

Aurora nodded. She stood up, mirroring the queen's movements automatically.

"And do me a favor?" The queen took Aurora's hand in her own. Rings pressed cold against her bare skin. "Do not leave this room until you are sent for. As much as it pains me to say it, things are not completely safe for you. We only want to protect you until the marriage is secure."

"I understand," Aurora said.

"I will have some books sent," the queen added. "Things you might find of interest. Some stories, some bits of history. I understand that you used to like reading."

"Yes, Your Majesty." She forced herself to raise her chin, her hair falling back so she could look the queen in the eye again. For the first time, her smile was almost natural. "Yes, I did." Perhaps the answers would come, as they always did, from the pages of a book.

"Excellent. Then I hope you enjoy yourself. It was lovely talking to you, my dear."

"Yes," Aurora said. She slipped into a curtsy. Her hands were numb. "You too, Your Majesty."

"Please," the queen said. "Call me Iris."

As promised, the queen sent Aurora a large chest of books. They were stylish volumes, wrapped in leather, with neat, uncreased spines. Aurora lined them up on the bookshelf, studying each cover as it came to the top of the pile, letting her thoughts fade away into the steady rhythm of bend, stretch, and place. Once all of the books were unpacked, she organized them by title, and then again by genre, constantly moving, constantly shuffling, unable to let herself sit still. When she could think of no other way to arrange them, she sat back on her heels and ran her hand along the spines.

She only recognized one of the books: a history about the first days of Alyssinia, so long ago that it felt more fantasy than truth. When she was younger, she had thumbed through her own copy so many times that the pages had fallen out, and she had scribbled her thoughts in the margins like a diary of her growing up. It must still be on the table beside her bed, up at the top of her tower, like the rest of her life from before. Almost untouched by a hundred years. For a moment, she considered going back, collecting it and her other books. But the thought made her stomach twist. She could not return to that place. Could not see the way the dust had gathered on the stairs, proof of the decades that had crept past while she slept. She could not move her things out of there and into here, like this bare room was her home now. Like she was accepting this.

She pulled the new copy off the shelf. Aurora had begged her parents, her nurses, everyone, to tell this story, the story of Alysse, over and over, in a million different ways, filling in every known detail of her life. Alysse, the namesake of Alyssinia. The beautiful princess who saved everyone, despite her youth. The girl whose kindness and empathy allowed her to understand their new land when they first fled from the magicless kingdom across the sea. Alysse the Good, who ruled after her father, wondrous fair and beloved by everyone who knew her. After every telling of the story, from when she was five until she was seventeen, Aurora had run to the window of her tower and peered out, desperate desire bubbling inside her. One day, she would be like Alysse. Wonderful, beautiful, and loved.

Now Aurora sat on the bare floor, the new volume heavy in her hands. According to the stories, Alysse had vanished into the forest a few years after being crowned queen, and so Aurora had pictured her as eternally young, as beautiful and delicate as a cobweb after a rainstorm. It seemed nonsense now. Alysse must have grown old, and Alysse must have died, just as Aurora's parents had grown old and died, and the faces she saw every day, and even the kingdom that had surrounded her as she grew up. Aurora was the only one stuck in a kind of forever.

She tossed the book to the ground, a bitter taste in the back of her mouth.

When the queen returned a few hours later, she strode into the room without knocking. "They're awaiting you in the throne room," she said. "Come along, quickly. It sets a poor example to be late."

"The throne room?" Aurora said. She stepped backward. "You said we weren't to be married for three weeks."

"Why would we marry you in the throne room?" she said. "My husband is holding court this afternoon. He requested that you attend."

"The king is holding court?" Aurora asked. "What does that mean?"

The queen shook her head almost imperceptibly. "He is hearing grievances, rewarding the worthy, punishing the guilty. You will not be expected to participate. Remember what we discussed."

Smile. Curtsy. Be silent and beautiful. Her presence would add wordless legitimacy to everything that the king said, but her input itself was unwanted.

Two guards stood on either side of huge brass doors. They bowed as Aurora and the queen approached. Through the doors was a large chamber, bursting with people. Nobles stood in rows and groups. The threads of their clothes echoed the finery fastened to the walls: golden swords and shields, standards and spears. A row of guards in red cloaks lined the wall behind the crowd, and between them, a set of oak doors stood open, reaching from floor to ceiling. When the queen crossed the threshold, the courtiers moved as one, bowing and curtsying her into the room.

Two thrones had been placed between the crowd and the brass doors. The king sat in the larger one, and the queen floated toward the smaller one, her head held high. She waved Aurora to the side with a flick of her wrist, to a spot where Rodric stood.

"Now that the princess and my dear wife have joined us at last," the king said, "we can finally begin. Bring the first petitioner in."

The guards led a tiny woman with stringy blonde hair into the room. When she knelt before the throne, her shoulder bones jutted out, visible through her dress. Her husband had died, she told the court, her wide eyes fixed on the ground, and she had been unable to find work or food since.

"He were a good man, Your Majesty," she said. "Worked too many hours and didn't eat near enough. A story you've heard many a time, I know. But it's been a long winter, Your Majesty, and any help, any at all . . ."

"We may have a position in the kitchen," the queen said, "if you are willing to work. And swear your loyalty."

"Of course, Your Majesty. I swear. That is very gracious of you, very kind."

"I will have you sent down to my head cook, Marie. She will see what can be done with you."

"Oh thank you, Your Majesty. Thank you so much."

The woman curtsied at least five more times as the guards led her out the door.

The next petitioner was clearly a noble. His clothes were tidy and neatly made, and his boots gleamed like new. Some of the courtiers murmured behind their hands as he entered, and no one greeted him with a smile. An infrequent visitor to court, perhaps, or else an unpopular one.

"Sir Gregory," the king said. "What an unexpected sight. I haven't seen you since I last visited Barton. How long has it been—two years? Three?"

"I believe nearly three now, Your Majesty."

"And you've joined us to celebrate our princess's return? It is a long journey."

"I wish it were for such good reasons," Sir Gregory said, "although I am delighted to see the princess, of course." He bowed in her direction. "But I am afraid I must report a revolt. Last week, a group of peasants gathered outside the gates of my home, demanding food. I have none to give them, of course, none beyond what I need to feed my own family. But they would not listen. In the end, they knocked down the gate, killed one of my guards, and stole more than half the grain in my stores. My own men and the local soldiers have attempted to hunt down the culprits, but without harsh punishment, I am afraid that they will strike again."

The king nodded. "I understand completely," he said. "We cannot have this sort of thing going unpunished. I will send a cohort of soldiers back to Barton with you. They will find the culprits, and protect you and your family. In recompense for this crime, all men and women farming on your lands must give you half of the food they gather in the next harvest, to compensate you for your loss. Anyone who protests will be executed."

Aurora wanted to argue, to point out that that didn't make sense, that taking their food would make the problem worse. Her lips moved in the beginnings of a protest, but her voice did not cooperate. Not with so many people around, so many eyes watching.

"I will ensure the soldiers are ready to leave by nightfall," the king said. Aurora bit her lip, her opportunity gone. "I wish I could invite you to remain and celebrate with us, Gregory, but I know you will be eager to return and protect your family."

"Yes, Your Majesty," he said. "Thank you, Your Majesty." With a deep bow to the king, he backed out of the room.

The third petitioner was an elderly woman with a mass of curly gray hair. She walked with her back bent double.

"Please, Your Majesty," she said. "I have traveled all the way from Wutherton to speak to you."

When Aurora had fallen asleep, Wutherton had been a tiny town, approximately a week's journey from the castle.

"I no longer feel safe in my home, Your Majesty. People in the town have been accusing me of witchcraft, blaming me for things I could have nothing to do with. The sickness has been with us this winter, and many children have died. I would never harm 'em, Your Majesty, never, but some people—they've convinced others. . . ."

The king leaned back, resting his elbows on the arms of the

throne. "And why do you think they've accused you?"

"I don't rightly know, Your Majesty," she said. "I think maybe—I run an apothecary, gathering herbs for minor ailments, infection, and breathing difficulties and the like. I don't pretend to be a doctor or a healer, never have, just use the knowledge my mother gave me to help people and earn a living as I can. But some of the people in the town . . . they were angry I could not provide a cure. Why help nettle stings and soothe us to sleep, they said, when I cannot save their children? I wish I could help, I do, but I don't have the knowledge, and now—"

The king raised a hand to silence her. "You gather herbs? You do not look in the shape for it."

"I did, Your Majesty, when I was young. Nowadays I have to hire apprentices to help me. The young things have good eyes, although they do sometimes dally about some. One of them succumbed as well, poor darling."

The king nodded. "And you come here—why, exactly?"

"I—I was hoping you could offer your protection, Your Majesty. You know all about the evil people who hoard magic and threaten us all. If you said I was innocent, that it was just a sickness . . . maybe I could go home."

"If I said? And why would I say that? You have nigh admitted your involvement."

The woman stood completely still. "Your Majesty?"

"You gather herbs and mix potions—what is that but some subtle form of magic?"

"The plants have the magic, Your Majesty. I only mix them like my mother taught me."

"And the apprentice who gathered the herbs for you fell sick from this curse too. Because the herbs poisoned her, perhaps? Or because she knew too much?"

The woman leaned away, shaking her head. Her eyes bulged. "No, Your Majesty! I would never do that. Never!"

The king glanced at Aurora. "Tell me, Aurora," he said. "You are the most affected by magic out of those here. What would you see done with this woman?"

She swallowed. When she spoke, her voice was raspy, almost too soft to hear. "Nothing, Your Majesty," she said.

"Nothing?"

"If she had magic, surely she would—she would use it to protect herself. Only an innocent person would come to plead for your help."

"Or one who wished to appear innocent." The king looked back at the shaking woman. "Do you hear that?" he said. "Our princess is touched by your tale. But just because you have charmed a sweet mind such as hers, does not mean you have succeeded." He leaned forward, hands on his knees. "However, in honor of the princess's return, I have decided to be merciful. I will protect you, as you have asked. Room will be made in the dungeon for you. We shall see if these deaths end along with your disappearance. If they do—well, I would reassess how you speak to me, old woman. We will talk again."

The king nodded to his guards, and one of them stepped forward to drag the woman away. She clawed at his hands, still shaking her head in disbelief, and when she turned to look at Aurora, terror filled her face. The terror settled in Aurora, too, a dreadful desperation that felt far more truthful than the king's dismissive anger. Aurora took another small step forward, watching the faces of the other onlookers. No one else seemed fazed. Some were fussing with their clothes, or fidgeting and whispering to the person next to them, as though this were a boring chore to withstand. Others were nodding in approval. The woman disappeared through the doors, and the king waved his hands to indicate that they should be closed behind her.

"I grow weary," the king said. "And I must deal with the soldiers for Barton. Tell our other visitors that I will hear them tomorrow." He stood up and strode out of the room. Iris beckoned for Aurora and Rodric to follow.

The antechamber felt close and too quiet after the grandeur of the throne room.

"I'm starving," the king said as the brass doors closed. "I think lunch is in order." He began to walk away, but Aurora found herself hurrying after him, questions bursting out of her.

"That woman," she said. "What will happen to her?"

"If we find her guilty—and we will—then we'll burn that magic out of her. It is the only way we can know we'll be safe."

Aurora's throat was dry. "And then—then you'll let her go?"

She knew it was an inane question, but she had to ask. She had to be sure.

The king laughed. "Such a sweet one, isn't she?" he said to the queen. "Of course we'll let her go. What's left of her, at least. I've never seen ashes walk very far, but there's a first time for everything! Especially when witches are involved."

And, still chuckling, he strode away.

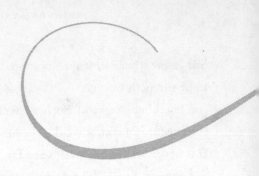

FIVE

AURORA COULD NOT SLEEP THAT NIGHT. Exhaustion burned her eyes, but every time she closed them, panic surged through her, the sense that she was drowning, smothered by the sheets, and her eyes would snap open again. The room was too small, too cold, too bare, the air stale and heavy on her tongue.

When she finally began to doze, the floor creaked, and blue eyes pierced through the dark. She sat up with a jolt, clutching the blankets to her chest. Nothing was there.

Aurora slipped out of bed. Her feet recoiled from the cold stone floor, but she pressed them down, savoring the shudder.

She pushed open the window and leaned out, letting the early spring breeze rustle through her hair. The chill pinched her cheeks.

The city seemed to glow, lights scattered across it like a reflection of the sky. Far below her, two girls ran along the street. She felt the sudden urge to run after them. To step outside, see the world she had fallen into, escape from these suffocating walls and breathe again.

Maybe if she saw it for herself, if she walked along the streets, she would start to understand what had happened to her kingdom while she slept. As she watched the lights glow across the city, she had to admit that she was hypnotized by their possibilities. Fascinated by the things she dreamed she might find.

Aurora doubted that anyone would recognize her from the brief glance of the day before, but she quickly changed into her plainest new dress, the one that seemed least likely to attract attention, and pulled a woolen cloak tightly around herself. Then she crept to the bedroom door and pushed it.

It was locked.

Aurora did not remember seeing a key or hearing a click, but the lock rattled when she pushed it again, holding the door in place. Sometime after Betsy had brought her supper, Aurora had been locked in.

Aurora swallowed her panic. She had been trapped behind many locked doors before. A single lock was much simpler than the heavy metal things that had once held her tower door in place. But then, the explanation had been plain. Sensible, even. The door must be locked to keep her safe. What was the explanation now? Was the queen protecting her?

Or was she keeping a valuable asset in?

Aurora hurried to her dressing table and picked up a couple of hairpins.

Her parents had locked her in her bedroom when their paranoia got particularly excessive. When they decided that two locked doors were safer than one, and that one room was harder to break into than a whole tower. She had been locked in at night, and some parts of the days, away from the other rooms in her tower, from the library and the old playroom and her instruments and all her books.

In her boredom, in the claustrophobia that had seized her, opening the door had seemed like the perfect challenge. She had little else to do with her time. She moved books with details on locks from her library into her bedroom, but even with careful study, it had taken her the better part of a year to master the trick, so that she could perform it every try. She was not the most dexterous person. But eventually, she had learned.

By then, of course, her father had stopped locking her bedroom door. He told her, with a guilty expression on his face, that he believed her trustworthy enough to have the run of the tower. She knew better. It seemed too much like real imprisonment if she was confined to one room, and her father always had been a gentle sort of soul.

The lock clicked, and Aurora gave the door an experimental push. It slid open a few inches, and she peered out. The corridor was deserted. She hurried along it, and the next, slipping through the shadows by instinct until she reached the door to her tower. It was an imposing thing, with ornate swirls carved into the wood and several heavy locks and bars. The handle was cold in her hand, and she pulled hard, half expecting the door to resist.

It swung open with a creak, and Aurora darted inside. When she closed the door behind her, the darkness became so thick that she could not tell where the walls ended and the air began. She bent down and groped in front of her until her hands brushed stone, then began to trace up and down, left and right with her fingertips. Somewhere, she had scratched a tiny star into the wall, marking the exact block she needed.

There. She pried her fingernails into the gap between the stones and tugged. The scraping set her teeth on edge, but the stone came loose, then the one next to it, and the one after that, until a small crawl space appeared.

It had been her escape route. She had spent years exploring every inch of her tower, hunting down secrets, but this one had been the hardest won, and by far the best. Every time the castle walls pressed too close around her, she would wrench the bricks free and crawl out into the forest, enchanted by the risk, the thrill of endless space. The tunnel had been built on purpose, she had told herself every time a voice insisted she should tell her father about its existence. He had included it in the tower himself, so that if anything terrible happened, she could slip out into the forest and escape. No one could see it from the outside. No one else could move the bricks. It was safe. So she told herself.

Now she paused at the edge of the space. Was this how Celestine had entered her tower, all those years ago? Through the tunnel that Aurora had kept secret, convinced that the freedom it offered was worth the risk? She swayed for a moment, staring in the blackness, and then shoved the thought aside. It was too late for those kinds of questions and regrets.

She wriggled inside. Dust clung to her clothes and her knees, but before she had crawled a few feet, the floor sloped downward, creating a narrow corridor she could stand in if she crouched. The tunnel was pitch black, apart from the occasional glint of light peeking in through the cracks in the stone. Cobwebs snatched at her hair, and there was a scuttling noise she did not want to think about, but her groping hands knew the way well, and soon fresh air fluttered at her face.

The exit was still open, covered with little more than ivy and grass and a few loose stones. She scraped at them with her nails, fighting her way through, and then she was outside, crouched on a slope that led onto the street.

She stepped onto the cobbled road, and her feet curled around the uneven stones. The streets wove in and out with no apparent logic, and Aurora followed them blindly, chasing the sound of activity and the distant movement of others. A century ago, she had always been too scared to visit the nearby town, certain that someone would recognize her. The same fear prickled the inside of her stomach now, the dreadful, thrilling feeling that she was doing something dangerous and forbidden, but she walked on, not entirely sure what she was looking for.

The larger roads near the castle were lit by lanterns, hanging from the walls like eyes gleaming in the dark. Not magic, she knew, but something like it, some strange power that let the fire burn bright and bold. The same power, perhaps, that held together this cramped, sprawling, impossible city. The buildings climbed on top of one another, chasing up into the darkness, and ropes hung from window to window, clothes fluttering underneath. Even at this late hour, the city was alive with people, pausing at market stalls, leaning against walls to chat and laugh, hurrying about their business. The smell of food filled the air, escaping from windows, wafting from a few stalls she passed.

One market holder caught her eye and began to yell. "Fabric!" he said. "Beautiful fabric, all the way from Eko." He held up a length of red material, too stiff and too shiny to be of true quality. His stall was illuminated by a lamp overhead, and the fabric glimmered in the dim light. "Worth its weight in gold, but I can cut a deal for a pretty lady like yourself. Two silver coins for a ream. Can't say fairer than that!"

"Don't listen to him," shouted a woman from across the way. She held up another length of fabric, green and translucent. "He buys his fabric in Alyssinia, tries to scam everyone.

But this stuff—this stuff is from Vanhelm. Inspired by the color of dragon eyes, it is."

"Sorry," she blurted, and she hurried away, her eyes fixed on the ground. Small paving stones covered the street, gray with dust. A groove had been worn into the brick. Another ran parallel to it, a few feet away.

"Move, girl!"

Something clattered toward her, and she jerked aside. A horse cantered past, held to a carriage with steel bars and a gleaming harness. The carriage itself was almost square, black lined with bronze, with a single lamp swinging ahead of it, and another behind. A man sat on the roof, whipping the reins.

The wheels ran through the ruts in the road, spitting dust in Aurora's face. She stepped back, coughing, then turned aside and ducked into a side street, away from the crowds.

There was no market here, only shuttered windows, hanging laundry, and the occasional person leaning against the walls. Not a trace remained of the forest that had stood here a hundred years ago, but some of the houses had boxes of flowers and plants hanging below their windows. Private patches of green amid the never-ending stone and dust.

Aurora took one turn, and then another, always heading downhill, following the curve of the streets, until they were so narrow that she could reach out and touch the walls on either side with her fingertips. Voices bounced out of the windows, laughter and chatter and the occasional shout. When Aurora glanced over her shoulder, only the tips of the castle towers were in sight.

A few people idled around a tatty building that jutted out of an alley. The Dancing Unicorn, the sign said. Aurora doubted that real unicorns were as fat and ungainly as the picture suggested. A woman's voice floated on the breeze as Aurora paused. She was singing, haunting notes that rose and fell like a sigh. The sound seemed to slip into Aurora's veins, as soft and delicate as silk. She had heard court singers and performers before, at the few celebrations she had attended as a child, and she played the harp herself in a clumsy, tentative sort of way, but she had never heard anything like this, nothing that sounded so raw and naked and sweet.

The music lingered in the air, tugging on some unknown part of her, the hollowness that had filled her ever since she awoke. She peered through the entrance and saw a large crowd of people, all moving, talking, laughing, dancing together. The rush of chatter made her pause, glance around warily, but there were so many people here that she truly was invisible. She could slip in, have a taste of that music, and no one would know.

She raised her chin and walked tentatively through the door.

The room inside was low and cramped, the air spiced with smoke. Lanterns hung from the rafters, swaying back and forth in time with the steps of the crowd, throwing scattered patches of the room into shadow. Mismatched furniture filled most of the floor—torn armchairs and stools of different colors and tables that rocked, seemingly without provocation—except for the space near the stage where people danced. And the people . . . they filled every inch, talking, playing games, dancing, arguing in more languages than Aurora could imagine. Several people around Aurora's age stood behind a roughly cut bar, and more were scurrying around, laughing and joking and ferrying drinks.

On the stage at the far end of the room, a tall girl played an alien instrument of wood and strings. She had a willowy look about her, with long black hair hanging over small, sharp eyes and pale brown skin. Half of her face was in shadow, the lines of her cheekbones sharpened by the distant lanterns. She swayed as she sang, her eyes closed against the hot buzz of the room. The music ached with a desire that Aurora could not name, a longing that loosened the knots in her stomach. She took a few steps toward the girl, weaving between the tables, letting the atmosphere of the place, the notes on the air, soak into her skin.

"Aurora—" Her name stuck out of the chatter as clearly as a shout. The speaker was an older woman, talking to a man who might have been her husband. She had a loud voice and animated hands, acting out every word with gestures and nods. "It's a miracle, is what it is," she said. "An absolute miracle. I told Maureen, I told her, I will never forget this day. I won't, and neither will she, I bet. I never thought, in my lifetime—" The woman stopped and looked up at Aurora. Her smile was almost toothless, welcoming. "Can I help you, dear?"

"Oh." Aurora's heart fluttered and warmth rushed into her cheeks. "No. I'm sorry."

"No need to be sorry, dear. Pull up a chair if you like. We were just talking about the ceremony."

"The—ceremony?"

"With the princess," the woman added, as though Aurora was rather slow. "Sleeping Beauty. Surely you saw it."

Aurora's stomach twisted. "I missed it," she said.

"Missed it?"

Aurora jerked her chin in an awkward imitation of a nod. She wanted to ask the woman to tell her about it, to spill every detail, share what she thought of the princess. But the words would not move off her tongue.

"Young people these days," the woman said to the man who might be her husband. "I've been waiting all my life for this, and these young things miss it. Tristan!" A boy, cleaning off a table a few paces away, looked up. "I've found you a friend."

The boy had scruffy brown hair and a lazy smile, like he was enjoying a joke that he hadn't yet shared. He walked over to them, balancing a tray of mugs in his hand. "A friend, Dolores?"

"Someone to get rid of that sullen look you've been wearing all night."

"It's not sullen! It's deep."

"Deep nonsense if you ask me. It's not like you." The woman shook her head. "How anyone can be miserable at a time like this, I really don't know. But don't you worry. I've found the only other person in Petrichor, if not all of Alyssinia, who missed the show. You can commiserate with each other, or complain, or whatever you young folk like to do."

He looked at Aurora, and there was a little hitch in his smile, as though something were tugging down at the corner of his lips. Aurora forced herself to look him in the eye, her heart pounding. Then his smile grew again, and he gave her a casual nod. "Glad to have you in the club."

"You'll regret it, you know," Dolores said with a knowing wave of her finger. "When you're old and gray like me, and your grandkids ask you where you were when Sleeping Beauty woke up. Tell them you missed it, and see what they say!"

"Don't worry, Dolores. I won't have grandkids. Are you finished with these?" He gestured toward the mugs on the table.

"Oh, yes, take them then, if you won't entertain an old lady's hopes."

"Sorry, Dolores," he said as he scooped them onto his tray. "I'm a hopeless cause." With a nod to each of them, he headed back to the bar.

"That boy," Dolores said, after he had gone. "If I ever see him care about anything, I'll be so shocked, it'll be the end of me." Aurora gave another awkward nod, and Dolores turned to her husband again.

With the conversation apparently over, Aurora drifted away, wandering closer to the stage. She leaned against a wall and closed her eyes, allowing the singer's voice to surround her. The sound was new and wistful and right, and as Aurora listened, it filled her empty stomach and soothed her throbbing head. One song melted into the next, and the next, until Aurora began to feel that she could breathe again.

"Good, isn't she?"

She opened her eyes. The boy she'd met earlier leaned against the wall beside her.

"Yes," she said. The music still filled her, leaving her oddly confident, almost bold. "I've never heard anything like her before."

"Yeah, Nettle's pretty new. Arrived in Petrichor maybe three weeks ago? One of those traveling performing types."

"Nettle?"

He shrugged. "Stage name. Don't ask me why. She's bristly enough for one, but the girl knows how to sing, so no more questions asked." He had a casual, comfortable air about him, like the whole world was his friend, and he was waiting for them to realize it. "Sorry about Dolores," he added. "She always thinks a 'nice young man' like me needs a friend. Seems to think I'm some kind of charity case, and ropes any pretty new girl into the cause."

"Oh." For some reason, the casual compliment seemed more genuine than all the voices that had ever called her beautiful. "That's okay."

"I lied, you know," he said. "To Dolores. I did make it to the ceremony. But her annoyance at the idea that I didn't was just too good to miss."

"Oh," she said again. She could feel him watching her out of the corner of his eye.

"How about you? What did you see?"

"Nothing," she said. "Only the crowds." It wasn't entirely a lie. "What was it like?"

"How about I tell you over a drink? My treat."

"Oh." It seemed to be the only thing she was capable of saying. "No, thank you."

"You can't come to an inn and not get a drink." He pushed himself up from the wall with one hand. "Don't worry. I won't actually be buying it. Bartender's privilege." When she did not move, he grabbed her hand. "Come on. We'll get you sorted out."

He set off toward the bar, and Aurora found herself following, suddenly conscious of her unbrushed hair and dusty knees. The boy didn't seem to notice. He gestured at a wobbly stool, and she pulled herself onto it without question.

"Made a new friend, Tristan?" The girl behind the bar had a mass of brown hair and a sternly cut mouth. Her expression was somewhere between an eye roll and a sigh.

Tristan laughed. "I'm always making new friends, Trudy."

"Don't I know it."

"Dolores says this one skipped the ceremony yesterday. Wanted to introduce me to the only other sensible person in this city."

Trudy glanced at the other customers and then across to the far wall. She frowned. "Don't let Nell hear you talking like that. You know how she gets."

"It won't hurt anyone," he said, but he stopped talking all the same.

"So what drew you in here?" Trudy said. "No offense, but you don't look like our usual clientele."

"I came in for Nettle," Aurora said. Her tongue tripped over the name. "I could hear her from outside. She's . . . she's really good."

Trudy smiled, revealing crooked teeth. "Got good taste then. I was beginning to wonder, seeing you come over here with this one." She tilted her head at Tristan, who promptly elbowed her in the side.

Aurora glanced back at Nettle, standing on the stage alone, now singing to an upbeat rhythm that made Aurora's toes twitch.

"There we go," Tristan said, pressing a large mug into her hands. "One mug of mead." She raised it slowly to her lips and took a sip. She was surprised to find it sweet and rich like honey. It warmed her throat, and she took a bigger gulp.

"Like it?" Tristan asked, and she nodded.

Another customer appeared at the end of the bar. "Evening, you two," he said. "Two pints of ale, please. And one for yourselves, in celebration of the princess's return."

"I'll take this one," Trudy said, and she bustled off, leaving Aurora alone with Tristan again. He swung himself over the bar and settled on the stool beside her.

"So," he said, "that was my dear, demented cousin, Prudence Middleton. But don't tell her I called her that."

"Demented?"

"Prudence. She thinks it sounds like the name of a shriveled-up old shrew. I think it suits her." Aurora tilted her head, unsure if he was joking, and he laughed. "And I'm Tristan Attwater." He stuck out a hand, and Aurora took it with tentative fingers. "So," he said again. "You got a name, or am I going to have to make one up for you?"

Aurora looked him in the eye. Her fingertips tingled. "What would you choose?"

"Let's see." He brushed her hair back from her face and looked at her with exaggerated care. "I dub thee . . . Mouse."

"Mouse?"

"Were you expecting something more regal?"

She shook her head and took another sip of mead. The sweet burn down her throat made her daring. "Why Mouse?"

"You look like you're hiding away."

He still offered her that lazy smile, but there was intensity in his eyes that hadn't been there before, a fleck of something that seemed to cut to the core of her. She stared down at the mug in her hands, but she could still feel his eyes on her. "I'm not hiding from anyone."

"Never said it was a person."

She gulped the mead to avoid a reply. Her heart pounded,

but it was a different sort of fear than the one she had felt in her tower. Thrilling. Nettle was still singing, and her music brushed against Aurora's skin like the heat from a flame. Here were people, treating her like she was normal, like she had no fate and no duty and no trauma around her. Someone to talk to, not protect or manipulate. It was, she thought, a first in her life. She wanted to dwell in it longer, in this freedom, where she could breathe and talk and listen and not hide everything behind expectations.

Yet Tristan was watching her closely, and his eyes seemed to see through it all, the myths and pretenses, to whatever lay curled beneath. The part of her that even Aurora could not see.

"You were going to tell me about the ceremony," she said. "What it was like."

"So you can paint a mental picture for your future grand-kids?"

"I just want to know what I was missing."

Tristan glanced over his shoulder, as though checking for lurking spies. "Not much," he said in a low voice. "It was all speech, smile, curtsy, cheer, speech again. The princess didn't say anything."

Aurora took another sip. "It must be pretty overwhelming for her," she said.

"Facing the crowd like that?"

"Everything," Aurora said. "They seem to expect so much from her."

"You're saying you don't?"

"I don't know. It seems a lot to ask one person who's been asleep for a hundred years." It was easier, somehow, to put her feelings into words when she could be anonymous, a nameless mouse instead of a lost princess. Not easy, but easier. "Do you think people really believe it? That everything will be better now she's back?"

Tristan frowned at her. "I think some of them do," he said. "The rest of them just want to believe." Their shoulders brushed. "People have to have something to hope for, don't they? Doesn't really matter what. It's better to believe in magic than think that we'll all be hungry and poor for the rest of our lives."

"And you? What do you believe?"

"Me?" He ran his fingers down the handle of his tankard, considering. "I realized a long time ago that no one's ever going to help anybody. You can't just sit around and wish. But perhaps we should talk about something else. Nell'll have my head if she thinks I'm talking trouble. And trust me. You don't want to make Nell mad."

"Who's Nell?"

"Owner of this great establishment," he said. "She's not a bad sort. Gave me a job when I needed it, even though I'm not exactly work material. But she likes to play it safe."

"And you don't?"

"Safe is boring, Mouse. It's for old folk with businesses to run, not people like me and you."

"Like me and you?" She smiled. "You barely know me."

"I know enough to know I want to know you. Does that count?"

"I'm not sure it does."

"Well, you're new in town," he said. "You could decide to be anybody! So I'll go with the hope you'll decide to be like me."

"I'll consider it," she said. She gripped her own tankard with both hands, pulling it closer to her chest. "How did you know I was new here?"

"I would remember if I'd seen you before."

She tilted her head to look at him. Blonde strands fell over her eyes. "And you've met everyone in this city, have you?"

"Everyone worth knowing," he said. He nudged her hand. A shiver ran across the points where their skin touched.

"Tristan Attwater!" A rather large woman with a mop of graying brown hair marched toward them. "I don't pay you to flirt, you know."

"You don't pay me at all, Nell," Tristan said. "But it's all part of the service."

"Well, customers are waiting."

He gave Aurora another smile and a shake of his head. "Duty calls. But it was nice chatting to you, little Mouse."

"You too." She smiled back at him, and a warm ache tugged in her stomach. "Tristan."

Then he was gone, and Aurora turned to the stage, letting the trembling music fill all the emptiness that formed whenever she sat still too long. She rolled the few words she had exchanged with Tristan through her mind, trying to decode the tone of his voice, the warm smile, the way he seemed to see right through her skin. Occasionally, her eyes wandered over to him as he served and cleaned and talked, seeming perfectly content with everything he did. Once, he caught her watching, and he shot her a grin.

She had no idea how much time had passed, minutes and hours of music and stolen snatches of chatter, before Nettle left the stage and the crowd began to thin. "Thank you," Aurora said as she passed the long-empty tankard across the bar to Tristan. She felt oddly peaceful, like all of her pain and stress belonged to some other girl.

"Nettle will be here tomorrow too, you know," Tristan said with a slight tilt of his head. "So—see you soon?"

She shouldn't. She knew she shouldn't. It wasn't safe, it wasn't allowed, and if anyone found out . . . but her heart was already beginning to pound at the thought of another night trapped in those castle walls, unable to sleep, staring at the ceiling and thinking of life happening below. The words slipped out before she could stop herself. "Yes," she said. Her voice trembled. "I'll see you soon."

SIX

AURORA'S DREAMS THAT NIGHT WERE FILLED WITH smiling, contorted faces and laughing eyes. She awoke before dawn and sat by the window, watching the beginnings of the day burn across the sky.

The click of the lock announced Betsy's arrival. Relocking the door had been beyond Aurora's skill, so she listened as Betsy unwittingly relocked it herself, then shook the handle of the unyielding door. After a few pushes, the lock clicked again, and the door swung open. A small frown marred Betsy's face, and she stared down at the key in her hand, as though trying to puzzle it out. When she noticed Aurora watching her, she slipped

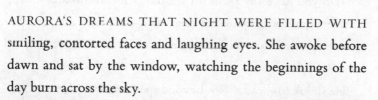

the key into her pocket and gave her a slightly uncertain smile. "Good morning, Princess," she said. "The queen says you're to have breakfast with Prince Rodric. Won't that be lovely?"

Lovely was not quite the word to describe it. Once they bumbled through the initial pleasantries, they fell into awkward silence, broken only by the scrape of knives and the crumbling of bread. Rodric looked everywhere except at Aurora. The declarations of true love had bothered her, but the silence was worse. It pressed heavily on her, as though Rodric had finally seen her true self and did not like what he'd found.

A thousand different conversation starters floated through her head, but it seemed too late to try any of them. They had been quiet for too long. She continued to pick at the food, not saying a word.

"Do you have any plans for the day?" she eventually asked, after servants had appeared to clear away the plates and crumbs. If he did not want to talk to her, at least she could give him an excuse to leave.

He shook his head. "Not beyond spending it with you. Getting to know you."

"Oh."

"Is there anything you would like to do?" He finally looked at her, and his voice rose hopefully. All it took were a few words on her part, and he appeared optimistic about the two of them again. Aurora could not muster the same enthusiasm. The prince seemed harmless enough, but the silence of the past half an hour felt far more truthful than his suddenly renewed friendliness. They were strangers, and pretending otherwise seemed ridiculous.

Yet things would be easier if they got along.

"Perhaps you could show me around," she said, staring down at her hands. "So much has changed since I slept. I would appreciate a guide."

"Around the city?" He looked alarmed. "I'm not sure that's—"

"No," she said quickly. "Not the city." She could still taste the sweet shadow of mead on her lips, feel the goose bumps on her skin from Nettle's song, and see the lamps, glowing like fairies along the paths, lighting up the darkness. They were her secrets, something that could not be tainted by curses or expectations. She did not want to trample through them with Rodric and guards and her story shouted before her. "Just inside the castle."

Rodric let out a breath. "I could do that," he said.

He led her through the half-familiar corridors, pointing out rooms and gifts from foreign guests, naming guards and servants who bowed as they passed. He parroted every word he must have heard from his parents, walking with an official air and a straight back. Although Aurora saw glimpses of the new, an eclectic mix of foreign tastes and sigils of rearing bears, the tour gave her no sense of the castle as Rodric saw it. Not unless the castle, to him, was the dullest place in all of Alyssinia.

"Is there still a garden?" she asked, after he pointed out the gilded chairs in the dining hall. "In the center of the castle?"

"Oh, yes," Rodric said. "It is my mother's. Would you like to see it?" She nodded. "I should have thought of it," he said. "Girls—girls like flowers."

And boys like fighting and mead, she thought with a snap, but she swallowed the words. Rodric was blushing enough already. "I don't know about girls," she said instead, "but I would like some fresh air."

Aurora remembered the gardens so clearly, so completely, that she could almost feel the brush of grass between her toes. The castle was hollow inside, its stone walls wrapped around a patch of undergrowth and trees, as though part of the outside world had settled within it, full of lush grass and clear skies above. But when she stepped out of the archway into the sunlight, she saw only paved paths, weaving their way around neat flower beds and the occasional fruit tree.

"My mother had flowers brought here from all over the land," Rodric said as he led her onto the path. "And she has a team of gardeners, the kingdom's best, to care for them. There aren't any flowers now, obviously. But there will be. Soon. When spring comes."

Aurora nodded. It was lovely, truly it was, but compared to the garden she remembered, it all looked so refined, almost restrained, as though even the winter grass had been bent to the queen's will.

"Is anything the same?" she asked. It was only a garden. She knew that. Nature did not wait for anyone. But it had always seemed so ancient and eternal, a living remnant of the land stretching back to the time of Alysse, full of ancient spirits and dreams that would reach out into forever. It was the only patch of the outside world she had been allowed to visit as a child, before confinement to the castle turned into confinement in the tower. "Has everything changed?"

"I don't know," Rodric said. "It's always been this way for me." He stared at the barren trees. "We still live in the castle," he said with an optimistic tilt to his voice. "And we—and you're here."

She stepped away from him, numbness tingling in her lips and fingers.

"There are some quite old apple trees," Rodric said, after a long, awkward pause. "Just over here. I'll show you—"

"What happened while I was gone?" The question burst out of nowhere, all of her unspoken desperation blurring into one simple thought. Rodric stopped, startled.

"I don't know. I mean—lots happened. What do you want to know?"

She knew what she wanted to ask. What had happened to make people obsess over a fairy tale? To make a prince believe a single kiss meant true love, and that a girl who knew so little could mean so much? People needed hope, Tristan had said. But he had not mentioned why. "Why do people like me so much?"

she said. "Why do they care?"

He opened his mouth, then closed it, then opened it again. "I'm not sure I'm the best person to ask, Princess," he said. He still would not look at her. His cheeks burned red.

"Your mother has told you not to tell me." It was only a guess, but his eyes shifted as though searching for an escape route, and she knew it was true.

"She does not want to overwhelm you," he said eventually. "She thinks that talking too much about the past would make it harder for you."

"The only thing overwhelming me right now is how little I know, about anything." She stared at him until he looked at her. "Tell me why you were so happy when I woke up," she said. "Let me be happy too."

"I'm not sure the past is happy, Princess." He stuck his hands in his pockets and set off along the path. She followed him, an arm's length to the side, her hands clasped in front of her so tightly her knuckles turned white. "Things were all right, I think, as long as your parents were alive. But once they died . . . what were people supposed to do? You were the heir, but you were fast asleep. No one knew whether there should be a regent, or a temporary king, or a new line—they still hoped you would wake up within the next month, the next year. Or some people hoped. My father says other people got greedy, saw the curse as the chance to take power for themselves."

"And if I woke up, the succession would be settled again?"

"Perhaps," Rodric said. He kicked the ground, scraping a groove in the dust. "Greedy people don't always step back, just because they run out of excuses."

"So that's it?" she said. "That's the reason everyone was so excited for me to wake up?"

"I don't know," Rodric said. "I mean—I don't think so. Not anymore. Of course, it's good that you're here. Fifteen different people have been king since you fell asleep, not including your father. Fifteen, in the past eighty years. My father tries his best, but it's not easy to keep the throne secure. So with you here, and me . . . it looks promising. It's more than that, though. It's . . . I don't know how to explain it." He stared at the ground, as though the answers hid among the stones. "I guess . . . people think that things were right when there was magic. And then there wasn't any. Except you, and you were far out of reach. And ever since you fell asleep, everything has gone wrong. Like things were right before you were cursed, and everything fell apart as soon as you pricked your finger. There used to be enough food, and now the weather is terrible almost every year, and nothing grows. People used to feel safe, and now they're terrified that someone else will claim the throne, that Vanhelm will threaten us, that Falreach will march across the mountains again . . ."

"They found a way across the mountains?" She had pored over the eastern maps herself, trying to imagine what it would be like to climb through the snow, to be utterly alone in the wilderness.

To be the first and only person to figure out a way across.

"They did. Although their last attack was many years ago."

Many years ago, but long after the world Aurora had known, where Falreach was a foreign, faraway place that could only be reached by sailing around the mountains, not a threat powerful enough to march across them. It took such an effort to communicate with them that few people ever did. When letters did travel across the sea, they always smelled of roses and honeysuckle. According to Aurora's mother, the court of Falreach had so many nigh contradictory rules of etiquette that a child had to be born there to ever understand them properly. When ambassadors for other kingdoms visited, they said the court would ridicule them in ways so subtle that it took them years to understand the intent. "My mother was from Falreach," Aurora said. She had always been jealous of her mother, her ability to leave her home and travel to somewhere entirely new. It seemed Alysse-like somehow.

"My mother is too."

"She is?"

Rodric nodded. "I think—" He turned away, looking up at the bare branches of a fruit tree. "It is hard. People are still distrustful. Of Falreach, and everything to do with it, after the invasion. Everyone is stuck in the past here." He shrugged, then stood up straighter, as though forcing himself back into brightness. "But now—now you're awake, Princess. Things will start moving again."

"I am stuck in the past too," she said, almost in a whisper. "Or . . . stuck here." She looked down at her feet. Her shoes seemed too bright and soft against the solid stone path. Her parents had feared the future, every second of every day. They let its possibilities control every part of Aurora's life, and all for nothing in the end. "I miss my family," she said. The words hung in the air, weak and useless, unable to capture even half of what she meant.

"I'm sorry," he said, so quietly she almost did not hear him. He was still looking away. "But—but you have a new family. With me." Another sigh, as though even he was aware of the uselessness of his words. Then a nod and a smile, even more decisive for the hesitation moments before. "You're going to tie things together. Old and new."

"Do you believe that?"

He looked her in the eyes. "It worked, didn't it? You woke up. Why wouldn't the rest of it be true?"

Not a shred of it seemed true. What did Celestine care for other people's happiness? No, Aurora could not believe it. Those promises had been invented in the years since her curse, and they would provide comfort, it seemed, to everyone but Aurora herself.

"You're wanted in court, Princess," Betsy said as she came into Aurora's room that afternoon. "Prince Finnegan has just arrived at the castle. He gave no notice or anything. The queen does not look happy."

"Prince Finnegan?" Aurora put down her book. "Who is he?"

"He is the prince of Vanhelm, Princess," Betsy said. "He hasn't been here for a couple of years at least, but now he's turned up out of the blue. It must be something to do with you."

Vanhelm. The land of Alyssinia's ancestors, many hundreds of years ago, before the steel and smoke drove them over the sea.

"What is he like?" Aurora asked as she stood up.

"I've never spoken to him, Princess," Betsy said. She began adjusting the pins in Aurora's hair. "I hear he's quite handsome."

The door swung open, and the queen strode into the room. Her hair seemed even more intricate than normal, with pearls woven into the braids that covered the top of her head. She pursed her lips when she saw Aurora. "Good," she said. "You are ready. We cannot keep the prince waiting." The queen looked rather rattled; the extra effort she had put into appearing digni-fied only increased the effect.

"The prince traveled far," Aurora said carefully as the queen steered her through the corridors. "Vanhelm is several days' journey across the sea, isn't it?"

"Yes," the queen said. "He must have been in Alyssinia already when he heard the news."

A hush fell over the court as Aurora and the queen walked through the brass doors. The queen settled in her throne, and gestured Aurora to a spot beside her.

Rodric entered the room through the door behind the

thrones. He smiled at Aurora, and she smiled back. Then he stopped to the left of his father's seat, a perfect reflection of Aurora's own stance.

"Enough of this waiting!" the king said. "Where is that prince?"

"I am here, Your Majesty. Just waiting for your word."

A young man with jet-black hair marched into the room. Dashing had always seemed a description that only applied to rogues and pirates in stories, men who swung swords and romanced girls with quick words and an impossibly good heart, yet the word fit this man perfectly. Handsome, oozing confidence, with green eyes that seemed to sparkle with delight. He seemed utterly convinced of his own attractiveness.

He knelt on the ground in front of the king. "It is wonderful to be here again, Your Majesty," he said. "I trust you are well?"

"Oh, none of that ceremony," the king said, waving Finnegan up with a sweep of his hand. "We're all old friends here." But if he did not want any ceremony—if he did not want Finnegan to kneel before him—why had he called them to court at all? He wanted Finnegan to kneel, Aurora realized. He wanted to show that he was the one with the power to toss propriety away.

Finnegan, however, did not seem concerned. His black hair tumbled across his eyebrows as he stood. He brushed it out of the way. "I hear that Alyssinia has had quite some good fortune."

"Indeed it has!" the king said. "Indeed it has, my lad. I know you were hoping for a similar blessing, but—well, I guess Rodric is just more of a man, eh?" He gave a booming laugh, as though he was teasing, as though it was all in good fun. Finnegan smiled in a good-natured sort of way, but Aurora noticed that his eyes had a hard glint to them.

"I am afraid we were not expecting you," the queen said. "So soon after the happy event occurred. The wedding is not for three weeks yet. You find us quite unprepared."

"I apologize, my dear Iris," Finnegan said. "I was hoping to arrive in time for the awakening ceremony, but we were delayed by rough seas. Once I heard of Rodric's success, I knew I could not wait until the wedding to give my congratulations and meet the famed princess for myself."

"Of course," the king said.

"We are blessed to have her," the queen said.

Finnegan fixed Aurora with an intense look. "It is a pleasure to meet you," he said. He walked toward her, took her hand, and pressed a kiss to her knuckles. "You are even more beautiful than they say."

Aurora bobbed into a curtsy, her head bowed. Finnegan's smile grew.

"So courteous too. What a delight." She got the strange feeling that he was mocking her. His eyes roved over her, and she fought the urge to step away.

The queen also seemed to have noticed Finnegan's gaze. "It is truly lovely to see you again, Finnegan," she said, "and I hope we will dine together soon. I trust the servants will make you comfortable until then? You must want to rest, after your journey." It was spoken like a dismissal, but Finnegan continued to smile.

"I always find that travel energizes me, especially when a long-lost princess is waiting at the end of it. I was rather hoping I could dine with you and the princess today. What better time to make up for one hundred lost years?"

The queen inclined her head. "I appreciate your enthusiasm," she said, "as does the princess, I am sure. But she is still rather overwhelmed after her own journey, and we are run off our feet with plans for the engagement ceremony in a few days. We so wanted to be here to greet you, but we cannot linger. You understand."

"Oh, yes," Finnegan said. He grinned at Aurora. "I understand perfectly."

The queen stood and offered Finnegan a slight inclination of her head. Aurora sank into another curtsy, executing the perfect sweep of her skirts. Finnegan's eyes followed the movement closely.

"Insufferable man," Iris said as she marched Aurora away from the room. "Stay away from him as much as you can, Aurora. He has expressed too much interest in you already."

"Stay away from him? Why?"

"That prince cannot be trusted."

"He's your guest," Aurora said as Iris steered her into another corridor. "If he is untrustworthy, why is he here?"

"Do you think we can trust half of the people here at court? Of course we cannot. And we need Finnegan appeased. He and his kingdom have too much power by far. But you must remember, for all he says, he has no interest in you. Only in what he can gain from you."

"Like you, you mean?" Aurora said.

The queen stopped. "No," she said. "We are trying to keep you safe. Keep the kingdom safe. So if you want to leave your rooms again, I suggest you listen to what I have said, and keep your impertinence to yourself."

Aurora refused to look away. She was going to have to fight to build her place, but not here, not where the queen could see. "Yes, Your Majesty," she said.

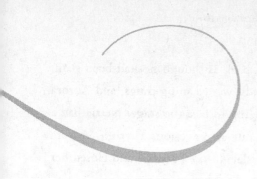

SEVEN

SHE WENT TO THE DANCING UNICORN AGAIN THAT night, her heart pounding in time with her footsteps.

The inn was full of people laughing and dancing. One large group of girls about Aurora's age held hands and danced together near the stage. A couple of young men lingered near their circle, but they could not get a glance from the girls. The inn's more sedate patrons sat farther away, gathered around tables and packs of cards, their conversations as loud as the music.

Tristan was leaning over the end of the bar, chatting to a group of older women. One of them raised a hand and slapped him lightly on the cheek, a coyly pleased "oh stop" kind of gesture, and Tristan reeled back as though he had been slain, grinning all the while. Trudy was cleaning mugs, and Aurora sank onto a barstool, swiveling to face the stage. Nettle had a band behind her, beating out an infectious rhythm. Aurora curled her toes around the slats of the barstool and closed her eyes.

"So," Tristan said, sauntering across to her behind the bar, "you're back."

"I said I would be."

"A girl who keeps her word," Tristan said. "I like that."

She smiled.

"You know," Tristan said as he wiped down the counter with a cloth, "it is customary on the second visit for new patrons to tell their story. Who they are. Where they're from."

She wrapped her toes tighter around the slat, pressing into the wood. "I'm not very interesting," she said. "I wouldn't want to put you to sleep when you're supposed to be working."

"Liar," he said, and he smiled again, like they were the best of friends. "Everyone's got a story. I see you sitting here, crazy blonde hair, covered in dust, and I think, wow, what a strange thing she is. She must have secrets worth discovering."

"I'm sorry to disappoint you," Aurora said, "but I've been told never to tell secrets to strangers. Maybe if you told me more about yourself, I'd be able to share."

"You already know who I am," he said. "Tristan, remember? But perhaps I can dig up some other stuff. If you insist."

"I do."

"Then let's see." He continued to clean, head tilted as though deep in thought. "First thing you should know about me is that I was born an orphan. Sounds impossible, I know, but it's true. I spent my early life alone, scrounging food from the streets of Palir, until a group of traveling acrobats took me under their metaphorical wing."

"Traveling acrobats?" She rested a hand on his arm, mouth open in feigned shock. "Not the famous acrobats of Palir?"

"The very same. Have you ever seen them, Mouse? They can spin twenty times in the air and land on their noses, all while singing folk songs of yore. A more impressive sight you'll never see. I, of course, became their star performer."

"Of course," she said. "Why lie about being an acrobat if you can't be the best?"

"Exactly," he said. "People would travel for hundreds of miles to see my signature move."

"Which was?"

"It can't be described with words, Mouse."

Aurora smiled. "Then I'd love to see it."

"Better not. Nell wouldn't be too happy if I kicked one of her customers in the head, and I'm all out of practice."

"How surprising," Aurora said. "Why did you stop?"

"I never intended to. But one day, when we were traveling to a distant land to perform, our ship was set upon by pirates."

"And they didn't appreciate your performance?"

"Strangely, no. They press-ganged us into service, and no number of backflips could change their minds. Luckily, I got on pretty well with them, once the ice was broken. I've got natural talent for more than just acrobatics, so it wasn't hard to move up through the ranks. It wasn't long before I was captain of the ship."

"Lead acrobat and captain of a pirate ship," Aurora said. "That's a lot of adventure in . . . seventeen years?"

"Nineteen," he said, "although you're right. I've spent the last two years here. Life on the high seas got tiring after a while. I blame the seasickness. So I decided to come to the capital and make an honest living for myself." His elbows landed on the bar with a thud. "So. Think you can beat that?"

"Of course I can. You see, my secrets are true." Aurora leaned forward, resting her own elbows inches in front of his. "I was born a princess," she began, "in a far-off land—"

"At least try to make it plausible."

"Like your pirate tale?"

"Exactly."

"I was born a princess," she said again, "but I was cursed by an evil warlock at birth. I must always wander the land, he said, never resting, never finding comfort, until—"

"Let me guess. You find true love?"

"Who's telling this story?"

"Well, me, by the looks of it," Tristan said, but she glared at him, and he lowered his head with an unrepentant grin. "Fine," he said. "Continue, please."

"Until," Aurora went on, her thoughts scrambling over every fairy tale she had ever read, "I find the answer to his impossible riddle."

"Which is?"

"I don't know. He never told me. That's why it's impossible."

"Perhaps," Tristan said, tilting forward so that his forearm brushed hers, "the lack of a riddle is the riddle itself. How do you solve a riddle that has not been asked?"

Trudy walked up to them, a tray in her hand. "You don't have to talk to him, you know," she said to Aurora. "I never do."

"Trudy finds my charm so completely overwhelming," Tristan said.

"I find your annoyingness so completely overwhelming. You've got things to do."

"Yes, Prudence."

"I'm serious, Tristan. A little help at some point would be nice."

"I'll help," he said. "I promise. Just—not right now. Okay?" Trudy glared at him, but then her expression softened.

"Soon," she said. "Or I'll leave all the cleanup to you."

"Yes, ma'am."

She shook her head and walked away.

"So," Tristan said, after she had gone. "Did you ever find the answer to the riddle?"

"Not yet."

"I wouldn't worry about it," he said. "Fairy tales seem full of rubbish to me. Better off being a pirate."

"I'll keep that in mind."

They fell silent, and the clear, quavering notes of Nettle's song wrapped around them like smoke. Aurora closed her eyes again, letting the sounds seep into her skin, words of love and hope and a joy so close you could almost taste it.

"She's really something, isn't she?"

Aurora opened her eyes. "It makes me sad."

"It's a happy song!"

"I know," she said. "It makes me sad all the same." She ran her fingers through her hair, but Tristan grabbed her hand before she had more than a second to muse.

"Well, we'll have to put an end to that," he said. "Trudy, mead please!"

"You work here too, you know," Trudy said, but she brought over two mugs of mead anyway. Tristan pressed one into Aurora's free hand and then raised the other in a toast. They clinked mugs and drank deep. Warmth settled in her belly, and she smiled. Even with all the jokes and lies, she felt part of something here, like she actually belonged.

"You know," she said slowly, "I haven't seen much of the city. I could use a guide."

"A guide?" he said. "And where would you find someone like that around here?"

"Well," she said. "I was hoping maybe you would show me. Sometime. If you don't mind."

"Sounds like a plan," he said. He dropped her hand and

hurried around the end of the bar. "Let's go."

"Now?"

"No time like the present."

She glanced over at the far side of the room, where Nell, the inn's owner, was chatting to customers. "Don't you have to work?" Now that she had what she wanted, she felt a little jolt of fear. She shouldn't go out alone with this boy, this stranger she knew nothing about. But a guide, a real guide, to show her the city as he saw it, show her the things that a royal escort would never show her . . . she could not say no to that. She could not say no to the way her heart was beating faster, the thrill of doing something that was so certainly forbidden.

"They won't miss me," he said.

"But Trudy—"

"She's joking," Tristan said. "And besides. I'd much rather spend time with you." He squeezed her hand, standing impossibly close. "Come on, Mouse. Don't you want a little adventure?"

Five minutes later, they were walking out of the pub, cloaks pulled tight around them.

"So," she whispered. "Where first?"

"I know just the place. Follow me."

He led her along the cobbles. A few people shouted greetings and comments at him as they passed, and he laughed and shouted back.

"Who's the girl?" one of them asked, as they turned onto another street.

"She's new in town," Tristan said. "I'm just showing her around."

"I'm sure you are, Tristan," the man said, and Tristan waved at him before striding on. He turned down a narrow path, and soon they were hurrying away from the crowds. The streets tumbled over one another, forming a crisscrossing, twisting, looping labyrinth that made Aurora's head spin. Gradually, the cobblestones faded away to beaten earth. Voices leaked through the gaps in the walls, but soon there were no lights at all, not even the glow of a candle through an open window, nothing to show the way except the gleam of the moon. Aurora reached out and clutched the back of Tristan's cloak, bunching the rough cloth between her fingers. "Don't worry, little Mouse. I won't lose you."

"Don't you dare."

His hand found hers. "Come on," he said. "We're nearly there."

The city walls loomed ahead. Aurora stared at them, watching the lights that flickered above the stone. She pulled her head back farther, trying to see the sky beyond, and almost tripped over a girl who was huddled against one of the buildings. Aurora could see the hollow shadows of her face in the moonlight. The girl looked up at Aurora reproachfully, but she did not even blink as Aurora rambled her apologies.

"Who was that?" Aurora asked as they moved away. "Why was she sitting out here in the dark?"

"Oh, nobody," Tristan said. "They built the city walls decades ago to keep the riffraff out, but, much to the king's surprise, they keep existing! So they sweep them out to the north edge here. Don't want them dirtying up the doorsteps of the good part of the city, now, do they?"

"Why do they come here?" Aurora asked. "If they're mistreated, then why—"

Tristan scowled, and when he spoke, he sounded almost angry. "Where else are they supposed to go? People think it's safer to live near the king. Invading armies don't tend to burn your house if you live here. Of course, rioters can do the job just as well, and these people don't exactly have houses to destroy. But even picking off the streets, there might well be more food here than outside the walls."

Aurora glanced back. The girl was already out of sight, but as they continued through the streets, she saw more faces, more shapes in the dark. One alley held so many people that they formed a single mass in the shadows. Aurora could only tell where one person ended and the next began by the way they shifted as they spoke.

"Someone should do something about this," she said. "Help them."

"But no one will." Tristan shrugged, but there was an edge to his voice. "Which part of the city did you say you live in now, Mouse?"

"Not near here."

"Shame," Tristan said. "It's such a lovely place."

They continued to move closer to the walls, weaving around wooden buildings that slumped together as though unable to stand up unaided. "Where exactly are we going?" Aurora asked as they turned into another raggedy alleyway.

"There's a lot to hate about this place," Tristan said. "So, before it gets to you, I thought I'd show you why it's worth staying." He stopped in front of a low, crooked house, on a street so dark that she could barely make out the shape of him beside her. The quiet hum of voices filled the air. "Now this," he said, "is the hard part. You're not afraid of heights, are you?"

She thought of her tower, of leaning out of the window, high above the world. "No," she said.

"Good. Watch this." With a scrape and a spring, he was gone, vaulting up into the air with the grace of a cat. A moment later, his face peered over the edge of the roof.

"Reach up and jump," he said.

She raised her hands and groped the air above her. The edge of the roof was barely in reach, slightly sharp against the inside of her knuckles. She strained onto her tiptoes, and her fingers scratched across the roof tiles, digging into one of the seams. She jumped. Her feet scraped the wall, struggling for a grip on the stone, and her arms ached from the effort. One hand slipped, and Tristan gripped it at the wrist, pulling her up and over.

"Okay?"

Aurora laughed. Adrenaline chased through her. "I'm on the

roof," she said. She was only a few feet off the ground, but she felt tall, impossible, powerful.

"I know," Tristan said. She could hear the amusement in his voice. "This way." They scrambled over the tiles, climbing higher and higher still. The buildings formed a giant's staircase, each roof in reach with a jump, a grab, and a jab of fear. Tristan crouched as he walked, slow and steady, each step precise. Aurora stuck close behind him, following his movements, feeling her way with the soles of her feet.

"Here should do it," he said. They stood on a small square roof, sloping down from a point in the center. "You can get around half the city this way, but this is the best spot. And I'd hate to take you the dangerous way. Little mouse like you might fall to her death."

"I'd hold my own."

"I don't doubt it." He grabbed Aurora's hand and sat down, pulling her with him.

She yelped. They were very far off the ground. "Tristan! Careful."

"I won't drop you. Look." And he stretched their arms outward, skin meeting skin, their hands pointing far into the city.

Lights. Hundreds and hundreds of lights, so many that the city glowed, casting glimmer and shadow over sloping roofs and weaving roads. Up ahead, frozen in the night, was the castle. The base of it glowed too, but the lights faded as it stretched upward, until finally, at the very top, Aurora's own tower stood, so dim that it seemed to melt into the sky. The moon loomed large overhead.

"Pretty good, huh?"

"It's beautiful." She slid her legs down the roof until they were hanging over the edge, swinging in the chilly night air. She still clutched Tristan's hand in her own. His heartbeat brushed against her skin.

"When I first moved to Petrichor, I missed everything." His fingers tightened around hers. "My home. My family. I'd never been to the city before, didn't even know Trudy, and I was going crazy with how loud and busy and insane it all was. So I started climbing on the roofs. It's a good place to think. Up here, the city doesn't seem so bad, you know?"

The wind caught Aurora's hair. It tickled her cheeks and tangled in her eyelashes. "Why did you leave home?"

He sighed and let go of her hand. Her fingers felt cold in his absence. "Why did you?"

She let her hand fall to her side and gripped the edge of the roof. "I didn't choose to."

He was quiet for a long moment. "Me either," he said.

They sat in silence for a while. Aurora's feet dangled in the cold air, the wind nipping at her ankles. While she had slept, the world had shifted and lit up like the stars. Tristan was right. This place was brutal and cold, but there was something beautiful, something wild, in the brick and stone. She looked behind her, wanting to follow the glow all around the city, to see all of this place that had swallowed her whole. A few specks of light peeked out of the darkness. The city walls stood watch, and beyond them, only shadow.

"What's over that way?"

He turned too, following her gaze. "It's just the forest."

"The forest?" Of course. Not everything was gone. She twisted until she was flat on her stomach, head propped on her elbows, her whole body pointing toward the darkness. "Have you ever been there?"

Tristan twisted with her, and then they were lying side by side, staring at the trees they could not see. "Of course I have," he said. "I wasn't born here, was I?"

"Oh," she said. "But since then? Since then, have you been?"

"Not in years," he said. "It's not the most inviting of places."

There was a taste of the world she knew, just beyond the walls. "Let's go," she said. "Now."

He laughed. "Are you crazy? Even I don't have that much of a death wish."

"Why?" she asked, the word rushing out of her. "Why is it crazy?"

"Because we have no way to get out, and no way to get back. Not without being seen. Not without breaking our necks. And of course," he added, when she didn't reply, "there are the ghosts to think about."

"Ghosts?"

"Ghosts," he said. "And monsters. Werewolves. Trees that

come alive and grab at you as you try to sneak past."

"Liar," she said. "There aren't any monsters."

"Oh really?"

"There are only bears. And wolves. And the occasional lion. But no monsters. Don't tell me you're afraid of them?"

"You're mad, Mouse. Completely, utterly mad. And yes, to answer your question. I don't fancy becoming supper for some ravenous beast."

She pressed her chin down into the palms of her hands and closed her eyes. "I'm not mad," she said. "It's just . . . it's somewhere I'd like to go. It reminds me of home."

"Do you miss it?"

"All the time. But . . ." She opened her eyes. Even in the darkness, she could see the outline of his face, the slight frown that curved his mouth. She shrugged. "There's no going back now."

"My parents are dead." He spoke so bluntly, so matter-of-factly, that it took Aurora a moment to realize what he had said. "That's why I had to move here. Why I live in an inn. I'm guessing that you're not particularly surrounded by family either."

She shook her head, unable to form the words. *My parents are dead.* It was too horrible, too undeniable, to say out loud. She sucked in a breath and let it out slowly, trying to blow away the tightness in her chest. They sat, silent except for their breathing and the occasional sound of life below.

"Does it get any easier?" she asked, after so much time had

passed that she was sure he had forgotten their conversation.

"No." The word fell heavy in the air, but it wasn't sad. Painfully, bluntly honest, but not sad. Aurora let the word roll in her mind, relishing its plainness. "It doesn't. But—I don't know. You find other reasons to live."

The lights flickered below them. With her eyes fixed on the forest, she reached out and grabbed Tristan's hand. For a heartbeat, he paused, and then he squeezed tight, his thumb tracing shivers across her skin.

EIGHT

"PRINCESS?" A HAND LAY ACROSS HERS. "PRINCESS, it's time to wake up."

Aurora dragged her eyes open, blinking in the bright light. Betsy stood in front of her, dark curls frizzing wildly around her face. "Princess, why are you sleeping here?"

"I was reading," she said. "I must have fallen asleep." *The Tale of Sleeping Beauty* lay open under her elbow, balanced precariously on the arm of the chair. The paintings of her mother and father smiled up at her. She tried to sit straighter, and her shoulder ached in protest.

"Oh, Princess, you must get some proper rest," Betsy said.

She placed her breakfast tray on the table nearby. "I worry about you. Sometimes you look like you never sleep at all."

"I've already slept more than I'll ever need to," Aurora said. She forced a small smile.

"But you still need real sleep, if I may say so."

"I'm adjusting."

Betsy put a plate down by Aurora's side. "At least you can eat." Aurora picked up a jam-covered roll and took a tentative bite, letting its sweetness fill her mouth.

"Where are you from, Betsy?" Aurora asked as the maid turned away to the wardrobe. "If you don't mind my asking."

"I don't mind," Betsy said. "But it's not very interesting. I was born in Petrichor. My mum has worked in the castle for as long as I remember—she worked for the old king, before that guard killed him. I didn't work here then, though. But my father, he was a blacksmith, and when he died, my mum moved us both here. Best place to be, she says, long as you keep your nose out of people's business and do what you're told." She blushed. "But you probably didn't want to know all that."

"I do," Aurora said. "I want to know. Is it—your mother didn't think it was safe outside the castle?"

"Well, my dad, he was killed during a riot a few years ago. Not everyone likes people with ties to the royal family, and he did work for them, shoeing the horses and the like. But where else could we work, except here? Better to live inside the walls and eat well and stay safe, than try to be in both worlds at once, out there and in here. Or so my mum says. Don't get me wrong, the people are good here, in the city and in the castle. But as I'm sure you've heard, Princess, it hasn't been the best of times while you were asleep." She turned back to the wardrobe. "How about the blue dress today?" she said. "I think it will look lovely for spring."

Aurora nodded.

Betsy fidgeted as she arranged Aurora's hair, taking the same pin in and out several times, as though uncertain what to do. "I have to tell you something, Princess," she said eventually. "The queen asked me to lock your door at night. For your own protection. You—you understand that, don't you?"

Of course, the door had been mysteriously unlocked for the second morning in a row. After the previous day, Betsy was sure to have double-checked the lock before she left for the night. But she did not sound accusing or reproachful. Just . . . warning. Concerned. Aurora felt a jolt of guilt. But she could not stop sneaking out now, not when she still had so much to see. Not when Tristan was waiting for her. "Yes," she said. "I understand."

Half an hour later, after Aurora was dressed and Betsy had left for her other duties, Rodric positively bounced into the room. A grin filled his normally pained, blushing face, and everything about him, from the tips of his hair to his footsteps on the stone floor, seemed to laugh in excitement.

"I had a thought!" he said, as though this were a rare and

celebratory occurrence. "I think you'll like it. I—" He looked at her face, and he paused. "Are you all right, Princess? You look tired." There was that distinctive pink flush again. "Not that you don't look lovely," he said. "You always look lovely. Even when you are tired. But you do look tired, Princess, if you don't mind my asking about it—"

My name isn't Princess, she thought, and suddenly she felt tireder still. But what was the point in explaining? "What was your thought?"

He hesitated, all the excitement lost in the moment's interruption. "It's a silly idea, really," he said. "I understand if you don't want to."

"I'm sure it will be wonderful," she said. "What is it?"

He smiled again, if a little cautiously. "Would you like to come and see my sister?"

Rodric's sister. Aurora knew nothing about her, except for that brief glimpse of a young girl, soon after she awoke. "Yes," she said steadily. "All right." When Rodric continued to look unsure, she added, "That would be nice."

"She might not say much," Rodric said, "but I know she'd be excited. She's read your story many times. It's one of her favorites."

Of course. Even now, she was to be paraded about. *Come and meet her for a gold piece. Gain affection from your siblings with her strange delights.* What if, after years of appearing in the girl's storybooks, she was a disappointment?

Rodric knocked on a door on the far side of the castle, several floors above Aurora's own. Beyond the wall, Aurora heard a rather stern, pinched-sounding woman pause in her lecture. Rodric eased the door open.

"Mrs. Benson," he said. "I am sorry to trouble you. I wondered if I might speak with Isabelle for a moment."

"We're in the middle of a lesson," Mrs. Benson said. "With all due respect, your sister's education is of the utmost importance—"

"I thought," Rodric said, "that the princess and I might take her into the gardens. Only a short break. I wish my—I mean, I wish for the princess and my sister to become acquainted with each other."

"Please!" said a soft, high voice from inside the room. "Please, Mrs. Benson. I'll concentrate hard afterward, I promise."

The woman sighed. "All right," she said. "But be quick about it. And don't you even think of getting your new dress dirty, young lady."

"I won't!" the girl said. "Thank you!"

Feet scurried across the floor, and then a small girl ducked around Rodric. Isabelle had brown hair, pinned at the back and then running straight down to her waist. Her face was thin, like her mother's, but she clearly also had her brother's propensity for embarrassment. When she saw Aurora, she stopped so suddenly that she might have hit an invisible wall. Her cheeks went from freckled and pale to a glowing, painful crimson in the space of a blink. She stared up at Aurora with huge, deerlike eyes, and when she bit her lip, Aurora saw that her front teeth crossed over slightly.

"Hello," she said. "I'm Aurora."

Isabelle nodded.

"This is my sister, Isabelle," Rodric said. "Isabelle?"

The little girl jolted back to life. She sank into a curtsy, bowing her head, letting her hair fall delicately forward over her face. It was a move Aurora had practiced herself many times in her life. Only Isabelle's shaking knees gave her inexperience away.

"You don't need to curtsy to me, Isabelle," she said softly. "It's lovely to meet you."

Isabelle stood up straight. She was still biting her lip.

"Come on," Rodric said. "Let's go to the garden."

They walked in silence, Rodric in the middle of their little group. Isabelle stared at the floor, her face still burning, tripping slightly over the long, tangled skirt of her dress. Every few seconds, she glanced sideways at Aurora through her eyelashes. Aurora pretended not to notice. She couldn't stop picturing this shy, blushing, proper little girl, bent over her storybooks, staring at paintings of Aurora, absorbing every detail. Each glance was an impossible evaluation. Did Aurora's hair curl like in the pictures? Was her smile as bright as Isabelle had hoped? Was she as sweet and kind as the stories had always said?

When they reached the door to the courtyard, it rattled

under Rodric's hand. Locked. "Oh," Rodric said, and there was that damned blush, like every little trip-up was a dreadful reflection on his character. "Sorry. I guess I didn't think—I'll go find someone with the key. Sorry."

He hurried away, leaving Aurora and Isabelle alone with the guards. The moments dragged past.

"You're very pretty," Isabelle said, so softly that Aurora almost didn't hear her.

"Oh," Aurora said. "You're very pretty too."

Isabelle shook her head so that her hair whipped from side to side. She sucked her lips over her slightly protruding teeth, hiding them from view.

"I mean it," Aurora said. "I think you look lovely."

"Mother says a princess has to be perfect," Isabelle said.

"Nobody's perfect."

Isabelle stared, her eyes earnest and intense. "You are."

For some reason, the assertion made Aurora feel unbearably sad. She bent her knees until her eyes were level with Isabelle's. "Nobody is perfect," she repeated. "I do all sorts of things wrong." Everything, if her mother's criticisms were to be believed. "I never put things away neatly. I'm terrible at talking to strangers, although I find," she said, "that a smile helps hide it." Isabelle's lips twitched. "I'm so bad at pinning my hair that one time I stabbed myself in the eye, and I play the harp so poorly that it sounds like a cat is singing. I crease down the pages of books, even ancient ones, where they're all yellowed and crinkled. I write in them too. And—" She paused. Past tense. She had done these things. Once. She had given herself these imperfections, locked away in her tower. Now her problems felt quite different.

"I crease the pages too," Isabelle said. "For the best bits. I—I read all the time."

"Me too." At least, she had. Once upon a time.

"Mrs. Benson says stories are silly," Isabelle said. "She says they aren't real. She says I should learn history instead."

Aurora thought of all the stories she had devoured, the histories, the fantasies, the hundreds of worlds and lives and adventures she had seen and lived and breathed while locked in that circle of stone. "If they're real to you," she said, "then they're real."

"Like yours," Isabelle said. "Yours was true."

Rodric returned with a key in his hand and a small, deep-green cloak hung over his arm. "Don't want you to get cold," he said, and he draped the cloth over Isabelle's shoulders and fastened the clasp with hands that looked well accustomed to the task. He held Isabelle's hand with one of his own and unlocked the door with the other. It swung open with a click.

Rodric and Isabelle stepped ahead, their feet firm on the path. Everything in the garden seemed still and orderly, tightly under the queen's control. Aurora followed a few paces behind.

Silence surrounded them. They walked deeper into the garden, and then, suddenly, Rodric dropped Isabelle's hand. "Race you to the apple tree!" Isabelle yelped and began to run, her small legs pounding the ground, her skirts flapping and tangling around her legs. Rodric lumbered behind her, running with exaggerated effort. Isabelle's hands slammed against the tree trunk, and she leapt with delight.

"You cheated!" Rodric said.

"Did not," she said. "You're just slow."

"I am not," Rodric said, and he swept his sister up in his arms, spinning her around. "You're just a cheater." Both of them laughed as he twisted her upside down. Her hair tumbled down, pins falling loose as she squirmed. He set her down on the ground, and she turned and ran toward him. He ran too, ducking behind the tree.

"Isabelle!" The queen's voice cut through the air. Aurora looked up. The queen stood by one of the windows on the second floor, glaring down at the scene. "Stop that nonsense at once. A princess does not behave like that."

Isabelle's smile vanished. Her lips parted slightly, revealing her large front teeth, and tears gathered in her eyes. She did not let them fall.

"Is Princess Aurora running and making a fool of herself?" the queen continued, and Aurora blushed and squeezed her hands before her. No, she thought. She was not running. Years of training had crushed the impulse well enough. But she did not want to be an example for the end of Isabelle's fun. "Show some propriety."

Rodric and Isabelle walked slowly over to Aurora. "We had better return you to Mrs. Benson," Rodric said to his sister. "She might worry. And I am sure the princess has other things to do."

The protest stuck in Aurora's throat.

Isabelle pressed a hand to her scalp. Pins were still tumbling left and right.

"Here," Aurora said softly. "Let me fix that."

She knelt behind the girl, repositioning the pins without a word. When she had finished, every hair looked perfect.

After lunch, Rodric led Aurora to the queen's chambers on the fourth floor of the castle. It was an airy suite of rooms, separated from the rest of the castle by guarded doors and connected by a private corridor that overflowed with flowers. *Honeysuckle,* Aurora thought.

The door to one room was ajar. The king, queen, and about twenty courtiers were gathered inside, some women chatting with the queen over their embroidery, others playing games with cards and stones. A plush red rug covered the floor, while paintings hung on every wall, depicting wild creatures and nobles at their feasts.

"Rodric!" The king had been talking to an older man, but he stepped forward when he saw the prince enter. "You finally joined us. Come here, come here. I was telling Sir Edward about your great victory. Maybe you could add in the details." Rodric glanced at Aurora, but the king laughed before he could speak.

"You two have had all morning together. Surely the princess can entertain herself for five minutes. She can spend some time with the ladies."

Rodric gave Aurora a bobbing bow and hurried to his father. Aurora hovered in the middle of the room, watching the women as they sewed. "I received a letter from dear Theodora this morning," one of them was saying. Their needles wove in and out of the fabric while the ladies barely glanced down. "Poor thing says she is sick."

"Nothing serious, I hope?" the queen said. She looked at Aurora, and the message was clear. Sit here.

Aurora began to walk toward the group. Then she sensed someone standing close behind her. She turned. It was Prince Finnegan.

"Princess Aurora," he said. "You look a little lost."

"I was deciding where to sit."

"A difficult choice," Finnegan said. "There are so many excellent options."

"What are you doing with our princess, Finnegan?" the king said. "Don't try to sweep her away, now."

"There will be no sweeping, I promise you that," Finnegan said. "But who could resist getting to know a girl so beautiful?"

"She is a gem, to be sure."

"Come on," Finnegan added to Aurora. "Join us for a game of cards. Alexandra has won the past four rounds, and we really need someone to intervene."

A girl with thick black curls laughed. "I can't help it if none of you know how to play."

"See how overconfident she has become?" Finnegan said. "Help us to defeat her."

"I'm afraid I won't be much help," Aurora said. "I don't even know the rules."

"Then I'll teach you. It's all very simple. I'm sure that a clever girl like yourself will pick them up in moments." She glanced up at him. Something about that phrase, "a clever girl like yourself," made her feel like he was poking fun at her. Subtly, politely, but a jab she was supposed to notice nonetheless.

"I have always heard that the skill of the student reflects the talent of the teacher. In your capable hands, I am sure I will be winning within the round."

"Excellent," he said. He pressed a hand into the small of her back and steered her to the group of card players. "Someone fetch the princess a chair."

A wooden chair was deposited beside Finnegan's, and Aurora sat. Another man Aurora did not know was gathering the cards. He shuffled them with hand movements so quick that they all blurred together.

"Alexandra must deal," Finnegan said. "Since she won the last fifty rounds. The princess and I will share a hand, so I can teach her how to play."

Alexandra plucked a card from the top of the deck and placed it faceup on the table. "The unicorn is the red four," she said.

"Shall we play with the hunter this round?"

"No, let's keep it simple," another woman said. She had straight brown hair flowing over her shoulders. "As it's the princess's first game."

Aurora would have thanked her for the consideration, if she had not suspected that this was the same woman who had called her "not quite bright" on the day she awoke.

"Considerate as ever, Carina," Finnegan said. "Shall we begin?"

The cards flew into piles around the table as Alexandra dealt. "The rules are straightforward," Finnegan continued. "On your turn, you can choose to take any single card from any player. If you have any matching pairs in your hand, you put them down. Whoever finishes the game holding the other unicorn"—he gestured at the red four in the center of the table—"is the winner. Trickery is, of course, encouraged."

"What kinds of trickery?"

"Anything you can get away with," Finnegan said. "If you're caught cheating, you must do a forfeit. But only if you're caught."

Aurora picked up her hand and spread the cards into a fan. The unicorn was not there.

Finnegan leaned over her shoulder, his fingers brushing hers as he rearranged their cards. "We have much to talk about," he murmured. "But we cannot say it here. Soon."

She forced herself to keep looking at her cards.

"Who has the two of clubs?" one man said.

"I do," said a woman with a brown braid hanging over one shoulder. She looked around, taking in all the expressions of her opponents, and then plucked a card from Alexandra's hand. "Seems like a safe bet, considering how many other games you've won," she said.

Cards moved back and forth quickly between players.

"Did you hear about what happened the other evening, down by the south gate? The road was barred, debris set on fire. I believe a few guards were injured." Carina laid a pair of cards on the table and gave a dramatic little shudder. "My husband told me they're concerned a rebellion is brewing again."

"Rebellion?" The man beside her laughed. "Don't be silly, my dear. A few bad-tempered peasants do not a rebellion make."

"Oh, let's not talk about such dreadful things," Alexandra said.

"Alexandra is of the opinion that if you don't think about something, it does not exist," Finnegan said. "I'm surprised there's anything left in her world at all."

Alexandra gave a high-pitched little laugh. "Oh, Finnegan," she said. "You're too cruel." She continued to smile, but her eyes looked furious.

The player to Finnegan's right shifted forward. Aurora caught a glimpse of her cards. No unicorn there.

"So," Finnegan said in her ear. "Who do you think has it?"

She glanced around as people battled over cards. She had little experience in reading people's faces. But Alexandra, she noticed, kept glancing left and right. Her chair had crept back a couple of inches, as though she was trying to get a better view of other people's cards. "Alexandra doesn't," she murmured back. "She's trying to find it."

"Anything else?"

She looked around again. "The man in the green cravat," she said. "He isn't paying attention to the cards he takes. It's as though he doesn't care, because he already has the one he wants."

"Perhaps," Finnegan said. "But unfortunately, that's just Andrew. He cannot lie, so he prefers to leave it up to chance."

"You two are quite off-putting with your whispering," Carina said. "I feel like I'm the subject of a plot. It makes me highly suspicious of both of you."

"She's on to us," Finnegan said in a stage whisper. "How will we hide?" Everyone around the table laughed. When play had moved on, he leaned even closer to Aurora's ear. "She has it," he said. "She's trying to keep a blank face, but every time someone takes one of her cards, she glances at the one two from the left. Just a flicker of movement, before she can stop herself. There's our unicorn, I promise you."

"And how do you know that isn't an incredibly advanced bluff?"

"Because, Aurora," he said. "I know."

Almost all the cards had disappeared by the time Finnegan reached out to take the suspected unicorn. He slipped it into Aurora's hand without a word. It was the red four.

As the turns moved on, he reached forward as though to consider their three remaining cards. With a flick of his finger, he slipped the unicorn behind another so that it could not be seen from the front. Aurora shifted her fingers so that it slid farther left.

When Carina moved to take it back, she took the wrong one.

Andrew dispatched the final pair of cards, and Aurora placed the unicorn on the table, smiling.

"A shame," Finnegan said. "The whole court beaten by a beginner. I think I'm going to enjoy having this one around."

Aurora fought back a frown. He had won the game, not her.

"I'm tired of this game," Carina said. "Why don't we play something else?"

Alexandra looked at Aurora. "Do you know any games, Princess? What did you used to play, before you came here?"

"Oh yes, something old-fashioned!"

"I am afraid," the queen said, "that Aurora will have to teach you another day." She stood behind Aurora's chair, although Aurora did not know when she had appeared. "I simply must steal her away to my embroidery table. We have a lot to talk about."

"Another time, then," Finnegan said.

The queen nodded her assent. "Come along, Aurora," she said.

Aurora stood up and followed her across the room. "I warned you to stay away from him," Iris murmured as soon as they were out of hearing. "Do not allow him to reel you in."

"We were only playing cards."

"Yes, well. Finnegan never *only* does anything. He has his motives, trust me."

The women glanced at them over their embroidery as they approached, but they offered little more than smiles and nods. The queen gestured at an empty chair and then sat down herself. She picked a piece of rough cotton off the table and passed it to Aurora.

"Practice on this, my dear," she said. "We will measure your skill and see where it can be put to use."

"I don't know how," Aurora said softly as she took the needle and cloth into her hands. A blush crept across her cheeks. "Needles . . . I wasn't allowed . . ."

"Then it is time you learned," the queen said. "You don't have to worry yourself about pricking your finger anymore, after all."

The needle felt cold and thin between her fingers. "That is true, Your Majesty."

"See if you can stitch your name," she said. "We can all guide you once we see your mistakes. Curses don't last forever, dear."

Aurora plucked at the material, trying to slide the needle through the cloth. The fabric snagged, and she pulled harder, keeping her eyes low. The women resumed their talk of courtiers and potential wedding guests, and Aurora dug the edge of the needle into the pad of her finger, rubbing it back and forth. It was too blunt to do more than dig a groove in her skin.

She glanced at the card table, now absorbed in another game. Finnegan had moved seats, so he faced her and the queen. He watched her over the top of his cards, an eyebrow raised.

She turned her attention back to her cloth, but she could still feel his eyes on her, long after she looked away.

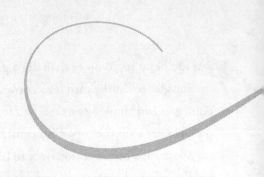

NINE

WHEN AURORA GOT TO THE DANCING UNICORN that night, Tristan was leaning against the wall outside the entrance, weaving a coin between his fingers. He smiled when he saw her approach. "Mouse!" he said. "You're here. Thought you were going to be late."

"Late for what? Standing around?"

"Better. You know about the night fair, the one on Market Street?" He held the coin between his thumb and forefinger like a symbol of triumph. "After I got back last night, Dolores decided to tip me extra well. Happy to see me with a nice girl, she said. Wanted me to be able to do something special." He grinned and flipped the coin in the air. "Who am I to refuse an old woman? So—want to go?"

Of course she wanted to go. But Aurora tilted her head, as though considering the offer. "I'm not sure," she said. "What's this night fair?"

"It's fun," he said. "Or as close to fun as you can get, for something in the fancy part of town. Jugglers and fire-eaters and fortune-tellers and music . . . I think Nettle's performing there somewhere."

"Don't you have to work?"

"Nope! Got the night off. Thought Nell wasn't going to give it to me after we ran off yesterday, but she's got a soft heart. That and I promised to do extra dish duty for a week. So, shall we?" He offered his arm. Aurora linked her elbow with his.

"All right," she said. "Lead the way."

They took a different route from the night before, weaving through the alleys until they stepped out onto crowded streets. The castle towers peeked over the rooftops. As Aurora and Tristan moved forward, they got swept up in the crowd, the rhythm of their feet, every step dictated by the people in front and behind.

The road opened into a wide square that was thick with people. Market stalls lined both sides of the street, lit with lanterns and draped with colored cloth. Paper garlands hung between the trees. The air was a jumble of noise, people laughing and shouting, running on the cobbles, arguing with the stallholders, singing and bickering as they went.

"Is it like this every night?" Aurora asked.

Tristan laughed. "Of course not. One night a month, they close the whole street down. Full moon festival."

"Full moon festival? Sounds a little witchy to me."

"That's the idea," Tristan said. "All in honor of the princess. I guess they thought this racket would finally wake her up. It was a pretty good excuse while it lasted."

"Does it need an excuse?"

"I hope not. Otherwise they'll have to come up with another one."

The market tables were full of impossible, wonderful things: reams of cloth, small brass figurines, bowls and shawls and neck-laces that gleamed in the lamplight. One stall was piled high with books, tattered old leather volumes and bunches of paper held together with string. They were piled so haphazardly that they looked as though any movement would send them tum-bling. One section had already collapsed into a mountain of books, spines facing in every direction. A woman rummaged through it, pulling them out almost at random, glancing at the titles, then setting them on top. Aurora leaned closer, her fingers itching to leaf through the pages.

Tristan followed her gaze. "You like books?" he said.

"Yes," she said. "I do. Do you?"

"Not overly. My dad taught me to read, said it was important, you know? But I don't come by many books these days. I'm kind of rusty."

"Best way to get better is to practice." She squeezed between other people's shoulders until she reached the table. She grabbed the first book off the pile, leaves of paper bound with string. *Devious Dan and the Treasure of Arak*, the title read. A few of the pages had come loose.

"I loved those when I was younger," Tristan said. "When I could get my hands on them, anyway."

"I've never heard of it."

"You've never heard of Devious Dan?" Tristan pressed his hand over his heart as if in shock. "He's only the most adventurous man in all of Alyssinia. There are, what, fifty books about him? A hundred? I thought you liked to read, Mouse."

"I guess I never came across them." She flicked the book open. The text inside was roughly printed, smudged in places, with crude outlines of drawings on a few of the pages. "He has adventures?"

"Lots of them. I had a set of the books back home, would always buy them when I had a spare penny. But I lost them. When I moved here."

Aurora held the book out to him. "You should buy it," she said. "Relive the adventure. Put that money from Dolores to good use."

Tristan shook his head. "I'm too busy having my own

adventures now," he said. "But I can buy it for you if you want. My treat."

"I couldn't possibly," she said, but her fingers curled tighter around the pages.

"Yes you could," Tristan said. "It'd be easy." He held up the coin. "Excuse us," he said to the shopkeeper. "How much for this one?"

As Tristan bargained over price, Aurora pressed the book against her stomach, a smile spreading across her lips.

"Thank you," she murmured, after money had changed hands and the pair of them had stepped away. "Really. You didn't have to do that."

"I did," Tristan said. "Can't have you deprived of a good story, now, can we?"

They kept walking, Aurora clutching the book tight. Musicians played on street corners, and groups of dancers performed to the beat, flipping in the air and whirling with ribbons as crowds of people watched. Aurora and Tristan paused at the edge of one group, watching a man balance on top of a long, thin pole. He began to juggle huge clubs, and the audience applauded.

Up ahead, a band stood elevated on the edge of a stone fountain, singing and beating out a jaunty rhythm, while dancers whirled in a circle around them.

Aurora bounced on the spot at the edge of the square, her heels rising and falling in time with the drumbeat.

"Want to dance?" Tristan asked.

She had never danced in her life. She had practiced a little, moving around her tower in slow motion while her mother dictated the steps, but never around other people, and never dancing like this, people spinning without any order to their movements. "I couldn't," she said, but Tristan was already pulling her forward, slipping into a gap in the crowd. A girl gripped Aurora's hand, their fingers meeting around the curled-up book, and she was swept into the circle, skipping, almost running, her legs tangling with strangers'. Hands released, and bodies twisted together and apart, spinning on the spot, Tristan's grip firm on her waist. Then another stranger grabbed her hand, and they were dancing in a circle again. Aurora's hair flew about her face, and all the colors of the street blurred together, the greens and browns of the clothes, the orange glow of the lamps. There was an ordered kind of chaos to the steps, movements dictated by the music and the will of the crowd, and Aurora closed her eyes, letting it sweep her along.

They spun until they were dizzy, and then Aurora pulled Tristan away, stumbling out of the square, laughing so hard that her side ached.

"I need a break," she said, between gasps for air.

"Can't keep up?"

Tristan's hair stood up in five different directions. Aurora batted one piece down. Her heart was still racing from the dancing, the world around them streaked with color and light. She felt like they had spun away from the rest of the city, like she could do anything and it would mean nothing, wouldn't have any consequences tomorrow. She looked at Tristan, and he looked back, all flushed and out of breath, grinning his stupid grin.

Aurora darted forward and kissed him.

His eyes widened, but as quickly as she had done it, Aurora jumped back. She bit her lip. Tristan's eyes followed the movement, but before he could lean closer again, she skipped away, giddy with her own boldness, but not quite bold enough to try again. She giggled. "Come on," she said. "We have to find Nettle."

They continued down the street. In the distance, Aurora heard Nettle's voice, weaving through the crowd. Her song was softer, slower, barely noticeable over the shouts and the clatter of footsteps on the streets. She stood on a makeshift stage in a square, performing to a small crowd. Her black hair was held away from her face with a pin in the shape of a butterfly, and she swayed as she sang, strands of hair escaping to curl around her chin.

Aurora pulled Tristan's hand until they were in the square, lost in the crowd, only feet from Nettle herself. Gently, Tristan tugged her closer, pressing his free hand into the small of her back.

Blood pounded in her ears, and his eyes gleamed in the dim light. She let go of his hand and raised her own, letting it skim along his shoulder before settling at the nape of his neck. Downy-soft curls brushed her skin, and she wrapped one around her finger.

His breath tickled her ear. She felt light-headed, so she closed her eyes, letting the music flow through her. Tristan's hand tightened against her back, and they swayed together.

The song shifted, and he leaned even closer, so that his lip brushed against her earlobe. When he spoke, his words were so quiet that she felt rather than heard them. "Are you ever going to tell me who you are, Mouse?"

Her heart pounded so forcefully that she was sure he could feel it. She shook her head, and he sighed against her skin. "Didn't think so."

She swallowed and squeezed her eyes tighter. The moments were slipping through her fingers like grains of sand. She wanted to say something, to entrust some secret part of herself to him, before it all tumbled away.

She pressed her face against Tristan's neck. He smelled of smoke and sweetness. She rose up on her tiptoes, until her nose traced the top of his ear. "I'm lost," she said.

Nettle continued to sing, words of longing and heartache. Aurora held her breath, and Tristan smiled against her cheek.

"Me too," he said. "Maybe we can be lost together."

TEN

AS SOON AS AURORA RETURNED TO HER ROOM, SHE curled up in her armchair and opened her new book. The story turned out to be as terrible as it was addictive. Devious Dan stole and swashbuckled his way across the kingdom, jumping from one danger to another with only his dagger and his wits to protect him. His enemies cackled and the girls swooned as Dan dodged peril after peril on his hunt for legendary treasure. Reading it, Aurora couldn't stop picturing Tristan as a ten-year-old boy, devouring the adventures at an impossible speed. Was this what had inspired his story of piracy and acrobatics?

His lips still seemed to linger against hers, all the excitement of the night captured in one fleeting moment. She did not want to sleep. She wanted to cling to the memory, to enjoy the way her heart still pounded. She wanted to read the book again and think, *This is Tristan's, too.*

When Betsy opened the unlocked door the following morning, she paused for a long moment, staring at the ground. Then she closed it softly behind her and crept over to where Aurora sat. "Princess," she said. "I know I am only your maid, so I hope you don't think I am speaking out of place. . . ."

"You're not *only* my maid, Betsy," Aurora said. "You're not *only* anything."

Betsy nodded. "The thing is—if someone has been unlocking your door, you must tell me. It's important. I don't know whether you're aware of it happening or not, but I'm worried for you."

"Please don't worry about me," Aurora said. "It's just sometimes—it's stifling in here at night. I like to walk the corridors. The guards are always nearby."

"Even so, Princess. It's dangerous for you to walk around alone."

Aurora wanted to promise her that she would stay put, that of course she would be safe. But the music of the night before still hummed in her ear, the pressure of Tristan's hand brushing against her lower back, and the words stuck in her throat. She needed to see him again. She would go mad, trapped here.

"Anyway, I'm glad you're awake," Betsy said, turning aside. "Prince Finnegan has requested breakfast with you. I thought maybe you could wear the gold dress, with the ribbon? It will look lovely on you—"

"Finnegan wants to eat breakfast with me?" After being berated by the queen for even playing cards with him, she had assumed she would not see much of him again.

"So I've been told. Isn't that exciting?" Betsy pulled a dress out of the wardrobe and brushed down its skirts.

Aurora bit back a smile. "You think spending time with Finnegan is exciting?"

Betsy blushed. She shook out the dress once more, and then scurried over to Aurora, holding it in front of her. "Well . . . he is very handsome, Princess. Not as lovely as Rodric, of course, but . . . handsome."

"Perhaps you should go instead. You seem far more excited than I am."

"Oh, don't be silly," Betsy said. "I wouldn't know what to do. I wouldn't be able to say a word."

"Now *that* I don't believe."

Betsy giggled. "No, no, Princess, I'd clam right up," she said. "So it's lucky it's you and not me who's got the pleasure. Now breathe in while I lace this up."

The queen strode into the room half an hour later. She ran an appraising eye over Aurora, from her cinched-in waist to the wide skirts that swallowed her feet. She nodded. "Come along. Prince Finnegan is waiting."

"I thought you didn't want me speaking with him."

The queen frowned. "Betsy, you are dismissed." The maid curtsied and scurried out of the room. Once the door closed behind her, the queen spoke again. "You would question me in front of a servant?"

"I think I have a right to ask," Aurora said. "Yesterday you warned me to stay away from him. You told me he was dangerous. And today I'm to eat breakfast with him as though we're the best of friends?"

"No," the queen snapped. "Not as though you are the best of friends. As though you are diplomatic allies. Which is what you are. Finnegan has requested a breakfast with you, and as he is our guest, we can hardly refuse him."

"But—" *You're the queen*, she wanted to say. Surely she could refuse whoever she pleased.

"Must you protest everything I say?" the queen said. "Come along. The sooner you go there, the sooner you can leave. And be on your best behavior. Do not treat him with the same impudence with which you treat me."

The queen shepherded her into a small, cozy room on one of the lower floors of the castle. Finnegan stood by the fire, staring up at a painting, unattended by guards. He smiled when he saw them approach.

"My dear Iris! It is wonderful to see you again. And Aurora." He bowed. "Thank you for coming to meet me this morning. I so very much wanted the chance to speak with you again."

The queen forced a smile. "One of my attendants will be outside if you need anything," she said. "I shall have breakfast sent to you momentarily." The prince bowed graciously, and, with a warning look at Aurora, Iris was gone.

"Now, isn't that better?" said the prince as soon as the door closed. "I cannot stand that woman."

She stared at him. She felt the sudden urge to defend the queen, even though the words were ones that she herself had thought.

"Oh, don't tell me you like her," he said. "She's such a miserable old bat. I don't think she's spoken a true word in her whole life."

He was confident to the point of cockiness, smug in his grin and seemingly delighted with every blunt word he spoke. *A lady is polite,* she told herself. It had been her mother's first rule: politeness could get you anything.

"Iris means well," she said eventually. A blush crept across her cheeks. "She has been a great help to me."

"She means well?" He laughed. "Is that the highest praise our dear Sleeping Beauty can muster for her?" He leaned back against the table, hands gripping it on either side. "You are a terrible liar, Aurora. Even that simple one has set your face on fire."

"I may be a bad liar," Aurora said, "but I can read people, the same as you. I won our card game yesterday, remember?"

"You did," he said. "With a little assistance from me. What a team we make." He pushed himself back to standing. "It has been too long since we were last alone."

"Since we were last alone?" she echoed.

He nodded. "Summer of 668 by Alyssinia's reckoning, my eighteenth birthday. One kiss, but you didn't seem to like it." He tilted his head. "I hope you find I improve with age." When she did not reply, he added, "See, you do not even remember. I am hurt, my lady."

"Well, you know," Aurora said, "I have kissed so many men. Few stand out." The words felt dangerous on her tongue, but she would not listen meekly while he taunted her with smiles.

"But were all of them as handsome as I?"

"I do not recall."

"The cruelty of unrequited love." He sighed. "I remember you, of course. I had never seen one so beautiful."

"Are the women so very ugly where you come from?"

"No," he said. "They are all pictures of elegance. But mere weeds compared to your beauty and wit."

"You flatter me."

"Is it working? Are you ready to abandon Prince Rodric and run away with me? Oh, the adventures we will have."

Aurora paused, thrown off the rhythm of their banter, and he laughed. "I forget myself, Aurora, of course. You love Prince Rodric. You are destined to live happily ever after and have many golden children to repopulate the throne."

She looked away, embarrassment and annoyance tensing her muscles. "If you've asked me here to mock me—"

"Mock you? What an insult to poor Rodric. I was simply describing the dream."

A knock on the door saved Aurora from replying. Finnegan moved to open it. A maid stood on the other side, with red hair falling around a pale, freckly face. She clutched a tray of tea and pastries. "I brought breakfast, my lord. If it pleases you."

"Oh it does, Sylvia," he said. "Bring it in, bring it in. Such a lovely girl like you shouldn't be kept hovering on the doorstep."

The maid blushed from the roots of her hair to the tip of her nose. Finnegan's eyes followed her as she placed the tray on the table and bobbed into a curtsy.

"Do you always hound all the girls?" Aurora asked as soon as the maid was gone.

"Only the lucky ones." He sank into an armchair in front of the tray. "Come. Eat breakfast with me. Normally a shared breakfast would imply something quite different, but I am willing to let it slide. Eat. Tell me about yourself."

She did not move. "I am sure you already know all about me."

"From the stories? My mother always told me, 'Don't believe everything you hear in fairy tales.' I'd rather get my information from the source. Why do you think I'm here? The chances of Rodric awakening you seemed slim, but I made sure I was close by, just in case. I wanted the opportunity to meet you as soon as I could." When she did not sit down, he added, "If you do not wish to tell me your story, perhaps you could tell me mine. I would love to know what an honest girl like you thinks of me."

"I barely know you."

"Oh, drop the princess act," he said. "We were having such fun earlier. Why go cold all of a sudden?"

She frowned. "I think you are ridiculous and arrogant," she said. "Some prince from some foreign land trying to mock and humiliate me for fun."

"Go on. First impressions are important."

"You're frivolous and disrespectful, and I don't know why Iris wanted me to meet with you."

"See? Isn't the truth much nicer? Trust me, Iris thinks the same, and if she had any choice, I wouldn't be here. But she doesn't." He took a bite out of a bread roll. "I'm too important to ignore. And when you're that important, you can do what you like. A lesson you don't seem to have learned. Or are you not as important as they claim?"

She forced herself to maintain a neutral expression and slipped into the armchair across from him, her chin pushed high. "I am myself," she said. "You can tell me whether that is important enough."

"That would be difficult," he said. "You haven't told me a word about who you are. If you want me to understand the real you, it'd be a great help."

"I'd rather not."

"Fine. Then I'll see what I can come up with on my own."
He leaned forward, and his eyes swept over her skin. "You're fed
up," he said. "You're forced to act all meek and lovely, but you
have fire in you, and brutality too, I bet. You want adventure.
The others say no, but you—you want something more. Am I
close?"

She swallowed, struggling not to look away. "You don't
know what you're talking about."

He raised his eyebrows. "Lies really do not become you."
He took another bite of bread, and the tension between them
dimmed slightly. Aurora looked down at her hands, clutched in
her lap. "You'd like Vanhelm," he said. "It's nothing like here.
Only a little sea between us, and our worlds are so very different. Our buildings tower, Aurora, in a way that puts your castles
to shame. While you sprawl out over this land, we build up into
the sky, squeezing into tiny spaces, the ones the dragons tend to
leave alone."

"Dragons?" Her breath caught. Dragons were the creatures
of books, of legends and dreams from long, long ago. They had
not existed for as long as Alyssinia had existed—possibly longer,
for who could tell if the myths had any truth in them at all?

"Oh, yes," he said. "You didn't know? One day, fifty years
ago, they awoke. Rather like you. They came out of the mountains and burned half my kingdom to ash. Why do you think
your king and queen fear us? If we ever figure out how to tame

the creatures . . ." He grinned. "Does that excite you, Aurora?"

Creatures of legend, ones that should never exist, living and breathing across the sea. Of course it excited her. "Why?" she said. "How did they wake up?"

"No one knows. Would you like to find out? If you came with me, we could make quite a story of it. None of this fairy-tale nonsense. Heart-pounding danger, and a bit of fire."

The worst part was that his offer sounded tempting. Just leave. Leave Prince Rodric and responsibility, run and see everything she had never seen. She felt a surge of anger, furious at him for intriguing her, furious at herself for feeling intrigued. "Are you so intent on seducing me?" she said. "Or is it that you are so inept you need to bring in fantastical beasts to sway me?"

"Is it working? My mother would be most pleased if it did. We share ancestors, you know. That's why I'm here, as fun as teasing you might be." He moved closer. "Unworthy men have ruled Alyssinia since your father died. My family has a much better claim. We want to unite the two kingdoms, bring some of our advances to this backward realm, find some new land to build on. With you back, of course, things change somewhat, but if you wished for such an alliance . . ."

"You mean, if I betrayed my people."

"*Betrayed* is such a harsh word," he said. "If you support King John, we can learn to live as things currently are. We all want to help such a lovely fairy-tale darling. If, however, you ever have any doubts—"

"I support him," she said as quickly as she dared.

"Your face gives you away. You will need to start wearing a mask, if you want to be more convincing."

She stood up, her food untouched. "Is there anything else you wish to say to me?"

"Even when storming off, she is polite. The offer is there, Aurora. Come with me, and you will have your kingdom and your adventure, too. Alyssinia is a starving backwater of a land. I can make it better. And you would be able to leave. I know that appeals to you, whatever you might say."

"You think you can trick me into betraying my kingdom with a few winks and a handsome grin?" No matter how uncomfortable she felt in these walls, she suddenly knew how lucky she was to get a humble boy like Rodric instead of an arrogant man like this. A man who thought he understood everything with a single glance and could say whatever he liked without consequence or care.

"Of course not," he said. "But I can't help but notice: you speak of Alyssinia, but nothing of your supposed beloved." He stood up and reached for her hand. "You have given me much to think about. Thank you for meeting with me." He pressed hot lips to her fingers in a whisper of a kiss. "I am sure we will see each other soon."

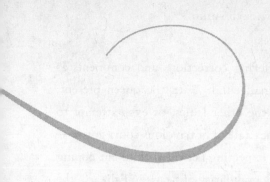

ELEVEN

AURORA SPENT THE AFTERNOON EMBROIDERING
handkerchiefs with the other women of court. The dullness of
their chatter left her plenty of opportunity to repeat Finnegan's
words in her head, to dwell on his subtle insults and invent the
perfect retorts. He had been so presumptuous, so overconfident,
like he expected Aurora to swoon at his feet and took her refusal
to do so as a particularly challenging delight. Every time she
remembered his smug smile, her anger bubbled up again, stronger than before.

The queen sat so close to Aurora that their elbows brushed
together each time she pulled her thread, and she watched the

princess's every stitch, offering corrections and comments as though Aurora were a small child. With the queen present, Aurora could not talk to the other ladies, or even attempt to enter the conversation. They talked of frivolous court gossip—how Lady So-and-So was expecting her third child but hoping to return to court, the new popularity of pearls in Falreach, the trouble that Young Whatshername was having finding a suitable maid. Topics changed without any apparent care for what the topic itself might be.

Iris must have known Finnegan was plotting to take the throne. Why else would she have warned Aurora away from him? Either she did not believe Aurora was safe with Finnegan, or she did not trust Aurora to resist whatever charms he was convinced he had.

She pricked her finger on her needle and gasped. The queen frowned at her. Aurora sucked the blood away, earning her a deeper frown.

Finnegan had offered to whisk her away, as though she were sitting and waiting for him to save her. He thought she would hide in his kingdom, stage a war against her own people. That she would put herself in debt to an arrogant prince who might well be her enemy, just so she could escape.

If she wanted to leave, she had another option. Tristan. A thrill ran through her at the thought. Vanishing into the inn, joking with Tristan, listening to Nettle sing, drinking mead and kissing him and never worrying about duty ever again.

She stabbed her needle through the cloth.

Tristan's kiss lingered on her lips. If she closed her eyes, she could still see the lights spinning around them. She could still feel his hand in the hollow of her back, so close it had seemed he would never let go.

In the end, it was all just a fantasy. But she would cling to it for as long as she could.

Aurora practically ran to the Dancing Unicorn that night, dizzy with nerves about seeing Tristan again. The inn was quieter than she had expected, but Tristan was there, wiping down the bar. For once, he wasn't smiling. He looked up almost as soon as she slipped in through the door, and he hurried over without a word to anyone. "Mouse," he said. "You're here." He rested a hand on her upper arm, and then looked over his shoulder. "I need to talk to you."

"I want to talk to you too!" she said. "I finished the book last night. You have to tell me what happens to Belinda. Is there more, or—"

"Now's not the time, Mouse. Come on."

He set off across the room, weaving through the crowd. Aurora followed. "What's wrong? Is this about last night?"

"No, not that," he said. "We just need to talk. But not here."

He grabbed a lamp from a table and led her through a door behind the bar into a messy storeroom, piled high with kegs and jars. Aurora could smell the alcohol in the air. The seemingly endless stock left little room to stand. He placed the lamp on the windowsill at the end of the room, casting glow and shadow across the floor. Then he turned to face her.

"I have to tell you something," he said. "But you can't tell anyone what I'm about to say. Not anyone."

The lamplight bounced off the side of Tristan's face. "All right," Aurora said. "What is it?"

"You have to promise," he said. "If you tell anyone, it won't be safe for any of us. Do you understand that?"

"Yes," she said. "I promise. Tell me."

He let out a breath. "I'm part of a movement," he said. "A group of people who aren't happy with the way things are. We want to change things."

"A movement?" she said. "You mean you're part of the rebels?" She glanced at the door. Her heart thudded against her ribs. Iris had warned her about rebels in the city. People who would be willing to tear her apart if they could. Aurora had never thought she meant Tristan.

"*Rebels* makes us sound like the enemy," he said. "We're not like that." He gripped her hand. "You've seen it, Mouse. You haven't been here long, but even you've seen it. How hungry people are. How cruel the king is. How he's shoved those who need help out to the edges of the city."

His hand seemed to burn against her skin. She swallowed. Her thoughts leapt too quickly for her to process them. "And you're trying to help them?"

"We're trying," he said. "I'm not sure if we're succeeding. We'd been making progress, more people had been willing to listen to us, but then . . . well. Things changed. With the princess."

His grip on her hand was too tight. "Why are you telling me this?"

"Because I trust you," he said. "Because I know you'll understand. And if you support us . . . things have been looking bad, but with you on our side, we'll have a chance. A real chance."

Aurora stepped back. Her lower back thudded against the doorknob. "You know who I am."

Tristan didn't move. "Yes," he said. "I know."

It wasn't possible. Her thoughts blurred together, struggling to pluck out anything she had said, anything she had done, that could have revealed the truth to him. "How?" she said.

"I've known since I met you," he said. "It wasn't hard to figure out."

She shook her head. "You didn't say anything."

"I'm telling you now."

She kept shaking her head, trying to grab on to her thoughts. "So you've been lying to me? This whole time?"

"I wasn't lying," he said. "If I'd said anything before, you wouldn't have come back. And I had to find out why you were here. I had to find out what you were up to."

"So that's why you've been spending time with me? Was all of this . . . was it just some game?"

"No," he said. "None of this is a game." He moved closer. "I didn't have to tell you the truth," he said. "But I wanted to. Because . . . because you're a good person. And because I care about you. And I know you'll want to help."

"Help?" she said. She tried to step backward again, fighting for some space to breathe, but the doorknob dug into her spine.

"I know you don't like the king and queen." His eyes gleamed. "I saw you, on that first day. You're not the sort of person who wants to marry some stuffy prince just because a story told you to. You're not going to want to stand there and act pretty and prop up every terrible thing they do." His words gathered speed. She could not look away from his face. "And that's all they'll do with you, you know. Make you a pretty little figurehead, until they have no more use for you."

"I know that," she said. "Of course I know that."

"Then this is your chance to change things. To fight them."

She couldn't think. The room was too small, and Tristan was too close. "Fight them how?"

"Just tell us what's going on in the castle, maybe speak to some people who might be sympathetic—"

"But why?" she said. "What do you intend to do?"

"Ultimately?" he said. "We want to overthrow the king."

"Overthrow him? You mean, rid him of his crown, arrest him, lock him up?"

Tristan did not answer.

Cold rushed through her. She slipped to the side, trying to

catch some air, but there was no space in the room, nothing but barrels and the smell of alcohol and him. "You want me to help you murder the king?"

"No," Tristan said. "It's not murder if he deserves it."

"Yes," she said. "It is."

"It's justice," Tristan said. "He's done so many terrible things, been responsible for so many deaths. He's the murderer. And killing him . . . killing him would be saving lives."

Aurora shook her head. It was too hard to breathe. "Sometimes kings have to make tough decisions," she said. "Sometimes criminals and soldiers die. That doesn't mean you can kill him."

"You have no idea what he's like, do you?"

"I know he's unpleasant," she said. "I know he's cruel. But—"

"He became king through murder. Did you know that? He convinced a guard to shoot the old king through the window with a crossbow, and then burned the guard on the castle steps for the crime." His voice was steady. He did not look away from her, not for a moment. Every word pierced her. "And then he killed all his enemies. All the troublemakers. Anyone who might claim the throne. He said that the reason we didn't have magic anymore was that a few people were hoarding it for themselves, making us suffer and starve. If we burned them, he said, their magic would be released back into the world. The princess would wake up. And within a year, anyone who might oppose him had been accused and burned, until everyone was either so convinced or so afraid that they could never stop him."

Aurora forced herself to look him in the eyes. A lump had gathered in her throat. "And then I woke up," she said. "So people think he was right after all."

"Yes," Tristan said. "That's why we need your support. If you speak out against him, more people will join us. And then he won't be able to stop us."

Nausea burned the back of her throat. "I can't," she said. "It's awful what he did, but—I can't. I can't help you murder him."

"It isn't murder," Tristan said. He gritted his teeth in frustration. Every muscle in his body was tense. His deep-buried anger was so clear, he practically burned with it.

"He did something to you," Aurora said. "Didn't he?"

"What does it matter?"

"It matters," Aurora said. "I'm right, aren't I?" *My parents are dead,* he had said. It was too awful to consider. But if what she suspected was true . . .

"I doubt there's anyone he hasn't hurt personally by now," he said. "But yes. Yes."

Aurora reached out, her hand resting on his wrist. "What happened?"

"He killed my parents." Tristan's voice was a hoarse whisper. "About five years ago. There was a bad winter; none of the crops grew. None except the ones my father owned. People in my village accused him of using magic and tore him apart. Literally tore him apart to get the magic out of him. And when my mother took me to the capital to ask for compensation, do you know what the king did? He executed her too, for working with him. And then he made me a servant in the castle, out of the kindness of his heart, so that I couldn't go wind up any more trouble." He pulled his wrist away. "And you're telling me he's fit to rule? I shouldn't want to get rid of him?"

"No," she said softly. "I would want him dead too, if he did that to me. But . . ." Everything in the room felt too close. "Killing him wouldn't make it right."

"It'd be a start."

She looked at the lamp on the windowsill. Lights burned across her eyes. "What will you do then?" she said. "Are you going to put Rodric on the throne? Or me?"

"We can't," he said. "If we do this, everything will have to change. People think you returned because of all the things he's done. If you become queen and save us, that's just proving him right. They'll remember him as a hero."

"So you want me to help you destroy myself."

"It wouldn't be like that. You wouldn't be a princess anymore, but you'd be so much more. More than their stupid little symbol. You could have a place here. You could have a life."

"I don't need you to give me a life. I can make my own." She closed her eyes, trying to shove back the anger rising inside her. She had to stay calm. "And what happens if you succeed?" she said slowly. "Who takes the throne then?"

"We have to kill him first," he said. "Then we'll work out the rest."

Her eyes snapped open. Disbelief burned inside her. "You don't have a plan? What if someone worse takes the king's place?"

"Anyone would be better than him."

"You can't believe that," she said. "You'd have to be stupid to believe that there couldn't be anything worse. There's always something worse." She stepped back, shifting toward the door, straining to increase the space between them. "I can't help you, Tristan," she said. "I can't be a part of this."

He clenched his fists. "So you're going to be selfish? Protect your own comfortable existence instead of helping?"

"That is not what I'm doing," she said. "But you haven't said a single word about the people. I thought you wanted to make things better."

"Getting rid of the king will make things better," he said. "You've got to get to the cause of the problems. Otherwise it won't make any difference at all."

"It's suicide, Tristan. For you and for the kingdom. You have to see that."

"I thought you would listen to me," he said. "I thought if I told you the truth—"

"I am listening to you," she said. "But you can't seriously mean this." The Tristan she knew was not a murderer. But, she was realizing, she did not really know Tristan at all.

"Of course I mean this," he said. "He killed my parents, Aurora."

"Don't call me that," she said. "Not now."

"Why not?" he said. "You're not Mouse, are you? The girl I thought I knew would care. Or would you prefer if I bowed and called you Your Majesty?"

She stared at him, taking in the fury on his face. "I guess you were wrong about me," she said. "I'm only a silly princess after all."

She tugged the door open, but he spoke again before she could move. "You're making a mistake. I won't be able to protect you."

She laughed. It wasn't funny, not really, but the idea that this was his parting message, half warning, half threat, that in the end it all came down to keeping her safe for others to manipulate . . . it was too painful to be serious. "I survived a hundred-year curse, Tristan," she said. "I don't need you to protect me."

She slipped through the door and let it click shut behind her. He did not follow her.

Outside, rain drizzled, forming a light mist along the alley. Aurora lingered in the doorway, her head buzzing. A customer bumped into her as he entered the inn, and she jerked aside.

Nettle, the singer, leaned against the wall. The slight overhang of the roof protected her from the rain. She looked willowy and angular, her long black hair falling over her eyes, her knees and elbows jutting out in points. She glanced across at Aurora. "Are you all right?" she said. Her voice was as smoky as when she sang, but it sounded slightly unnatural and as angular as her body, as though the words were sharp in her mouth.

"Oh," Aurora said. "Yes. I'm sorry if I disturbed you."

Nettle stood up straighter. "No," she said. "You did not disturb me. You look like you have had a shock." Nettle was watching her with barely a flicker of an expression on her face, as though merely commenting on the weather.

"I guess that's true."

"Tristan told you that he knows?"

Aurora stared, too startled to pretend she did not understand what the singer meant.

"You are surprised that I know too? Do not worry. I doubt any one else has noticed."

"Tristan noticed," she said. "Right away, he noticed."

Nettle tilted her head to the side. Tristan had described the singer as prickly, but that wasn't quite the word for the way she tossed her head, carefully pronouncing each word. She was aloof, but sincere, watching Aurora like she was a curiosity that had stumbled into her path and needed to be decoded. "I believe he found you hard to miss," she said. "The girl destroying all his hopes."

"I am not destroying his hopes," Aurora said. "I don't even know what I'm doing."

"Neither does he," Nettle said. "At least you are able to admit it." She sat. Her long dress darkened as it fell in a puddle, and her legs would be brown with mud by the time she stood, but Nettle either did not notice or did not care. She stared straight ahead, the picture of calm. "Will you sit with me? It is too cold and quiet out here to be alone, but I do not want to return inside just yet."

Aurora hesitated. But the singer was right. She did not want to be alone.

She sank down beside Nettle. The rainwater soaked into her skirts.

"Do you want to talk about it?"

"I don't know," Aurora said. "I just . . ." She stared at the wall across the alley, watching the way the rain trickled down the stones. She tightened her grip on her knees, pulling them under her chin. "Tristan said some things that . . . I don't know."

"He has a lot of bitterness in him," Nettle said. "He tries to hide it with jokes, but he is always angry. It is a dangerous way to be."

The sound of conversation from the inn hummed behind them, and the rain patted out a rhythm on her bare arms. "He's not who I thought he was."

Nettle continued to watch her. "You have known him—how long?"

The nights all blurred together, a mess of smiles and fear and mead warming her lips. "Four days, maybe."

"So. You meet a boy, and you imagine he is everything you want to find. Comforting. But now the real boy is fighting back."

"It's not that," she said. "He was keeping secrets from me. All the time, he was thinking . . ."

"But you were keeping secrets from him too, were you not?"

"It's different," Aurora said. "My secrets . . . I needed to stay quiet. It was the only way to keep me safe."

"Maybe he felt the same way."

"No," she said. "He made it quite clear that safety isn't the issue here, his or mine."

"Tristan is a fool," Nettle said. "He does not know what he means. He is so full of his own plans and ideas that he cannot see anything else."

Aurora rested her head against the wall, letting it scrape her scalp. The rain pattered out a rhythm by their feet. She needed to talk about something else, to shift the attention away from herself. "Is Nettle your real name?" she asked.

Nettle looked at her. A single strand of black hair brushed across her nose. "That is what I have told people to call me," she said. "Does that not make it my real name?"

"I'm sorry," Aurora said. "I did not mean to offend you."

"It takes more than that to offend me. But you must know that names do not mean everything." She shifted, pulling her right knee toward her chin. "It is not the name my mother gave me, nor a translation of it, although some people once told me otherwise. Boys like your Tristan, and yet not like Tristan at all. When I had only just begun traveling outside my kingdom, when I did not speak your language so well, they named me. Nettle. Like the flower that was my name before. They said it suited me. It was not until later that I found out what it meant.

They thought me a weed. Something unwelcome, to be torn out."

Aurora tilted her head to look at her. Her hair tangled on the stone. "Why did you keep using it?"

"You have seen flowers, have you not? Such delicate things. A rough hand, a strong breeze, the slightest frost . . . they die so easily. Even left to their own devices, they shrivel and die so quickly. But a weed . . . a weed is strong. Almost impossible to kill. And if someone tries to destroy a weed, it will hurt them back." She stood up, as abruptly as she had sat down. "Let me give you some advice," she said. "Don't trust anyone except yourself."

"Why do you say that?"

"I was you, once." Nettle shifted on her feet. From Aurora's angle on the ground, she looked disheveled, cold, and utterly beautiful. "People do not hear me in my songs. They only hear themselves. Selfish, self-centered, each thinking this is about me. This is about my life. And that is not a bad thing. But right now, I am not trying to tell you how you feel. I am telling you how things are. And the truth is that you must not expect others to be the way you would like inside your head. You must not let them in." Nettle turned to look at the open door. "I must return to sing. But think about what I said." She slipped inside before Aurora could reply.

Aurora rested her chin on her knees, shivering slightly. The rain had stopped, leaving a cool mist and sharp, fresh air in its wake. Soon Nettle's music laced its way out of the inn. She took a deep breath, then another, savoring the sting of hurt that nestled in her chest. She closed her eyes and soaked in the music, trying to make the moment last. She could not come back, she knew. But even now, Nettle's voice filled some emptiness inside her, and she did not want to let go. Not yet.

TWELVE

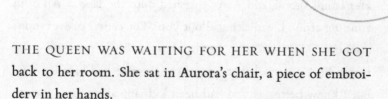

THE QUEEN WAS WAITING FOR HER WHEN SHE GOT back to her room. She sat in Aurora's chair, a piece of embroidery in her hands.

"I am glad you finally decided to rejoin us," she said. "Do close the door."

Aurora shut the door behind her and stepped farther into the room. How could the queen have known that she left her room? Had Betsy told her she was gone?

"I admit, I was curious," the queen said, and she placed the embroidery aside. The chair scraped the floor as she stood. "I wanted to be the first to see you when you returned." She sounded almost friendly. "Where have you been?"

"I went for a walk," Aurora said. "Around the castle."

"That is strange. I did not know it was raining inside the castle. And I do believe the door was locked."

"Somebody must have forgotten to lock it, Your Majesty."

"Do not lie to me, Aurora. It does not become you." The queen brushed her skirts, smoothing out invisible wrinkles. "Betsy came to me, after she returned to your room and found the door unlocked and you absent. She was most concerned."

Aurora wrapped her fingers in the folds of her cloak. "I am sorry if I worried you, Your Majesty."

"Worried me? Would you have liked that?" The queen reached for a crystal decanter and poured herself a glass of water. Her hands shook, and water splashed onto the floor. "All of us running around, panicking about you? The center of everyone's attention?" She took a sip, her lips pursed. "No. Your silly maid might have assumed that something terrible had befallen you, but I knew better. If you had been kidnapped by some vicious group of rebels, it would be unfortunate, of course, but something we could work with. You leaving your room at night and getting into all sorts of trouble . . . that is, I think, less acceptable."

"Less acceptable?" Aurora said. "You locked me in, like a prisoner. All I did was go for a walk."

"All you did? You could have ruined everything." The queen's knuckles were white against the glass. "I have told you that the world is dangerous. I told you that it was not safe. Do you think I say these things for my own amusement? I locked this door for your own protection, and you break through it, like it means nothing, like you know better."

The worst part was that the queen was right. Aurora had escaped from the castle, and the first person she met was a rebel. A boy who planned to kill Iris's husband, who attempted to recruit her. Her stomach twisted with guilt. "I'm sorry," she said. "But—"

"But?" The queen raised her eyebrows. "You should be begging my forgiveness, Aurora, not contradicting me again. You have a willful, stubborn, spoiled mind, and we do not have the time or space for your mistakes."

Aurora balled her fists at her sides. First Tristan, now the queen, treating her like she had no valid thoughts of her own. "If you think so little of me, why keep me here at all? If the idea that I was kidnapped is so much more convenient to you, then why even bother with me?"

The queen frowned, as though seriously considering the question. "I do not think little of you," she said. "You do not factor into things much at all. You may despise that, but it is the way of things." She closed her eyes as if in pain. "I know you think I am some wicked woman, forcing you to bend to my whims. But I am only trying to help you. You do not know what is best." When she opened her eyes again, she looked weary, her expression tinged with distaste. "This is not how I would have liked things to be. But we have no choice. You are going to have to listen to me, or you are going to suffer for it. Everyone will. For goodness' sake, Aurora"—and her hand slammed down on the table—"all you have to do is smile and curtsy. The people will fill in the rest! Why is that so difficult for you?"

"Are you asking me why it's so difficult to pretend to be nothing? To just be this blank little smiling thing? You don't know what it's like."

"I don't know what it's like?" The queen's laugh was like shattering glass. "I was living it before you were. Lost all your family? Far from home? I know what it is like, Aurora, so do not try the poor-soul act with me. Life is hard. We do not get what we want. We do not get to be who we want. And we have to deal with it. You think intentions are good enough for these people? You think anyone in this world cares what you meant to do?" The queen, usually so full of polite smiles and cold shows of affection, almost burned with intensity. "I have always been an outsider. But the people want to love you. Let them."

"I didn't ask for this." Aurora felt stupid even for saying it, but she could not stop the defiance in her from issuing a final plea. "I didn't want this."

"I did not ask to be queen," Iris said. "I did not ask them all to hate me, or to have you in my charge. Yet here we are."

"They hate you?"

"I am from Falreach," she said. "Of course they hate me. But things are quieter now. People have hope, for the first time in years. Do you want to destroy that? Do you want Rodric to be torn apart in the streets? Because I promise you, Aurora, people have suffered for too long. And if you fail them—"

"But what if they want more than I can give?"

"Well." The queen smiled her narrow, icy smile. "You had better give your all then, don't you think?"

Aurora turned to look out of the window. If things were as terrible as Tristan claimed—and she had no reason to doubt that they were—then she needed to help. Somehow.

"Luckily," the queen continued, "no one else knows that you were gone. Rodric does not know. John does not know. This is between you and me, Aurora. I am giving you that chance."

Aurora knew she should thank the queen, for that discretion at least, but the words would not come. Her limbs felt heavy and strangely faraway.

"The maid will be punished, of course, for allowing you to leave in the first place."

Betsy? She had never shown anything but care for Aurora. The queen could not punish Betsy. "But it's not her fault—"

"You are right. But I cannot punish you." She placed her glass on the table and stood up. "It will not be too arduous. But if you wish her to stay safe, I would not do anything so reckless again. Is that understood?"

"Yes." Aurora could barely hear the word herself.

"From now on, my own personal guard will stand outside

your door. You are not to leave unless accompanied. Whatever you may feel, it will not be worth the consequences if you disobey me again. Am I being perfectly clear here?"

Aurora forced herself to look Iris in the eyes. "Yes, Your Majesty," she said.

THIRTEEN

"GOOD MORNING, PRINCESS." BETSY LOOKED AT THE floor as she slipped into the room. Her hair was pulled back into a sloppy bun, and her normally rosy skin was blotchy. "I am sorry I am late."

"Betsy." Aurora stood up and hurried toward her. "I'm so sorry—"

"There is no need to apologize to me, Princess," Betsy said in a flat, steady voice. "I am only the maid."

"That's not true," Aurora said. Betsy still did not look at her. "I didn't mean for you to get hurt. I didn't think—"

"Prince Rodric will be here soon," Betsy said, as though

she had not heard her. "The queen wishes you to take a walk together. Which dress would you prefer to wear?"

"Anything," Aurora said. "It doesn't matter."

"I cannot choose one for you, Princess. Please make a choice."

Aurora stared at Betsy's back. One of the few people she could count as a friend here, lost through her own idiocy. "The green one," she said. "The green one is fine."

Betsy helped her dress and styled her hair in silence. Then she left with a small curtsy, still not looking Aurora in the eye. Aurora sat by her dressing table, braiding and unbraiding the ends of her hair. She should have been more careful. Betsy had warned her, but she had stupidly, blindly gone on. And for what? A few dances, a kiss in the dark? She had been a fool to trust him, and this was her reward.

"Are you ready for our walk?" Rodric said when he appeared half an hour later. "The garden is looking lovely today."

Aurora watched him, all stiff back and burning cheeks, as he bowed his way into the room. He was, she thought, rather sweet. He did not keep things hidden, like Tristan, or smile and flirt and manipulate, like Finnegan. It was a naïve sort of honesty, but honesty nonetheless.

Maybe, if she took Rodric someplace where she could be her old self, just a girl in a tower, waiting for the day when she would be freed from the curse . . . maybe then, she would feel more comfortable around him. "Actually, I was hoping we could go somewhere else," she said. "I want to show you something."

"Do you not like the garden?" Rodric asked. "I am not sure my mother would approve if we went too far. . . ."

"I do like the garden," Aurora said quickly. "I just—please. Let me show you."

Rodric gave her a small, tentative smile. "Okay," he said.

She strode down the halls, Rodric falling in step behind her. Aurora's heart pounded as she approached the heavy wooden door that led to the tower, seized by a fear she could not quite define. This place had been her prison and her escape, all at once. Frozen remnants of her old life were scattered through its rooms.

She climbed the spiral staircase slowly, pressing her feet into the worn carpet. She kept her eyes fixed directly ahead, trying to ignore the tapestries that adorned the walls. Rodric followed, not saying a word.

She paused one landing from the top. She could not go back into the bedroom where she had slept for over a hundred years. She did not want to look at the dust-free fireplace and still-rumpled covers, and think of how she had slept while the rest of the world continued on. Instead, she turned to another door: the playroom she had not entered for years, even in her own time. Its hinges were stiff from lack of use, and when she shoved it, a cloud of dust burst into the air. She stumbled forward with a hand pressed over her mouth, coughing.

"Princess? Perhaps this is not a good idea."

Aurora brushed a cobweb aside and peered into the gloomy room. "It'll only take a moment." Speckles of dust spun and danced in the beam of light that fell from the window. Beneath the decay of a hundred years, the playroom looked exactly as Aurora remembered it. A rocking horse waited in one corner, his mane tattered and worn, the glorious red saddle faded to a shade that was not really a color at all. Her old dollhouse stood by another wall, and wooden games and balls were strewn across the floor. Aurora picked her way through them, her skirts dragging and catching on the mess. Once she had made it across, she sat on the rocking horse, balanced sidesaddle, her toes brushing the ground. She rested her hand between his ears and closed her eyes tight, trying to imagine that she was six years old again, hidden away in this room for hours on end.

It smelled all wrong. The dust, the rotting wood, the neglect that clung to everything . . . it scratched her nose and the back of her throat, and she could not forget.

"Is this what you wanted to show me?"

Aurora opened her eyes. Rodric stood at the edge of the room, staring around with a mix of trepidation and curiosity on his face. "I guess," she said. What had she thought this would achieve? "I don't know."

"He's lovely." Rodric stepped toward her, his eyes fixed on the horse. "I wanted one when I was little—a rocking horse, I mean—but . . . well. My father wouldn't let me. He said I should be busy learning to ride a real horse. If I'd known one was here . . ."

"I never rode a real horse." Aurora ran her fingers through the remnants of his mane. It caught in knots, and she tugged her fingers free. "My parents didn't like me to leave the castle."

"Never?"

She ran her fingers through the mane again. "I visited the stables once," she said, "but when my father found out, he was furious, and it never happened again."

"I can teach you. If you like." Rodric did not look at her, and his cheeks flushed red, but he sounded sincere.

"Thank you," she said. "That would be nice." When she was little, she had imagined galloping across fields, ducking under trees and leaping gorges as the heroes always did in books. The wind would whip her hair back, and mud would splatter over her dress, and she would laugh, free and uncatchable. Perhaps not all of her dreams were completely lost. She slid off the horse. "Would you like to try?"

"Oh," Rodric said. "I couldn't—I am too tall. . . ."

She smiled. "Please. Sit." She patted the saddle.

He placed his hands on the horse's shoulders, watching it with uncertain eyes as it rocked slightly. He drew in a breath, as though steeling his courage, and then swung his leg over the back of the horse so that he sat on it like an overgrown knight. Even with his knees bent, his feet were planted firmly on the ground.

"You have to put your feet in the stirrups," Aurora said. He nodded and pressed his knees up toward his chest, squeezing his toes into the metal rings on either side of the horse. The movement made the horse rock forward, then back, and Rodric snatched up the rope reins with a jump.

Aurora couldn't help it. He looked so ridiculous, squeezed on a child's toy less than half his size, all determination and unease. She giggled. Rodric looked up at her. He was smiling. "Do I look that silly?"

"Worse," she said, "but I don't think Franksworth minds. Must have been lonely, sitting up here by himself."

"Franksworth?"

She shrugged. "A horse has to have a name. It was in a book, and it seemed suitably regal. To a five-year-old."

Rodric nodded, and the horse rocked again. From his unsteady seat, the prince almost flew over the horse's head; he grabbed a handful of mane just in time, and swung himself to the ground with a nervous laugh. "Perhaps I can keep him company on the floor."

The pressure in Aurora's chest returned as soon as his feet touched the ground. Without the horse, without a focus for conversation, everything felt awkward and clumsy again, made worse by the memory of their silliness not a moment before. His blush deepened, and he looked around the room, at anything and anywhere but Aurora herself. "This was your playroom?"

"Yes." Aurora moved a wooden doll from a chair and sat down. "I spent a lot of time here."

"It's hard to picture it," Rodric said. "You as a young girl."

Aurora looked down at the doll in her hand. It still had both glass eyes. They stared up at the princess in an accusatory manner. "I wasn't allowed playmates, so I spent a lot of time here alone." She brushed her fingers through the doll's hair, trying to recall the feel of it, the smoothness that flowed past and vanished like silk.

Rodric still stood beside the rocking horse, his tall frame completely out of place among the girlish toys. He stared at the floor now. Their footsteps had left marks in the dust. *Make an effort*, she told herself. *He is. Why can't you?*

"Did you have a playroom?" she asked.

Rodric shook his head. "A nursery, and a few toys, but . . . my father wanted me to grow up as fast as possible. It was swords and horses for me. Not that I was any good at any of it."

"No?"

"I shouldn't be telling you this," he said. "You'll think less of me."

"I won't." That much was true. There was something deeply human about the lanky, blushing prince that made her like him far more than any godlike figure on a tapestry.

"I always dropped my sword during practice," he said. "One clash, and it flew out of my hands. And I used to be scared of the horses. The real ones, I mean. They would bite my toes when I tried to ride them. I think my father gave me the meanest ones on purpose."

"Your father—" She broke off, hunting down the right words. She did not know how to approach the whispers of his cruelty without insulting Rodric or giving her indiscretions away. "He sounds very strict."

"He wanted me to be strong, like he is." Rodric ran a hand down the horse's back, tugging on the loose threads of the saddle. "I never lived up to his expectations."

"That can't be true."

"It is," he said. "I will never be a fighter."

"Fighting is not the only way you can be strong. I am sure your father knows that."

"No," Rodric said. "He does not. But I studied hard. He made sure of that, too. I hope I've done enough to make a good king."

Aurora tilted her head, examining him closely, from the splayed strands of brown hair down to the large, booted feet. He did not look like a king. But, she supposed, she did not always look like much of a princess either. "Your father became king ten years ago," she said. "But he was preparing you to be king before that?"

If Rodric noticed that she had changed the subject, he did not comment on it. "My father believes there's only one way for a boy to be, be he a prince, a noble, or anyone. And he was advisor to the king for many years, through all the famines and the uprisings and many other terrible things. Strength and knowledge were how he thought I would survive."

Aurora ran her fingers through the doll's hair again. Her hands shook. "Were things truly so terrible back then?"

"I don't remember a lot of it," Rodric said. "My father became king when I was eight, so the trouble before then . . . my parents tried to keep me out of it. But I remember being afraid. There was an uprising when I was six. I remember looking out of my window in the castle and seeing the city burning, and all the people, hundreds of them, filling the streets. They crowded around the castle and started hammering on the doors, screaming."

"What did they want?"

"Food, I think. I told my mother, they can have some of my food. Give them some of ours. But she said no, it wasn't really about food at all. They hated us, she said, and they were just looking for an excuse. The whole castle seemed to shake from the way they pounded on the doors. I don't know what would have happened if they'd got in. They were there for days."

"What happened?"

He turned to look out of the window. The narrow shaft of light fell over his face, making his hair glow. "The king—the old king—he called in the soldiers. They killed everyone who fought back."

Aurora swallowed. "But if they had got in," she said. "If they had broken through the doors—"

"They probably would have killed us all. They killed the guards. They killed the servants unlucky enough to be outside the castle walls. And the things they shouted . . ."

Aurora shivered. She could almost hear the screaming, almost see the hate in the people's eyes as they surged toward the castle. It was the same hate she had seen in Tristan's once-affectionate face as he spoke of the king. It could not happen again.

"After that," Rodric said, "the king imprisoned my father for failing to save the kingdom from famine. He was the king's chief advisor at the time, so the king assumed he must have been scheming against him, giving him bad advice to undermine him. He accused my mother of being a foreign spy. For a while, it was just me and my tutors, locked up in a tower. I wasn't told what was going on, or where my parents were, or if I would see them again." He bowed his head, staring at the faded, fraying saddle.

"I'm sorry," she said. "That sounds awful."

"It's over now," he said. "And it will be worth it, if—well. It will be worth it."

The silence was like a living thing, creeping between them, crawling over their skin.

Rodric stepped abruptly away from the horse and walked toward a large chest at the edge of the room. Two wooden swords stuck out of the top. "Are these yours too?" he asked. He freed one with a tug.

"Yes," she said. "Not that my mother approved. They're not very ladylike."

"This is more like the toys I knew," Rodric said, holding up the blade for examination. It was a roughly cut, simple thing, given to her by one of her guards on her birthday. "Of course, my father would have filled them with lead, to make practice that much harder."

"I never got much practice," Aurora said. She stood up and placed the doll beside her. "I would swing it around by myself, but I never really had anyone to play with."

"No one?"

"You're not allowed to make many friends when your father is afraid you might be attacked at any moment."

He handed her one of the swords. It felt lighter than she remembered, but calming, somehow, to hold. She swished it through the air, her fingers tight around the hilt. "That's not quite—I mean, if you don't mind, Princess . . ." Rodric walked closer and rested his hand over hers. "Like this." He adjusted the placement of her fingers. "If you loosen your grip, it'll be easier," he said. "Think of it as part of your arm. You don't have to cling to keep it there."

She attempted another swipe, and he smiled. "That's good," he said. "You're better than you think. Not much force behind it, but you could be quick. Dangerously quick."

He stepped back, opening up the space between them.

"Shall we practice?" Aurora said.

Rodric shook his head. "We shouldn't," he said. "If I hurt you, I wouldn't—we should not risk it."

"You said I wasn't that bad."

"It's not your lack of skill I'm worried about."

She turned away, letting the sword hang loose by her side. "I thought I'd be like one of the girls in the stories," she said. "Swinging swords, fighting dragons, having adventures. But . . ." She stared down at the ragged old doll. "Nothing turned out as I thought."

"For me, either." She looked up. Rodric was staring into the air again, his lips pressed tightly together.

"What about you?" Aurora asked. She stepped toward him. "What did you want?"

"I don't know," he said. "It always seemed that my future would be decided for me."

Aurora looked at the sword in her hand. The little girl who had run around this room, slashing at ghosts and shadows, had never felt that way. The present was fixed, but the future . . . anything had seemed possible then.

"It must have been lonely," Rodric said, still not looking at her. "Playing in this tower by yourself."

"Yes," she said softly. "I suppose it was."

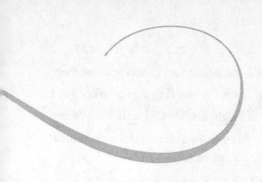

FOURTEEN

THE FOLLOWING AFTERNOON, AURORA WAS summoned to the queen's private rooms. Light poured in through large, high windows, making the space seem cheerful and airy. The queen sat at a round table, staring at papers laid before her. Aurora's stomach clenched at the sight of her. Three older ladies waited behind the queen, their hair tied up in neat buns.

"Ah, Aurora," the queen said, smiling her thin-lipped smile as though they had not argued the last time they'd spoken. "How lovely to see you. We were just looking at the design for your wedding dress. Come. Take a look."

The dress was sketched out on a large piece of parchment, in charcoal first, then in pencil, and finally, a version washed over with delicate colored inks. It was an ethereal thing, layers of gossamer floating outward from a tight bodice and reflecting every color of the light, like something from a dream. Old-fashioned yet fantastical, impossible to touch.

"It's lovely," Aurora said. She ran her finger over the page, tracing each pencil stroke and splash of color.

"I am glad it pleases you, Princess," said one of the women. She bowed as she spoke, a stiff jerk of her neck.

"These," the queen said, standing up with a flourish, "are the best seamstresses in Alyssinia. They have come here especially for you and will be taking your measurements today."

The women all bowed again, and one murmured, "Your Majesty is too kind."

They wrapped tapes across every inch of Aurora, squeezing so tightly around her waist that she had to hitch in her breath. Once they had scribbled down every measurement on a long piece of parchment, they began to fuss with her hair, piling it on top of her head, twisting it around, inspecting her earlobes and wrists while the queen looked on.

"We will leave her hair loose," the queen said. "For purity. But perhaps some garlands . . ."

"A line of flowers," one of the women—the tallest one—said. She ran a finger from the middle of Aurora's forehead to the back of her ear. "Here."

"No, no," said the austere one who seemed to be their leader.

"A single lily, tucked behind her right ear. Beauty, purity, grace."

The queen nodded. Aurora forced herself to stand still, her face carefully blank. No one asked her opinion. Finally, the prodding and poking ended. The seamstresses collected their piles of papers, covered in measurements and notes and little sketches of thoughts, thanked the queen profusely for her patronage, and promised, with a severity that prevented any sliver of doubt, that they would start work immediately and meet with the queen to discuss further details on the morrow. The queen dismissed them with a delicate smile. With a few more bows and curtsies, they departed, leaving Aurora and the queen alone.

"Now that went well," the queen said, and her smile was broader than usual, as though she felt genuine relief at the proceedings. "These ladies made my coronation gown ten years ago, and they have only grown more talented with age. You will have a wedding dress that all the world will remember."

"Yes," Aurora said. "Thank you, Your Majesty."

"I have told you to call me Iris," the queen said. "We will soon be family, after all. Now, come." She held out her hand. "Sit with me a moment, my dear. I wish to speak with you privately." Aurora sat down carefully in a high-backed wooden chair. "I have been thinking of our last conversation," the queen said. "I hope you have taken my words to heart."

Aurora nodded. Her hair itched the back of her neck, and she longed to brush it away, but she did not dare move, in case she attracted more of the queen's attention. If she stayed still, and silent, perhaps the conversation would end quickly, and she could escape from the queen's piercing gaze.

"Good," the queen said. She settled in a chair opposite Aurora. "I do not do this to hurt you, Aurora. I hope you know that. It is the only way."

"I know," Aurora said.

"I am glad. But if there is some problem, it would be better to resolve it now, before it becomes too troublesome. So please tell me, my dear. How have things been?"

Aurora stared at her for a long moment. She could not imagine that the queen wanted an honest answer, or that she intended to help if she received one. "It is hard to sleep," she said eventually.

"I imagine so," the queen said, "when you do not even try."

"I try," Aurora said, the injustice forcing defiance out of her. "But it is difficult. I have lost everything."

"What have you lost, my dear?" the queen said. Her expression remained neutral, but she raised her eyebrows almost imperceptibly as she spoke. "You have a home and a kingdom. And you have your true love." Her tone made clear that she would accept no arguments on that point.

"I have lost my family," Aurora said.

"Everyone loses their family in the end. And really, dear. Were they that good to you before?"

Of course, Aurora wanted to say. She could not get the words out.

"But that is no longer relevant," Iris said. "We cannot change the past, and we cannot have it disrupting your beauty sleep. We don't want you to look too haggard during your engagement ceremony."

No, Aurora thought. *We would not want that.* No one would want to see her as she really was, confused and exhausted and grieving for a life lost. How terribly unfestive that would be.

Iris stood. "I will have more books sent to you, and I will suggest that my son lengthen your daytime walks together." It sounded like a dismissal. Aurora stood as well, forcing her chin to remain high.

"Thank you, Iris."

The queen smiled. "Don't you worry, Aurora. We'll tire you so that you'll want to do nothing but sleep until the wedding. You'll get your rest."

Aurora bobbed into a curtsy. The drawing of her wedding dress lay unfurled on the table, the parchment curling at the ends. So delicate, so perfect, like a dream captured on the page. In her imagination, the walls lurched inward once again.

She was almost out of the room when the queen spoke. "Remember, Aurora. My guards are watching."

As Aurora wove her way back through the corridors, shadowed by a guard on either side, anger pounded in her chest.

Someone darted into the corridor, a blur of silk at chest height, and Aurora was so wrapped up in her thoughts that she almost crashed into her. Isabelle jumped backward. "Sorry!" she squeaked.

"No," Aurora said. "Don't be sorry. It was my fault."

Isabelle was still scrambling away, tumbling over her own feet. She stared up at Aurora, and then paused, her cheeks pink. "What's wrong?" she said.

"I'm fine," Aurora said. Her voice was a little quieter and less sure than she would have liked. "Thank you."

Isabelle frowned. "You don't look fine." She glanced behind Aurora, as though checking for any ghosts or goblins that might be looming behind her. "Were you talking to my mother?" she asked. Aurora nodded. "Sometimes," Isabelle added, in a matter-of-fact sort of voice, "I get sad after talking to her too."

The contrast between Isabelle's words and her practical tone made Aurora pause. "Why does she make you feel sad?" she asked.

Isabelle looked at her feet. They just poked out underneath her skirts. The dress was too long on purpose, Aurora thought. She remembered that trick well. It forced you to walk slowly, take tiny steps, like a well-bred young lady should. When no one was looking, she had picked up her skirts and run too.

"You don't have to tell me," Aurora said. "Sometimes I didn't get along so well with my mother either."

Isabelle looked up at her. "Why not?"

She had tried. She really had. But her mother had always watched her with careful eyes, picking out every little wrinkle in her dress and flaw in her stance. She had never been cold, not exactly, but a little bit distant, as though scared to get too close. Her mother always spoke precisely, dressed precisely, lived precisely, and although Aurora missed her with an ache that squeezed her insides into nothing, her mother had never quite seemed to approve of her. She had always been one step away. "She wanted me to be more of a princess," Aurora said.

"What did you do?"

"I became more of a princess."

Isabelle bit her lip and nodded, as though Aurora had imparted some deep life lesson that she needed to absorb. *What a horrid thing to tell her*, Aurora thought. That she had to smile and curtsy and pretend. But it was the truth, as Aurora had lived it.

"I suppose—" Isabelle said, "I suppose it worked. In the end. Because now you have Rodric."

"Yes," Aurora said. "I have Rodric. But not because of that." Not because of anything she had done.

"Mother says I have to behave better, since Finnegan is here." It seemed like a strange change in topic, until Isabelle added, "She wants me to marry him."

"Marry him?"

"When I'm older. She says it's the best thing for Alyssinia, and it would be my—my greatest achievement"—she spoke those words carefully, picking out each syllable—"if I got his support."

Aurora could not imagine this sweet girl married to that arrogant, scheming man. Even if Isabelle were older, it would not be a match she'd want to think about. Then again, things like compatibility and likeability would not matter to the queen, as long as it was best for the kingdom.

"You could achieve much more than that," Aurora said, "with or without Finnegan." She was not entirely sure it was true, but it seemed the right thing to say. Maybe if Isabelle believed it, it could become true.

"Isabelle!" The little princess jumped. "What are you doing?" A woman appeared in the doorway, hands on her hips. She seemed slightly out of breath. "Running away from me like that. You shouldn't be bothering the princess."

"She's not bothering me," Aurora said, but the woman ignored her. She stepped forward and grabbed Isabelle by the crook of her arm.

"Get back in here this instant."

"Good-bye," Aurora said softly. The woman hurried Isabelle away, and the corridor turned quiet again. Aurora stared at the closed door. It was like her past self had come to life, uncertain and hopeful and eager to do the right thing. Isabelle would learn, as she had learned. For some reason, the thought made her sad, and she quickly turned away.

Perhaps her own mother had been like Iris, Aurora thought as she hurried back to her rooms. Aurora seemed to disappoint both of them in the same way.

A memory bubbled up, long ignored and unwelcome. Her mother, the foreign queen, brushing through Aurora's hair as she stood by the window, just tall enough to see over the ledge.

Aurora had been chattering about something, about books and adventure and her impossible dreams. "I'm going to travel," she said. "Like you, mother. See everything. Everywhere."

"No, dear," her mother said. "It isn't safe."

Aurora craned her neck, ducking free of the tug and pull of the brush. "Not now," she said. "After."

Everything had always been before and after in her head. Cursed and free.

"Not even then," her mother said. "Why go far away, when you can be safe and loved with us?"

Aurora stayed silent then, but she kept dreaming until the end. Planning, wishing, poring over maps and books, right up until her eighteenth birthday and the finger prick that ended it all. She had gotten her wish, she supposed. She was a story of her own now. But it was not as she had imagined. Still the rest of the world was locked away.

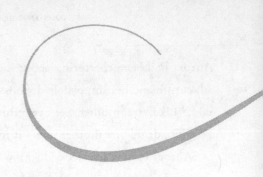

FIFTEEN

WHEN AURORA FINALLY SLEPT THAT NIGHT, SHE dreamed in fitful snatches. A crowd chasing her down the street, Tristan pulling her along before shoving her to the ground. Hands snatching at her hair, her clothes, as she struggled to regain her feet.

She woke up drenched in cold sweat. She forced her aching legs out from under the covers and paced the room. She wanted to see Tristan. She wanted to escape from these walls, to drink mead, to forget who she was meant to be for one more night. But she couldn't. She knew she couldn't. She had been a fool to ever trust him.

She pulled the book he had given her from its hiding place at the back of the bookshelf and began to read, trying to remember the thrill of that night. Every word of adventure seemed tainted now. It all made her think of Tristan's face as he told her his secrets and of the brutal hero he thought he could be.

She grabbed the cover, ready to tear some of the pages away, but then stopped and tucked it back where it had been before.

"Goodness, Princess," Betsy said, when she arrived with breakfast. "You look a sight. Are you all right?"

"Yes," Aurora said. "Yes. I just had a bad dream."

"Oh," Betsy said. She ducked her head, as though suddenly remembering that they were not friends after all. "At least you've been getting some sleep."

Aurora received no summons from the queen that day, and Rodric did not appear. She assumed that they were busy preparing for the engagement presentation the next day, that Rodric was learning a speech while his mother picked over every word choice, every intonation, every thread of his clothes. Aurora had not been invited. Why would she be needed, when no one expected her to say a word, when the queen could dictate the details of her every move? She picked up a book and tried to read it, but the words would not stick in her head.

Tomorrow, she would be officially engaged. She would stand before the crowd again, and they would cheer, and Rodric would smile, and happily ever after would begin. Tomorrow.

Someone knocked on the door. "Come in," Aurora said.

The door creaked open, and Isabelle slipped through the narrow gap.

"Isabelle. What are you doing here?"

"Sorry," Isabelle said quickly, almost tripping over her own feet in her hurry to back through the door. "I didn't mean to bother you. I just thought—"

"No," Aurora said. She hurried to close the door before Isabelle disappeared entirely. "You just surprised me. Don't you have lessons?"

Isabelle looked at the ground. She definitely wasn't supposed to be here. "Only history," she said quietly. "Mrs. Benson was going to test me."

"Sounds like something you wouldn't want to miss."

"It's boring," Isabelle said. "I'd rather talk to you."

"You don't like history?" Isabelle shook her head. "I thought you loved stories."

"I love stories," she said, energy appearing in her expression almost instantly. "Ogres and swordfights and romance and—and everything! But history isn't like that." She tilted her head, watching Aurora closely. "Except you," she added. "Without the ogres and swordfights. But you're not history. You're here."

"Everything in history was here once," Aurora said. "That's what makes it interesting." Isabelle did not look convinced. "My favorite story is true," she added. Or at least, it had always seemed true to her, when she'd pored over the pages, soaking in every word. When she had pretended to be the great Queen Alysse, alone in her playroom. "Have you heard the story of Alysse?"

Isabelle sighed, that painful, world-weary sigh of an over-burdened eight-year-old. "Alysse was one of the first settlers in Alyssinia," she said in a dragging monotone. "She made the land hospitable and was a great queen."

"Ah," Aurora said, grabbing Isabelle's hands and pulling her toward the chairs in the center of the room. "But do you know the real story?"

Isabelle shook her head. Aurora nodded sagely and sank into her chair. Isabelle settled at her feet, her skirt forming a bubble around her. The book sat on her bookshelf with the others, perfect and unread, but Aurora didn't need it. She could still remember every word. "Long ago," she said, running her fingers through Isabelle's hair, "the people of Alyssinia lived across the sea, in a land of metal and smoke. Once, the land had been beautiful and full of magic, but the wicked kings had choked its beauty, and the magic died away."

"Like here," Isabelle said.

"Yes," Aurora said softly. "Like here. Disgusted by their rulers, and full of despair, a group of bold adventurers set off across the sea, until they saw land that seemed to glow with natural power. Enchanted by its stormy skies, wild forests, and glassy lakes, the adventurers decided to settle in this land, naming it after their leader's beautiful young daughter, Alysse.

"But the land had a mind of its own," she continued. "Cutting down trees seemed to turn the creatures against them, and the land seemed to need cajoling more than taming. If they did not figure out how to get Alyssinia on their side, the people would surely die, but no one, not a soul among all those men, knew what to do. But Alysse was different. She was just your age, you know, and when she walked in the forests, she said she heard the whispering of the trees. And she knew how to whisper back."

"With magic?"

"A kind of magic, I suppose," Aurora said. "She soothed the way for her people and led them deeper and deeper into the forest, pointing out each place where a few of them could live. Not in cities, not walled up and locked away. But little villages, and one castle, hidden among the trees, where no one else could harm them."

As Aurora told the story, about the good, patient, kind-hearted Alysse, who brought peace between the people and the land and made everything possible, the familiar words began to feel twisted and foreign. Like they did not quite fit in the air. Alysse had always seemed so strong to her as a child: a future queen, loved by everyone she met, an adventurer in a new land and the only one who understood it. She had been so *good*. So gentle. All the regal traits her mother had impressed on her, long ago.

"What happened to her?" Isabelle asked.

"She vanished. They say that one day, she was wandering in the woods, and she disappeared into the mist. The forest reclaiming its own."

What nonsense, Aurora thought. *She died*. Everyone died.

"Will she come back?"

"No one knows."

"Maybe she's you," Isabelle said, bouncing on the spot. "Everyone says you're going to save us. That you'll bring magic back!"

Magic. For the first time, she heard the word and felt a twist in her stomach, a little thrill. Having that kind of power, that kind of influence . . . it was a wicked thing. Yet she could not deny the satisfaction she felt at the thought of it. At the idea of having importance, having true influence, the ability to do as she pleased.

It was impossible, of course. She was not a long-dead queen reborn, and she was as likely to restore magic as she was to see her parents again. But she could not crush Isabelle's dreams. She could not crush that feeling in herself.

"Maybe," she said. "Maybe."

That evening, the entire court gathered in the banquet hall for a pre-engagement celebration. A silk curtain hung across one end of the room, hiding a makeshift stage from view. Members of the court waited on slanted wooden benches, whispering and joking among themselves. The benches formed a *V*, with two red-and-gold thrones in the center for the guests of honor. Aurora sat in the one on the left, her hands clasped neatly in her lap. Next to her, Rodric fidgeted with his sleeve. Neither of them spoke.

Finnegan sat to Aurora's left. She did not look at him, but she could feel his eyes on her.

A short man stepped around the curtain and addressed the crowd. "My company and I are honored to perform before you tonight. At our beautiful queen's request, we will be presenting a dumb show of a story that I am sure you all know well, reviving this old form of entertainment in honor of our princess." He bowed at Aurora.

"Excellent," the king shouted. "Let the play begin."

The curtains slid open, revealing two figures, a king and a queen, covered in finery. The queen rocked a baby in her arms, and peaceful music rang out from a harp. Aurora pressed her hands into her lap. She should have expected this blind cruelty. They were going to perform her life back to her, as though it were nothing more than light entertainment.

Finnegan leaned closer, hissing below her ear. "Oh, good," he said. "This is my favorite story. Don't you agree?"

She ignored him.

One by one, actors approached the woman and child, their faces hidden by masks. They each bowed or curtsied and placed a gift by the baby's feet. Then a drum rolled, echoing like thunder off the stone walls, and another player appeared, dressed in black from head to toe and wearing a bird-like mask with dark feathers and red scales around the eyes. The figure pointed at the child, her chin thrown back in defiance as the music swelled. The king pulled out his sword and advanced, but the woman waved a hand, and the sword vanished. The audience gasped.

"The blade retracted through the hilt, of course," Finnegan murmured. "It has vanished up the actor's sleeve. Ingenious, really."

"Thank you for the explanation," Aurora said, the words scraping through her teeth. "I would not have noticed it myself."

"You are very welcome," he said. "I know that illusions must be quite out of your depth, innocent as you are." She jerked around to look at him, but he shook his head. "Shh," he said. "Watch the play. I want to see how it ends."

Onstage, the witch threw back her head and laughed. The music rose, and the room plunged into darkness. When the light returned, a young woman was standing on the edge of the stage, brushing her long blonde hair. Her golden mask only covered her eyes, and the actress's lips had been painted rose red. The court watched as the girl flitted about the stage, pressing a hand to her heart, tilting her head and reaching into the air. Every movement was graceful, every twitch of the lips delicate and refined. A flower of a girl, silent and pure.

"You know," Finnegan said, "I think I like you better."

The stage princess fluttered like a bird, dancing with an

imaginary partner, curtsying to no one. The music ached with loneliness, and then jolted, as the pretend Aurora turned to find the dark bird-masked woman behind her. The woman beckoned.

The strings shuddered in fear as the princess stepped back and shook her head, her hands reaching for help that was not there. The woman beckoned again, and this time the princess slid toward her.

Aurora closed her eyes. It was only a play. A story of her life, nothing like it had been. But as the strings shrieked in her ears, something flickered in her memory. Some kind of music, a bobbing light, and a pull—not like a trance, but like an urge, a need to follow her curiosity and face whatever lay beyond. Her fingertip burned at the memory, and she ran her thumb over it.

The lights flashed again. When Aurora opened her eyes, the princess was reaching for a spinning wheel, one finger outstretched.

Rodric slid his hand into hers and squeezed. She squeezed back, her fingers tightening around his knuckles.

The curtains closed, and after a brief interlude for applause, they opened again to reveal a new set of characters. A great king, his crown even larger than the last, his mask snarling like a bear. A queen, her mask an echo of the previous queen's. And a prince, wearing a red mask that only covered his eyes.

Rodric slid his hand out of her grip.

"It was my birthday," he murmured. She could barely hear

him over the music. "I'd been dreading it for years. Disappointing everyone on my eighteenth birthday—not the best way to come of age."

"It was your birthday?" Aurora looked at him. "I didn't know."

"It's all right," Rodric said. "I didn't tell you."

Onstage, the prince approached the sleeping princess. The music swelled.

"Happy birthday," Aurora said.

The fictional prince kissed the girl. She awoke and swooned in his arms. How much simpler things would be, if that were true. One kiss, and they would live happily ever after.

The play ended, the court applauded, and the king stood up. "Excellent," he said. "Excellent! How quaint. After the wedding, I will have to ask you to prepare it as a masque for us. I'm sure the court would love to play parts, and Rodric and Aurora as well."

"Yes, Your Majesty," the lead actor said. "Thank you, Your Majesty."

"What's a masque?" Aurora asked Rodric as they moved into a neighboring room full of comfier chairs and the smell of wine. "A new type of play?"

"Yes, Princess," Rodric said. "It's a bit more elaborate. There's singing and dancing, and big speeches, and of course everyone wears masks. I dread them, if I'm honest with you. But you'll be wonderful."

"Why do you dread them?"

"Because we all have to be in them. We don't have lines, but they always want us to dance. I'm not a good dancer."

"If everyone wears masks," Aurora said, "then it doesn't matter. How will they know that it's you?"

"I know that it's me," he said. "That's bad enough."

Aurora stuck close to Rodric's side as the court buzzed around them, commenting on the play, expressing their delight, always speaking at them instead of to them. Aurora nodded as they spoke, the back of her hand brushing against Rodric's. No one cared that she was not in love with her future husband, or that she had shown little sign of being their savior. But for the first time, she knew that Rodric was trapped in this too. She felt it like a fist clenching beneath her ribs. The play had misrepresented them both.

One of the court ladies, Alexandra, slipped her arm through Aurora's and turned her aside. "Such a lovely play," she said. "Did you see the like often, in the past?"

"Not often," Aurora said. "I was not allowed to leave my tower much, and my father would not invite actors to the castle. They travel so much that it's impossible to keep track of who they really are."

"And of course, they are the masters of pretense," Alexandra said. "Any actor who isn't would not be worth seeing." She smiled.

"Perhaps you should be an actress, Alexandra." Finnegan

had appeared behind them. "A beauty like you."

Alexandra leaned closer to Aurora. "Shall we ignore him?" she whispered. "Nothing is more likely to infuriate him than a little silence."

"Ignore me? Why would you do such a terrible thing? Surely the princess is too kindhearted for that. All I want is your adoration."

"I'm afraid that all my adoration is spent on Rodric," Aurora said. "You'll have to rely on Alexandra, and she doesn't seem inclined to give it."

"You wound me, the both of you." He pressed a hand on his heart, as though they had stabbed him there. "I'll leave if you wish, but know you'll be torturing me, as I imagine all the things you are saying behind my back."

Alexandra only curtsied, and Finnegan bowed and walked away.

"Infuriating man," Alexandra said. She didn't criticize him the way Iris did, full of barely controlled loathing. She smiled as she spoke, sounding almost amused.

Aurora arranged her features into the most innocent expression she could muster. "You don't like him?"

"Oh, I like him fine enough," Alexandra said. "But you can't let him think that. It's much more fun to let him think we dislike him. It will only infuriate him, and make him try harder for our approval."

Aurora doubted that Finnegan was under any illusion about

how much Alexandra liked him.

"I hear he is engaged to Princess Isabelle."

Alexandra wafted a hand through the air. "For now," she said. "Who knows how these things will turn out?" She sighed, and her grip on Aurora's elbow tightened. "It must be so nice to have everything laid out for you. To marry Rodric, and know it is the right thing. Nothing can go wrong. Are you excited for the engagement presentation tomorrow?"

"Of course," Aurora said. "Excited, and nervous."

"Don't be nervous," Alexandra said. "It's all been decided, hasn't it? You know how things will go. And it's all so romantic."

"Yes," Aurora said. "It is very romantic."

"Alexandra!" A group of three ladies called from across the room. "Come play whist with us. We need another person to make up the table!"

Alexandra glanced at Aurora. "But the princess—"

"Go," Aurora said. "I don't mind. Besides, if you are busy on a full card table, Finnegan won't have a chance to talk to you. It's perfect."

Alexandra smiled. "If you're sure—"

"Of course," Aurora said. "Make him mad with envy."

Alexandra curtsied and glided across the room. Aurora lingered where they had been standing, casting around for Rodric or another familiar face. The prince had been pulled into conversation on the other side of the room, the king beside him. Aurora did not want to interrupt. But before she could find another option, Finnegan was beside her again.

"You did not fancy putting together a card set, Princess?"

"And miss the opportunity to talk to you? Your words to me during the play were so delightful."

"The play did lack a little something, didn't it? I couldn't quite put my finger on it."

"Perhaps it lacked silence," Aurora said. "I hear that was meant to be the point." She turned away, bristling with annoyance. He was so confident, so smug. Yet the most frustrating thing was that she almost enjoyed talking to him. She had never met anyone who annoyed her before, who made it their goal to get under her skin.

"No, what I think it lacked was realism," Finnegan said. "Although I suppose that suits this place. I often think that Alyssinia's courtiers would make excellent actors themselves."

"And you?"

"Oh, Princess," he said. "I do believe it's my specialty."

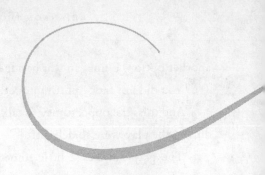

SIXTEEN

AS SHE GOT READY THE NEXT MORNING, EVERY ONE of Aurora's muscles screamed the same word at her, over and over: run.

I could do it, she thought, as Betsy tugged in her waist and straightened her skirts. *I could run.* Tristan had offered her a way out. She could leave the castle behind, hide out in the inn, and never worry about fate or duty or promised love again. Until she was caught, at least. Until his rebels murdered everyone in the castle. Until the king's men fought back or the whole kingdom descended into civil war. Her stomach lurched, and she pressed her tongue against the roof of her mouth to hold back the wave of nausea that rushed through her. She could not leave. The risk was too great.

Rodric waited in a large chamber, empty except for a single table and mirrors along one wall. He blushed when he saw her, and his hand jerked up to rub the skin behind his ear. "Princess," he said. She gave him a nod that was almost a curtsy, and he bowed in return. "You look beautiful." He was a good person, she told herself. But she did not love him, and every beat of her heart thudded through her, telling her that this was wrong, wrong, all wrong.

The queen had given her an old-fashioned dress, with long, flowing sleeves and a tiny lace-up waist. It was something out of a dream, a picture of life as it had been in "the olden days." Her hair hung loose around her shoulders in a shower of curls. She brushed one back from her face and ducked her head. "Thank you."

"I brought you something," he said. "A gift. For our engagement." He pulled a necklace out of his pocket and held it up. A chain of diamonds, running in a loop and then dropping down to a star that glittered in the light. It looked like a jewel snatched from a treasure trove, ancient and magnificent. Clearly an heirloom. Had the queen told him to give it to her? "Do—do you like it?"

"Yes," she said, all far-off, perfected politeness. "It's wonderful. But I cannot accept it."

"Nonsense." The queen swept into the room. Her hair was

piled on her head in a bunch of elaborate twists, decorated with tiny glints that might have been diamonds too. "It will suit you."

"May I?" Rodric said. Aurora nodded. With a gentle hand, he lifted her hair. A few strands tumbled down to scratch her neck. He placed the necklace around her throat and fumbled with the clasp. Not so much as a whisper of his skin touched hers. The chain was heavy and cold, dragging her shoulders forward and pressing on her already tight chest. When Rodric released her hair, it tickled her skin.

"Let me have a look at you," the queen said. She grabbed Aurora's hands and held them out in front of her so she could scrutinize every crease and curl. She raised her arms higher, so that Aurora had to stretch up on tiptoe like a dancing doll. "Perfect. The people will love you." She tightened her hold on Aurora's hands, as though trying to squeeze every last drop of beauty out of her. Aurora fought back a wince. "Smile, my dear, and everything will be fine." A threat nestled in the words.

The queen released her hands, and Aurora's heels dropped to the ground.

"Rodric, do you remember the speech I gave you?"

The prince nodded. His skin had turned pale.

"Good." The queen looked as smooth and unruffled as ever, but tension darted through her features as she turned away. "I have a couple of final things to attend to. A guard will fetch you when we are ready." She marched away without another word, leaving Rodric and Aurora alone.

Aurora followed the edge of her necklace with her fingertips, following the cut of the jewels. Every nerve stood on edge, and her breaths did not seem to fill her lungs. At least the ceremony would be outside, away from these stern walls. Rodric shifted from foot to foot, his mouth running through his speech, lips tracing the same words over and over until Aurora felt dizzy watching him. Her legs itched to run. She clutched her skirts in her fists to steady the shaking, forcing back the threatening tears with a gulp of air.

"Prince Rodric, Princess Aurora?" A man in a bright-red uniform stood by the door. "Please come with me." She glanced back at Rodric. He looked almost green with nerves, but he nodded once and held out his arm to her. She rested her hand over his elbow, her fingers curling into the fabric of his tunic. She was not sure she could walk forward alone.

The guard hurried them down corridors and around to the front entrance of the castle, the place where Aurora had been presented to the people. The hum of the crowd grew louder and louder with every step, and over it, the king spoke in his booming, jovial voice. The words bounced off the walls, blurring together into meaningless cheer.

The guard led them toward an alcove to the left of the main doors, tucked out of sight. The space was so narrow that Aurora could almost feel Rodric's chest rise and fall beside her. Beyond the open doors, she could hear the crowd, thousands of voices muttering and cheering and pressing in, all there to catch another glimpse of their precious princess.

Breathe in. Breathe out.

"They love you," Rodric said under his breath. Was he talking to himself or to her? The lie cut into her, and something like panic bubbled up in her throat. They could not love her. No one could, not here, not really. Not the prince, not the crowd, not anyone. They were all deceived, by her face or her silence or their own desires. Her whole body tingled, as if tiny needles were diving into every inch of her skin.

She reached out and clutched Rodric's hand. He squeezed, his fingers warm around hers. She tightened her hold until her knuckles strained white, but he did not let go.

"Aurora—" Rodric began, but the guard stepped forward before he could finish the thought.

"It is time," he said. He ushered them out of the alcove, sweeping them toward the doors. They paused on the threshold as a fanfare blared and a herald stepped ahead of them.

"Presenting Prince Rodric and Princess Aurora."

The crowd roared in approval, and Aurora and Rodric walked through the doors, hands clutched together. People clambered on the walls and sat on roofs, shouting and cheering and waving banners that whirled in a flash of color. Aurora stretched her lips into a smile so wide that her face felt it might tear in two. The frenzy of excitement snatched her breath away, and she looked down at the stone steps, struggling to steady her spinning head. She felt sick with the lie of it.

Keep smiling. She sank into a curtsy, her head bowed, and the roar increased. Her eyes skimmed over the crowd, trying to take in the eager faces, the delighted grins. One woman was not smiling. Tall and thin, with long blonde hair and a familiar, heart-shaped face. Her ice-blue eyes seemed to burn into Aurora's skin. Aurora took a step backward, slipping on the smooth stone.

Rodric tugged on her hand, and the shouts of the crowd broke through the haze, rattling in her ears. Her lips ached, like two fingers were yanking them apart.

"Kiss her!" shouted a boy. The crowd laughed and cheered in approval, and soon the cry had been taken up by every voice. "Kiss the princess!"

Rodric's smile was almost apologetic, and his face burned as pink as ever. Hundreds of eyes seemed to scald Aurora's cheeks, and she knew the queen's were among them, judging their performance. Aurora's heart constricted, each frantic pound screaming *run, run, run,* but she had nowhere to go. The moment lingered on. She could not leave, could not turn her head away, but neither could she bring herself to stand up on tiptoe and touch her lips to his, declaring their love for everyone to see.

Slowly, Rodric pressed a shaking hand against her cheek. It was hot—or maybe that was her own blushing skin—and then his lips brushed hers.

She closed her eyes and counted the seconds. Her heartbeat did not slow, and the roar of the crowd did not fade.

One. Two. Three.

An explosion rocked the courtyard. The cheering turned to screams. Aurora, her ears ringing, leapt away from the sound in time to see a spray of golden sparks bursting from a shell on one side of the steps. The thing skidded across the stones, spitting fire. The crowd squealed and shoved one another to get away, but Aurora did not move, her eyes fixed on the flame. It burned like panic, like fever, cutting through the numbness in her fingertips.

The shell exploded again, louder than the first time, and the sparks were blinding red. Aurora screamed this time too and leapt backward. The sparks burned into the stone a few feet from where she stood.

Another explosion came from behind her. People screamed again, and Rodric grabbed her hand, pulling her back to the castle. Guards poured out of every crevice, seeming to step out of the air itself. They pulled out their swords, and people scrambled farther away as they caught the glint of the steel.

"Fireworks in honor of this joyous day!" The cry carried over the chaos, echoing from somewhere in the very midst of the crowd. The guards plunged toward the voice, shoving people out of the way. Some leapt back from the gleam of the blades, but at the back of the square, others pushed closer to watch the show. The crowd jostled back and forth, rippling and buzzing, elbows flailing. A girl fell in front of a guard. He kicked her in the stomach and drew his leg back again to toss her aside.

"Stop!"

Rodric's grip on Aurora's hand slackened, and she wrenched herself free. She ran forward, down the steps, and grasped the guard by the arm. "Stop!"

The guard swung his blade. She jerked back, and the tip caught her side, cutting through her dress as if it were air. In the time it took the guard to blink, the square went still. No one screamed; no one struggled. No one moved at all, except for Aurora. She collapsed onto the hard cobbles. The guard stared at her, horror spreading across his face. Red stained the corset of her dress. She pressed her fingers over the wound. Hot blood pulsed between them. The world twisted sideways. She raised her fingers in front of her face and stared at the blood, bright red against the whiteness of her skin. It dripped down the palm of her hand, stroking her wrist and disappearing under her sleeve. Blood burned in her ears. It raced through her fingertips.

She pushed herself to her feet. Everything was distorted, faraway, except for the red.

A hand grabbed her arm. "Princess!" Rodric said. "Come on." She pulled her arm away, but he did not let go, so she spun around and shoved his shoulder backward, anger racing up out of nowhere. Another explosion, loud and fiery red, burst around them. The prince jumped backward, his feet dancing away from the scorched stone. His hair smelled of smoke.

Her whole body shook. A bright red handprint stuck to his tunic. She clutched the spot on her arm where he had held her.

That would be stained too. It was only a little blood, she knew that, she knew, but she felt like it was spilling all over her, staining every little patch of skin. For a wild moment, she wanted to smear it over her face, hide that oh-so-beloved beauty under a taste of her messy insides.

Rodric stared at her, his eyes wide, as though seeing her for the first time.

"That's right," she said. "You don't know me." She could not tell if he heard her. She did not care. The fire was in her veins now, all that tension, all the fear, pounding and chasing and burning through her.

"Princess, please forgive me. I didn't know—" The guard moved forward, but several others grabbed him, jolting him to a halt. Aurora stared at his desperate face, her lips slightly parted. As quickly as it had come, the strength and wildness dropped out of her, and she swayed. The world spun. She shook her head. "Are you all right?" she asked the girl she had rushed to save. The girl was standing up now, pressing backward into the crowd. When she looked at Aurora, her eyes were full of fear.

"It'll be all right," Aurora said, but the girl's eyes flickered between Aurora's bloodstained dress and the scorch marks below Rodric's feet, and she stumbled back again, as though anything would be better than facing Aurora in this moment.

Off to her left, the blonde woman still watched her. Her eyes were filled with hunger.

Another shout echoed over the crowd. "Long live the Useless Prince and his Bloodstained Bride. May they sleep together always."

She knew that voice. She turned, searching the crowd, even as the guards swept them backward again. Another hand—she did not know whose—grabbed her and tried to lead her up the steps, but she refused to turn. Not until she saw.

He was perched on a roof at the very edge of the square, watching. Their eyes met.

Tristan nodded and ducked away.

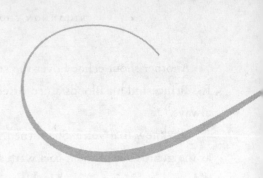

SEVENTEEN

"IT IS ONLY A SHALLOW CUT," THE HEALING WOMAN said as she pressed a cloth to Aurora's side. The wound stung under the pressure, but Aurora refused to wince. "It looks a lot worse than it is."

"Good," the queen said. She stood behind Aurora, her face pale. "What needs to be done?"

"Very little," the woman said, and she peered at the cut again. "I will clean it and bandage it, and as long as she doesn't do anything strenuous over the next few days, it should heal fine."

Aurora nodded. What strenuous things could she possibly do? Move the furniture around her locked room? The light poured in through the queen's high windows, making the room look unnaturally cheerful. Aurora felt cold and faraway. She had to wait up here until the healer gave her permission to move, until the square had been emptied and the guards had searched the castle, hunting for any lingering threats. Rodric had been swept away as soon as they reentered the castle, leaving Aurora with her fretting future mother-in-law. The queen's lips were thinner than Aurora had ever seen before, and she seemed to be having trouble standing still. She paced the room frequently, and even when she stood in one place, she twitched her skirts every few seconds.

"Will it leave a scar?" the queen asked.

"I do not think so, Your Majesty. But perhaps."

They talked back and forth, the queen sounding increasingly peevish, but Aurora stopped listening. She glanced toward the sunny windows. Had the guards caught Tristan, or was she the only person who had seen him, watching the scene from the rooftop?

She had been such a fool to trust him. Even after he had told her his intentions, she had done nothing to stop him. She had not thought he would hurt innocent people. She had not thought he would hurt *her*.

The healer dabbed a wet cloth against Aurora's side, cleaning the blood away.

The queen continued to pace the room. Her knuckles were white where she gripped her skirts.

The healer tied the bandages in place. They covered Aurora's whole stomach, crisp and white against her pale skin.

"Thank you," Iris said as soon as she was done. "You may leave us. Please attend the princess again this evening." The healer curtsied and shuffled away.

"Do you believe me now?" Iris said as soon as the door closed again. "I knew something like this would happen."

"Yes," Aurora said. "I believe you."

"There will have to be some new rules," she said, sweeping across the room to look out of the window. "This cannot be allowed to happen again." Now that the only other witness was gone, she did not even pretend to be calm.

"What's going to happen?" Aurora asked. "Is there still to be a wedding?"

"Of course there is still to be a wedding," the queen snapped. "We are not going to let a few noxious weeds destroy the most important day this kingdom has seen in a hundred years. But we are going to need to take extra precautions to ensure your safety." She spoke quickly and precisely. "Once the castle has been properly searched, you are to remain in your room until further notice. No walks in the garden. No afternoons with the court. No brunches outside. If you must leave, you will be provided with a guard to accompany you at all times."

"But—"

"Do not interrupt me, Aurora." Iris's face turned red. "You must listen and be silent, for once. Do you understand me?"

Aurora nodded.

"Good," the queen said. "I am glad you will cooperate." She stepped away from the window. "I wish they had given us more guards here," she said. "We really do not have enough. We must search every inch of this castle, and interrogate all the people they caught in the square—"

"Is that necessary?" Aurora asked. She did not want more innocent people arrested or punished because of her.

"Do you think we would be making such a fuss if it were not?"

"It's just—" She looked down at the ground, remembering the people huddled by the city wall on that dark night, their faces blank with hunger. "They must think what they're doing is right."

Aurora half expected Iris to snap at her, call her a naïve idiot of a girl, but instead, she sighed. "I was once like you," she said. "Trusting. It didn't work out well."

"What do you—"

"Four years ago was our last big rebellion," she said. "The biggest one since my husband became king. Drunken crowds stampeded the castle. They killed our guards. Our servants. Innocent people outside were crushed in the rush. My own personal maid was murdered in the street, just because I sent her out on an errand. They are animals, Aurora. They don't have morals. They want to ruin us, and they don't care who else they destroy in the process."

Aurora swallowed. She could not stomach the thought of Tristan's involvement in something like that. In murders and mobs screaming for blood.

Someone rapped on the door.

"Come in," Iris said. A messenger stepped into the room.

"The guard who attacked the princess is in the dungeons," he said. "We have arranged a public execution for tomorrow morning."

"No!" Aurora said. She stepped forward with a jerk, and her side throbbed in protest. "It was an accident." She did not want him to die for her.

"He was reckless," Iris said. "We cannot have people hurting you without consequence."

"Then choose a smaller consequence."

"Do not talk about things you do not understand," the queen said. "A smaller consequence is no consequence at all. If we show leniency, this will happen again."

This is my fault, Aurora thought. If she had not run into the crowd, the guard would be safe.

But then the girl he attacked might well be dead, and no one would have punished him for that.

"It is wrong," Aurora said. "You cannot kill him."

"I can," the queen said, "and I will. Thank you, Stefan. That will be all."

The messenger bowed.

"Did you catch who was responsible?" Aurora said quickly. "For the disturbance?"

The messenger glanced at the queen. "We will, Princess," he said. "Do not worry."

So they had not yet. Aurora felt a spike of relief. Tristan was not the person she had thought he was. But she could not wish him dead.

If she told anyone what she knew, she would be slipping the noose around his neck.

The sun had set before Aurora was allowed back to her room. She walked with two guards on either side, their footsteps echoing along the empty corridors. One floor above Aurora's own, one of the guards paused.

"Why are you stopping?" a second guard said. "This isn't her room."

"No, I know." The guard frowned, as though he wasn't sure why he had stopped either. "I—I heard something." He glanced behind him.

"I didn't hear anything." The other guards looked back too. At first, Aurora could hear nothing but the dim sounds of the castle, the whistle of wind through the stone and the sound of faraway footsteps. Then she heard a whisper mingling with the wind, half singing, half laughter. The song crept along the inside of her skin, a memory of a memory.

When the guards glanced back, their faces were blank, like

they were focused on something much farther away than the end of the hall.

"What's wrong?" Aurora asked. They did not respond. She grabbed the arm of the nearest one and tugged, shaking it. The guard was still breathing, but he did not react. His mind seemed to have been sucked away.

Aurora stumbled backward. She turned, preparing to shout.

A light glowed at the end of the corridor. Green, indistinct, shifting like water.

The song, the light . . . she knew them.

Celestine.

The memory tugged at Aurora, light bobbing out of reach, the urge, deep in her stomach, to see where it led. Her finger slipping against something sharp.

It was impossible. The witch could not be here, not after a hundred years had passed. But the light slid closer, so familiar, so certain. If Celestine could make Aurora sleep a century away without aging a day, her own survival could not be beyond her power.

Aurora followed the light. Torches on either side of the passageway dimmed as she passed. With every step, the green orb floated another step away, guiding her down the corridor, around the corner, farther from the guards.

She knew she should stop. She knew she should turn back. But what could Celestine do to her? There was nothing left for the witch to take away. And if she was here, Aurora needed to know what she had to say. She needed to see her.

The light paused in front of a blank expanse of wall. Aurora walked closer, her arm outstretched, until her fingers were inches away. Then the light melted into the wall itself, making the stone glow for a heartbeat before fading back into darkness.

Still Aurora followed. Her fingers met a hint of resistance as they brushed the stone, more a memory of a barrier than a barrier itself, and then she was stepping through the wall, the corridor slipping away.

The room beyond was round and bare, without windows, without doors, without anything but dust and stone. The green light hovered in the center, just above Aurora's head, casting shadows across the walls.

A woman stood beside it, her fingertips dancing across the light as though caressing the feathers of a bird. Her blonde hair curled around her elbows, and the light emphasized the cheekbones in her heart-shaped face. Everything about her was either sharp or soft, from her tiny, pointed nose to the long nails at the end of her delicate fingers. All so familiar, but it took Aurora a moment to place her. She was the woman from the square, the one who had watched her with hunger in her eyes.

"Aurora," she said, stretching her red lips into a smile. "How good of you to join me."

"Celestine," Aurora said. The witch nodded. "You're alive."

"Of course," she said. "You didn't think something as fleeting as time would stop me, did you? I have been watching you since you awoke."

Aurora screwed her hands into fists, digging her fingernails into the soft skin of her palms. The pain helped to keep her focused. She could not be afraid. "Watching, but not speaking to me?" she said. "You should have introduced yourself."

"I did not think you would welcome my presence," Celestine said. "And I admit, I wanted to see what you would do alone. It was rather unimpressive, I must say."

"And yet you're talking to me now."

Celestine tilted her head. Her blonde hair cascaded over her shoulders, seeming to flow in the green light. "Well, you finally showed some potential. I wanted to congratulate you. You put on quite a show today. It made my skin buzz to see it." Her smile felt like it was nestled under Aurora's skin. "It was good to feel that way again, after so many years."

Aurora's fists tightened. "I don't know what you're talking about."

"That little explosion," she said. "Attacking your true love . . . not the sweetest of things to do on your engagement day. It is lucky you are not more powerful, or you might have set the boy on fire."

"Those explosions weren't me."

"Not at first," she said. "But the last one. Oh, your anger was something to behold. I knew you had the strength of it in you. You hated him in that moment, didn't you, Aurora?" She spoke lightly, as though it were all theoretical, a mild curiosity she had observed. "Hated him and his family and all this ridiculous show? And you could not stop it. You did not mean to, but it burst out of you."

"I do not hate him," Aurora said. And it was true. But, she realized, only partly true. She could not hate Rodric, the sweet, awkward prince, but she could hate Rodric, the prince who awoke her, who spoke of true love and happily ever after and forced her into this fate. She could hate everything he represented, and in that moment, with the chaos of the crowd, her panic and anger at the guard, her fear for the girl, it had come out. She had, for the briefest of moments, hated him.

And the ground exploded around him.

But that was a coincidence.

"I did not want to come to you before you had proved yourself," Celestine said. "I cannot abide useless people, Aurora, and I did not want to do everything for you myself. But now you have done this, now you've shown the fire in you . . . I think it is time we came to an arrangement."

Aurora stepped back, moving slowly, keeping her weight on the balls of her feet. "An arrangement?"

"Each of us has things that the other needs. You have magic, Aurora, burning inside you. And there is so very little of that left, even for me. But I know how to use it. I know how to make it count."

Aurora could not look away. Celestine was lying, she had to be lying. But a tightness had formed in Aurora's chest, compelling her to listen. "What are you offering me?"

Celestine slid closer, her footsteps so light that she seemed to float on the stone. "A choice," she said. "If you wished to use this power, to make these people suffer for every indignity they've given you . . . I could give that to you. And if you don't want it, I can make all of this go away. I could send you back to your family, let you be with them again."

Aurora's heartbeat pounded through her, counting out the seconds. The witch was trying to ensnare her, she knew it. She knew, but she could not look away. "What would I have to do?"

"Come with me," Celestine said. She was so close now that Aurora could see every dip in her smooth, porcelain skin. She ran her fingers through Aurora's hair, tangling the strands around her knuckles. "Let me teach you. Allow your power to strengthen me, return me to the woman I was before. I am a mere shadow of myself, Aurora. But you are the key. They are not lying when they say you can bring magic back. And once you have learned all I have to tell you, once you have done as I wish, you can make your own choice. You can stay with me, or you can return to your family, and never have to worry about me again."

"But others would," Aurora said. "If I help you, you'll hurt others."

"Perhaps," Celestine said. "But only those who deserve it."

Aurora still did not move. "You're a liar," she said. "Do you think I don't know what you've done, how many broken deals you've made? Why would I ever trust you?"

"I never once broke an agreement," Celestine said. She freed her fingers from Aurora's hair and brushed one sharp fingernail along the sweep of Aurora's jaw. "It is not my fault if people chose their bargains badly, or if they broke them once they were made. But you are clever, are you not, Aurora? You were meant for this. You will not have to marry the prince. You will not have to continue here, pretending that you can be happy, when we both know you cannot. I can offer you everything, Aurora. You could be with your family again."

Aurora stepped back, jerking away from the witch's touch.

"My family is dead," she said. "I should be dead too, if not for your curse. I would help you, and you would kill me, and call it a fair bargain. Isn't that right?"

"Perhaps," Celestine said. "If you did not join me. But you will want to join me. With me, you'll be who you were meant to be. You have so much potential inside you, and I would help you."

Aurora's throat was dry. "I will not help you," she said. "Not ever. Do you understand?"

"Poor, naïve girl." Celestine reached for Aurora, her fingers sliding through her hair, and Aurora jerked away. Her back thudded against the wall. "I am all there is for you now." Her voice was still soft, almost ethereal, like nothing she said mattered much to her at all, but then she moved, snatching both of Aurora's wrists. She squeezed so tightly that Aurora felt like her bones would snap. "Come with me, and you can avoid a lot of death and heartache. Wait, and this world will grind you up until you are begging for me to help you. You do not want that, now, do you? I am offering you an easier path, Aurora. An easier life."

"I don't want anything you have to offer me." Aurora pulled her arms away, but she could not loosen Celestine's grip. The witch's fingernails dug into her wrists, prying between the bones.

"A pity," Celestine said. "You will look back on this moment and regret it, I promise you."

"I will not." She yanked her wrists away again, but Celestine did not let go. "If you want me to go with you, you'll have to force me. And I will fight you every moment if you do. You cursed me. If you're looking for an ally, you won't ever find one in me."

Celestine sighed. The breath brushed against Aurora's cheek. "I am not the monster you think me to be," she said. "I have rules, Aurora, and there is no satisfaction in forcing anyone to do anything. I always give people the choice to refuse me. Even on the rare occasions, like today, when they would be fools to say no."

"You did not give me a choice when you cursed me."

"Did I not?" Celestine tilted her head again, a mockery of puzzlement. "I remember it differently." She released Aurora's wrists and glided back. Her eyes glinted in the darkness, blue and unforgiving. "Go then, if you must," she said. "When you change your mind, remember I will be close. You will come to me. Together, we will be wonderful." The green light sputtered behind her, and the wall behind Aurora's back seemed less solid, her shoulder slipping into the stone. "You will see, my dear," Celestine said, and her voice echoed in Aurora's head. "You will see."

Aurora closed her eyes for a fraction of a moment, sucking in a breath. When she opened them again, she stood in the corridor. Celestine was gone.

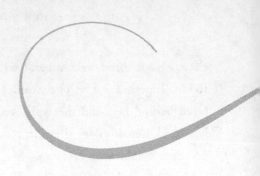

EIGHTEEN

THE GUARDS DID NOT SEEM TO HAVE NOTICED
Aurora's absence. As soon as she stepped into their midst, they
began walking again, the alert expressions back on their faces.

Aurora sat awake all night, her eyes fixed on the locked door.
She could still feel the witch's nails digging into her arm; little
half-moon crescents remained, red and fierce against her pale
skin.

Celestine was alive. Everyone Aurora had ever known was
dead, but Celestine was alive, lurking in the shadows, talking
in riddles about powers that Aurora could not possibly pos-
sess. Aurora wrapped her arms around her knees, every muscle

tense. She would not be afraid of her. But she could not let herself rest.

Betsy appeared the following morning, as she always did, but she did not say a word beyond the required pleasantries. She brought breakfast and helped Aurora into a simple dress, and then she left, the lock clicking behind her.

Aurora sank into a chair, slightly feverish from lack of sleep. Her eyes fell closed, and then snapped open again. She did not move for what felt like hours.

Then she heard the buzz and chatter of a crowd outside her window. Drums resounded through the castle. *The guard's execution,* she thought. After the shock of seeing Celestine, she had forgotten it.

She hurried across the room and banged on the door. She could not pick the lock with Iris's men on the other side, but if she made it down to the square, then surely they would have to listen to her. The king and queen would not want to seem in disagreement with her. But her guards ignored her, and the door held firm.

The drums rolled, the crowd gasped, and Aurora's opportunity was over.

She wavered in front of the door. Her bookshelf caught her eye, and she hurried over to it, pulling books out almost at random. Hunting for something, anything, to distract herself.

Her hand grasped the story of Alysse, founder of the kingdom, Aurora's favorite book for as long as she could remember.

The book said Alysse had been so good, so noble, beloved by all. Someone who had always done the right thing. Yet the books suggested the same things about Aurora, and not a word of it was true. It was all smiles and curtsies and promises, and Aurora chafing behind them, suffocating with expectations. Was that all Alysse had been too? Some girl, useless and confused, forced into an image by everyone else's hopes?

Aurora grabbed a page at random and tore it away, crumpling all its promises inside her fist. She ripped out another, and another, until they littered the floor. Every dream, every lie she had believed as a child, crushed in her hands.

"Princess?"

Rodric stood in the doorway. His mouth hung open as he took in the scene. "Are—are you all right?"

Blood rushed into her cheeks. Her display suddenly seemed foolish, now that she had an audience. "Yes," she said. She bent over, ignoring the twinge in her side, and gathered the crushed pages.

"Disappointing story?"

"You could say that." She tossed the fragments into the fire. Each one curled up instantly, the edges blackening, shrinking as though hiding from the heat, before the entire piece vanished in the flames.

"Do—do you mind if I come in?"

She shrugged, keeping close to the fire. The blaze warmed her skin. "It's not like I can go anywhere."

His footsteps crossed the floor. "I brought a game." His voice rose like it was a question. "I thought you might like company, but if you'd rather be left alone . . ."

"No," she said. She turned back to look at him. "I'd love to play."

The game involved multicolored squares and round pieces that leapt across the board. Aurora barely grasped the rules, but she won the first game, and the second. Either Rodric was an appalling player, or he was letting her win. Apart from explanations of the rules, and his corrections whenever she made a mistake, they played without speaking. No mention of the day before. No mention of the wedding. He didn't make any demands on her attention, and she no longer felt like she had to chatter aimlessly to please him. Yet the walls of her room loomed around them, and every time he shot her a nervous smile, she was reminded that they still did not fit together. Neither of them had chosen this.

She picked up a piece, and then put it back where she found it. "Why are you marrying me?"

He rubbed a hand across the back of his neck. "What do you mean?"

"You don't—you don't know me. And . . . I just don't understand."

Every tick of the clock jolted in her chest as she waited for him to speak. He stared down at the game board. "I guess—when I was little, I always wanted to do something. I don't know. When my father was arrested, and I was locked up in that tower, and the king was killed . . . I wanted to help. But . . . well, look at me." He shot the game board a self-deprecating smile. "Not exactly the noble prince. People always said the realm was broken, and the only thing that could fix things was—you. You, and now I guess me." He looked up. "If we have a chance to bring goodness and magic back, just by getting married—I want to do it. I want that chance. And if the promises are true, and if we will have true love, then that would be wonderful, but I would choose to do it either way, because I think you are good, and the people think you are good, and we have a real chance to make things the way they were before everything fell to pieces." He sounded so open, so honest, that Aurora blushed again. "Do you—do you not want that?"

She clutched her hands in her lap, twisting them tight. She could not be like him, so accepting and optimistic. "I guess—I guess I just want to be myself while I do it," she said.

"You can be yourself."

She moved a piece on the board without looking at it. "Your move," she said.

This time, Rodric won.

"I'd better go," Rodric said, once the game was over. "My father said he wished to speak to me before it got too late." Aurora nodded. He swept the pieces back into their box.

"Thank you," she said, the words tumbling over one another

in her hurry to get them out. "For coming here. Playing with me. It's been—it's lonely, sitting and waiting for things to happen."

He nodded. "I know how that feels." He raised a hand, as though reaching for hers, but stopped midgesture and turned away.

He was almost at the door when he paused. He did not look back. "Why did you do it?" he said.

She frowned. "Do what?"

"Prick your finger. If you knew the spinning wheel was cursed, why did you use it?"

She had never wondered that, not once. Fate decreed, and she had acted, like so much else in her life. "I didn't have a choice," she said. "Celestine enchanted me."

"There's always a choice, Princess."

He hurried out of the room before she could reply.

That night was particularly cold, mocking any dreams of the approaching spring. Aurora tightened the blankets around her, but the chill crept in through every gap, and she shivered. Her eyes refused to close. Whenever she blinked, the world filled with blood and needles stabbing into her skin, princes leaning down to kiss her and ice-cold bars everywhere she turned. She was so tired. She stared up at the ceiling, watching dark, imagined shapes flit across it. Rodric's words echoed in her head as she followed the shadows. *There's always a choice.* He sounded so convinced, but he was, in the end, like her, his life dictated by expectations and something they all called fate. Aurora wasn't sure she'd ever had a choice. It had all been laid out before her, by Celestine, by her parents' fear, by locked doors and fairy tales. Even now, as her wedding approached, she did not have space to choose. She was their savior, they said, and she had to obey them.

But Rodric's assertion would not leave her thoughts. She could choose to disobey the king and queen, to leave and accept everything that came with it . . . the loneliness, and the destruction that might follow. Or she could stay.

Yet what was the point, when she had no power of her own?

She sat up suddenly. Celestine had told her she had caused an explosion in the square in her anger. It was a terrifying thought. Impossible. But she had felt something in that moment that was not quite like herself. Anger that felt like madness, fury vanishing in a snap like the kick of a horse, and something that might be called magic, at least by a lying, manipulative tongue. And Celestine had seemed so convinced.

A spark lingered inside her.

If she had magic, and she could use it, she could help people. She could prevent Celestine from ever controlling her again.

The possibility took hold of her. Even if it was dangerous, even if the very thought of it made her feel sick . . . she had to know. She slid from her bed in one fluid motion and clutched at her dresser. A brush. Papers. A quill. Then the unmistakable smoothness of a candle. She tugged it free from its stand, cupping the base in her palms and wrapping her fingers around the stem.

Staring at the shape in the darkness, she willed it to light. *Burn*, she thought, and then she said it, whispering the word over and over like an incantation. "Burn, burn, burn."

Nothing. She squeezed the wax so tightly that she was sure it would snap, and pictured fire. Flames licking upward, tantalizing, hypnotic, sinful. The smell of smoke. Warmth on her face. She could almost hear the crackle and burn of it in the cool night air.

Nothing happened.

Frustration surged through her. *Useless,* she thought. She was a useless, stupid, sleeping princess, back then and now as well, playing at freedom while the bars crushed into her skin. Weak and willing to be manipulated by everyone around her. Sadness and curiosity and duty and fear had all at once seized her, but for a heartbeat, they were battered away, gone, lost under this hopeless fury. Hate stole her breath and scraped against her teeth, hate for the castle, hate for the darkness, hate for Tristan for deceiving her, hate for the queen and her stern, unbending expectations, hate for Celestine, for destroying her life and putting terrifying hopes in her head, and hate for herself, her weakness, her meekness, a life spent doing nothing.

For one bubbling, burning heartbeat, she allowed it to consume her.

The burn danced across her skin, chasing up her fingers. The smell of fire brushed her nose.

She gasped. The whole candle blazed.

NINETEEN

"PRINCESS, WHAT DID YOU DO TO YOUR HANDS?" BETSY turned Aurora's burned palms over, examining the raw flesh and barely formed scabs in the early morning light.

"I knocked over a candle," Aurora said. Betsy tutted and fetched a salve to soothe the pain, but she accepted the explanation without question. Aurora could not forget the incident so easily.

She flicked through books, trying to lose herself in the words, but every time she turned a page, her fingers ached, and she wondered whether these tales, too, were lies. A servant brought in a harp, and she plucked at it with stiff fingers, but the strings hurt her burns so much that she had to stop.

Although Rodric came every day to play, they did not talk about anything more compelling than the weather and the delicious food Rodric heard the servants were preparing for their engagement banquet. Once, Aurora dared to ask if anyone had caught the instigators of the violence at their ceremony. Rodric shook his head.

She ran her thumb along the healing burns, over and over, tracing the raw smoothness and the fierce blisters. The candle had left a spark of something in her. Not boldness, not resolve, and not a part of her old self—meek and adventurous, loving and resentful, hiding and smiling and curtsying and reading—but something secret and dangerous and entirely her own.

Or entirely its own. Although Aurora tried, again and again, to set something else on fire, shatter the vase on her table, knock a book off her shelf, she could not create even the slightest shift in the air. The hope of it flickered inside her, that spark that promised she was not as weak as she seemed, but it was unwilling to bow to her demands. If not for the red blisters that still covered her skin, she might have called it a dream, another moment of madness and flame.

She ran her fingers through her own story, *The Tale of Sleeping Beauty*, once again. She had spent a hundred years under a spell. Perhaps that magic had seeped into her, giving her power that she could not entirely control. Power that the witch now wanted back.

"Good morning, Princess," Rodric said when he arrived at her door a few days later. He hovered at the threshold, his cheeks pink. "I hope I'm not disturbing you."

"No," she said. She pushed her breakfast tray away and stood. "Of course you aren't."

"I have a surprise for you," he said.

"A surprise?"

"I thought it must be getting a little tiring," he said. "Being stuck in here all the time. So I thought we might go into the gardens."

Aurora smiled. The gardens were not exactly her idea of an adventure, but even embroidery with the queen would have been preferable to staying locked up in her room for another day. The fresh air would clear her head.

"That would be lovely," she said.

"I know it might be a bit cold," Rodric continued. "The sun won't be fully over the castle walls for another couple of hours, but . . . well, my mother is otherwise engaged this morning. She won't be wanting us for hours."

"And she wouldn't approve of what you've got planned?"

"I don't think she would *not* approve," Rodric said carefully. "But it may be better if she doesn't know until after it's done."

Rodric, being mysterious? Aurora had not imagined it possible. "What exactly are you planning?" she asked.

Rodric only smiled. "You'll see. Shall we go?"

As they walked through the corridors, followed by guards, Aurora tried to puzzle out what Rodric intended. It was too cold for a picnic, and they could play most games inside easily enough. Perhaps they would be taking Isabelle for an outing, but surely he could have told her that before.

When she finally glimpsed the garden, she paused, a smile spreading across her face.

Two horses stood on the path, held in place by a groom. The one farthest from Aurora was pure black with a lush mane and tail. The horse tossed its head, as though it were fully aware of its beauty and eager for everyone to appreciate it. The one nearer to Aurora was smaller and a little stockier, with a creamy gold coat and a white mane and tail that fell in rough waves. It had a pale splotch on its nose, and it was nuzzling the back of the groom's hand with its upper lip.

"You said before that you'd always wanted to ride a horse," Rodric said. "So I thought—I mean, it isn't exactly riding through the forest, that wouldn't be safe, but—we could try it. For a little bit. If you'd like."

"Yes," she said, and the word came out more like a breath. "Yes, it's wonderful. Thank you." Gratitude rushed through her. She spun on her toes and threw her arms around his neck, hugging him tight. He touched her gingerly on the back in return.

"Really," she said. "Thank you." She let go and turned back to the horses. "Which one is for me?"

"The smaller one. Her name's Polly. The black one is my horse, Shadow. Best horse in the kingdom. But she's a bit big for you."

Aurora crept closer, her arm outstretched. Polly stopped chewing on the groom's knuckles and turned to look at her. Aurora brushed her fingertips down the horse's nose, feeling the softness of her fur.

"She likes it if you scratch under her chin," the groom said. Aurora tried it, slightly scared that the horse would nip at her fingers. Instead, Polly's lower lip shook, and she tilted her head to butt Aurora lightly with her nose.

"How did you get them here?" she asked. The garden was entirely enclosed, solid castle walls on all sides.

"Well, to be honest," Rodric said, "I just led them through the corridors and hoped no one would tell me not to."

"And they didn't?"

"No," Rodric said. "One of the advantages of being a prince, I suppose."

"Ready to ride her, Princess?" the groom said, and Aurora felt a jolt of panic. The idea of riding had always excited her, but now that the opportunity was before her, with a horse whose back was higher than her head, she realized she hadn't the first clue how to go about it.

"All right," she said. "If you'll help me."

The groom held the horse's head while Rodric helped guide Aurora's left foot into the stirrup. Aurora jumped up, putting all her weight in the metal loop, and felt the saddle shift slightly as she scrambled with her right leg, trying to find her balance. Then she was sitting on the horse, reins loose in her hands, her skirt tangled around her.

"Now swing your right leg back this way," the groom said, "and put it between these two pommels here." She did what he asked, wobbling as her foot brushed across the horse's neck. Her leg slipped between the grips, and she sat back. It was a lot more comfortable than it had looked. As the groom adjusted the saddle straps on either side of her and fetched her a whip, he explained the basics to her: pull back to stop, kick to go, steer with your feet on one side and the crop on the other.

Polly turned her head and nibbled Aurora's toe.

For all his talk about being afraid of horses, Rodric hopped into his own saddle without any apparent problems. He adjusted the straps from where he sat, and then turned to Aurora with an expectant look on his face.

"After you," he said.

The groom still held the front of Aurora's bridle, but Aurora dug her heels into Polly's side anyway, and Polly plodded forward. Her footsteps clopped on the cobblestones, her whole body tilting from side to side as she walked. Aurora grabbed the front of the saddle.

"Are you all right?" Rodric asked. He was smiling, but he at least tried to sound concerned.

"Yes," Aurora said. "She just surprised me."

"Hold your reins a little tighter," Rodric said. "So that you can feel tension in her mouth, just a little bit. And then relax your hands in front of you. Yes, like that, that's good."

The reins rubbed against Aurora's burns, but Aurora found she did not mind. She could feel the horse's body heat beneath her, the sway of her steps, the way she nodded her head slightly as she walked. She felt connected, and even though they were moving slowly, even though they were still locked within the castle walls, she felt lighter, freer. She dared to lower her reins slightly and run her fingers through the fur at the nape of Polly's neck.

Rodric urged his horse alongside her.

She had clearly been given the gentlest, slowest horse in the stables. Polly followed Aurora's every tentative instruction without complaint, and her simple lack of majesty was almost comforting. Occasionally, she would yank her head to the side to chew on flower buds or tree branches, almost pulling Aurora's arms out of their sockets in the process, but the groom would pull her firmly in the other direction. "If she eats any of those flowers," he mumbled, "the queen'll have my head."

After a couple of loops of the gardens, Rodric suggested, with slight trepidation in his voice, that Aurora might like to try a canter. "You only have to sit back," he said. "Put all your weight in your saddle. Kick her on, one big kick, and then pull back when you want to stop. Polly's a good mount. She'll take care of you."

"All right," Aurora said. "Yes. I'll try it."

The groom frowned. "I can't run with you, Princess, if you do. It'll be too fast for my old legs."

"I'll be all right," Aurora said, although she did not feel as sure as she sounded. "Polly and I seem to be getting along well, don't we, Polly?" Polly blew air through her nose, as though in agreement.

On Rodric's shout, she sat down firmly in the saddle and kicked Polly forward. The horse leapt into a steady canter, her movements suddenly smooth, a flowing rise and fall. They came to a low-hanging branch. Aurora ducked. Twigs scraped the top of her head, and Aurora laughed. As though urged on by Aurora's glee, Polly picked up speed, her feet thrumming on the ground.

They reached a corner. Polly turned, leaning to the side to maintain speed. Aurora's foot slipped out of her stirrup. The metal clanged against her ankle a couple of times, and then Aurora was slipping too, her weight falling more and more to the left. She snatched for Polly's mane, but by the time she had realized what was happening, it was too late to stop it. The sky blurred before her eyes, and then she hit the flowerbeds with a thump.

"Princess! Princess, are you all right?"

Aurora took a moment to stare at the clouds. Her back was

slightly sore, but otherwise, she felt unhurt. She pushed herself into a sitting position.

Rodric had dismounted Shadow and was hurrying toward her, the horse's reins in his hands. The groom was running to grab Polly, but that seemed unnecessary. The cream horse was standing a few paces from Aurora, looking at her as though wondering what she was doing on the ground.

"Princess," Rodric said again. "Are you hurt?"

"I'm all right," she said, and she stood up to prove her point, brushing the dust from her skirts. "It was only a little fall."

But Rodric still looked pale. "Maybe we should stop for now."

"I promise I'm fine," Aurora said, but Rodric was chewing his lip, and she could tell that every possible riding-related disaster was now filling his head. "Another day?" she said. "With Polly? I just got ahead of myself. I'll be more careful next time."

"Of course," Rodric said. "I promise. After—after the wedding, we'll give you real lessons. And then you can ride out beyond the walls."

After the wedding. Her happiness ebbed at the thought. There would be many good things to marrying Rodric, she knew that. The freedom to finally leave the castle and ride a horse would be one of them. Rodric's extreme kindness and consideration would be another. But despite all that, he still only felt like a friend, and the looming wedding seemed like the day when all her possibilities would finally be taken away.

"Shall I help you back to your rooms?" Rodric asked.

"No," she said softly. "No, you help deal with the horses. I am sure the guards will walk me."

"I'm happy to—"

"No, it's all right," she said firmly. "I would like some time to think."

Rodric nodded, but she could not help noticing his disappointed expression as she walked away.

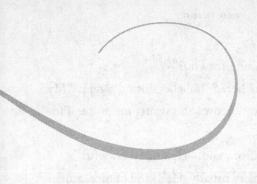

TWENTY

AURORA WAS READYING HERSELF FOR BED THAT NIGHT
when she heard a quiet voice in the doorway.

"Hello."

Aurora looked up. Isabelle was peering around the door.
Aurora placed her brush on the table and stared at her. "Hello,
Isabelle," she said.

The girl slipped into the room. "Rod said you were hurt. He
said that's why you aren't around anymore."

"I'm okay," Aurora said. "It's—it's just safer if I stay here."

Isabelle moved closer, eyes fixed on the ground. "Can I stay
here?" she said. "For a little while?"

"Won't someone be looking for you?"

"The guards know I'm here." Isabelle shifted again. "My mother wants to see me tomorrow. She wants me to see Finnegan."

"It will be all right," Aurora said. "He's not too awful."

Isabelle giggled. "He's okay usually. He's kind of nice. Smiles and tells jokes. But when my mother is there, it's like it's not really him anymore. All his smiles are too big."

Aurora sat down on a stool, and waved Isabelle over to her. "I think your mother has that effect on a lot of people."

Isabelle offered a small smile. She sat down by Aurora's feet, her chin resting on her knees. "I don't think he wants to marry me very much."

"It sounds like he likes you," Aurora said. "But you are a lot younger than he is. And I don't think Finnegan's the sort of person who would let anyone tell him what to do. No one would mind if he refused."

Isabelle was quiet for a long moment. "Mother would mind," she said. "She would say I failed."

"It wouldn't be your fault."

"But it would, wouldn't it?" Isabelle craned her neck to look at Aurora. "Mother says it would be the greatest thing I could do, and if it's the right thing, then shouldn't I do it? And if I didn't do it, doesn't that mean I wasn't good enough for him? So I failed."

Aurora ran her fingers through Isabelle's hair. "No," she said softly. "That's not true."

"It's all right for you," Isabelle said. "You have Rodric. Everything's already worked out."

"That's not entirely true either," Aurora said. "My mother told me the same things too, you know. I didn't have to meet princes, but she always told me—she said, it was my duty to be good and admired. If I did as I ought, happiness would come to me." The words had been so promising at the time. If she did her duty, if she waited in her tower until she turned eighteen, happiness would come after.

"I think she had suitors in mind for me too," she said. "I remember, on the day I—on my last day at home, she was preparing me for a big ball. For my birthday. And she kept telling me about all the princes who would attend. I think she intended me to marry one of them."

"But you're going to marry Rodric, aren't you?"

Aurora nodded. "Those princes—they are long dead now."

"And you—you love him. Don't you?" Isabelle peered over her shoulder with wide, meek eyes, as though desperate for the answer. Desperate, and a little afraid. "Because the princesses always love the princes in the stories, but Mother says that's silly. She says we have to marry whoever's best for the realm and we'll be happy later. But—but you love Rodric, don't you? Like in the book."

Isabelle trembled at the end of her speech. She continued to stare at Aurora, all hope and fear, and Aurora's reply stuck in her throat. How could she tell her the truth? How could she tell her that she had felt more for a rebel in an inn than for Isabelle's kindhearted older brother? Rodric deserved her affection, and Tristan did not, yet Tristan's betrayal still ached, while Rodric's kindness felt like nothing more than friendship. "Your brother is a good man," she said eventually, each word slow and careful. "But I barely know him yet. Perhaps, in the future . . . if the story is true . . ."

Isabelle did not flinch or look away, but the corners of her mouth turned down a fraction of an inch. She nodded. "It has to be," she said.

No, Aurora thought, staring down at the strands of Isabelle's hair caught between her fingers. The story was not true. She had awoken, out of need, or coincidence, or Celestine deciding it was time, or simply magic too weak to hold her any longer. Not because of fated love.

It did not matter, though. Others believed in it, and that, it seemed, was reason enough.

Aurora stayed up reading by the light of a candle. Her feet were tucked inside her nightgown, a blanket wrapped around her shoulders. The castle had been silent for hours. Even the servants were asleep, but Aurora's mind was still too full of her conversation with Isabelle to rest. She stared at the pages, but she could not process the words.

She was about to give up and try to sleep when she heard movement outside her room. Footsteps, and a few whispered words. She stared at the door.

The handle shook.

Aurora stood up. She had nothing that even vaguely looked like a weapon, so she tightened her grip on the book, feeling its weight. If Celestine had come for her again, she did not know how she would defend herself.

But when the door inched open, it wasn't the witch who entered.

It was Finnegan.

"Good," he said. "You're awake."

She stepped back, suddenly very aware of the way her nightgown brushed below her knees. "Finnegan," she said. "What are you doing here?"

"I have something to show you."

She shook her head. Her fingers tightened around the book. "My guards—"

"They let me in."

"They let you in?"

"It's surprising what people will do if you give them enough coins. I'm doing you a favor, coming here."

"You're doing me a favor?" she echoed. "By breaking into my room at night?"

"Something is happening," he said. "Down in the dungeons. Something you need to see."

Aurora shivered. She wrapped her free arm across her stomach, clutching her elbow. Explosions in the square, innocent people arrested, rebels who wanted the king dead. Dread crawled up her spine.

"Show me," she said.

Apart from her guards, her corridor was deserted, but she could hear voices and people running, the sounds echoing up from lower floors.

Finnegan took her hand. His palm was warm, his fingers sliding between hers. "This way," he said.

He led her down the corridor until they reached a battered tapestry at the top of the stairs. He lifted it with his free hand, revealing a narrow passageway. The torchlight illuminated the first few feet, showing rough stone coated with dust, but the darkness beyond was impenetrable. Anything could lurk within.

Aurora hesitated.

"Only way to get around unnoticed," Finnegan said. "Come on." She stepped under his arm into the tunnel. He followed her, dropping the tapestry as he went, so the material slapped against their backs, plunging them into darkness. Aurora tightened her hold on his hand. He squeezed back.

"Don't worry," he said. "I won't let the monsters get you."

"I wasn't worried," she said. "I don't want to lose you in the dark."

"Of course not. I wouldn't want to lose me either."

He walked on. Aurora's toes curled as she stepped in dust, the occasional cobweb sticking to her skin. She could barely make out the shape of Finnegan's shoulder ahead of her, the arm stretching back to hold her hand. Apart from their movements, the hiss of their breath, the passage was still.

"There are stairs down here," Finnegan said. "Be careful."

The stairs twisted beneath them. She tested each movement with her toes, turning her feet so they fit on the worn steps. Finnegan walked without hesitation, as though he had taken this path many times before.

A light glowed ahead. She could hear voices again, faint ones, but the echo made it impossible to understand the words. They paused a few steps from the bottom, listening.

She recognized one of the speakers. Tristan.

Aurora hurried past Finnegan, her feet slipping in her haste. The stairs opened onto a small alcove. Beyond, Aurora could only see an unlit stone wall, the light of nearby sconces spilling across the uneven floor. Aurora clung to the wall with her fingertips, peering around the corner.

Tristan stood toward the end of the corridor, dressed in the garb of the castle servants. A guard held his arms behind his back, while another leaned into his face. "It's like I told you," Tristan said. "I was passing through on my way to bed, and I heard a commotion. I rushed to see what was happening."

"Strange that I haven't seen your face before, dutiful servant as you are," the guard said.

"Ask the king," Tristan said. "He'll vouch for me. He gave me the job himself. I've worked for him for years."

Aurora's fingers tightened around the stone. Her first

instinct was to help him. To provide a distraction, to run up to the guards and order them to release him, to do *something*. If he did not escape, he would surely be killed. But doubt made her pause. She could not think of a single innocent reason why he might be here, dressed as a servant in the middle of the night.

Finnegan rested a hand on her shoulder, pulling her back. She shrugged him off.

"It's your lucky day, then, isn't it?" the guard said. "The king'll be here any moment, to deal with the lot of yeh. I don't think he'll be too pleased. Springing prisoners from the dungeon and all."

Aurora bit her lip. She remembered the old woman who had been arrested on her first day in court, the healing woman accused of poisoning her village and locked down here to rot. If Tristan had been rescuing people like her, helping them escape . . .

Sounds of fighting burst down the corridor. Grunts. Yells. Metal crashing against stone.

The guard who had been interrogating Tristan turned at the noise and reached for his sword. As soon as he looked away, Tristan moved. His arms slipped free of the second guard, almost as if he had been released, and his foot snaked around the distracted man's ankle, knocking him off-balance. As the guard stumbled, still reaching for his sword, Tristan yanked a knife out of his boot. He plunged it into the guard's side. The guard yelled, twisting toward the wound, and Tristan ran, toward the fighting, toward Aurora and Finnegan. He did not even glance at them as he passed. He skidded around the corner, swerving left, and then he was gone.

Aurora stepped after him as though she could catch him and demand to know what was happening, but Finnegan's hand tightened on her shoulder, yanking her back into the shadows.

"Careful," he whispered. "Don't let them see you."

"But—" She did not know how to process what she had seen. "The guard."

"He will live," Finnegan said. "That was a wound to slow him, not to kill him."

"And you know the difference?"

He jerked his head in a nod. More footsteps were coming down the corridor. The bleeding guard lurched to his feet and ran after Tristan, his partner trailing behind. But with the guard's injury, Tristan had gained a decent head start. He might escape, if he did not join the other fight.

Aurora leaned toward the noise, but she couldn't see anything. "We should get closer," she whispered to Finnegan.

He shook his head. "Any closer and they might see us."

Then another voice she recognized drifted down the corridor. "Have all the traitors been apprehended?"

The king.

"The fighting is continuing in the north wing of the dungeons," his attendant said. They marched into view. Aurora shrank back, pressing closer to Finnegan, trying to melt into the shadows. "But they're outnumbered. We will overpower them quickly. A weak attempt, in all."

"Any casualties in our ranks?"

"Not as far as I have heard. Except for the cost of the traitors among us, of course."

"Indeed."

The pair strode past Aurora and Finnegan's hiding place. Aurora held her breath, wishing that she could vanish into the stone itself.

"We cannot let word of this get out," the king continued. "We must deal with this tonight."

"Of course, Your Majesty."

They turned right, heading in the direction where swords had clashed only moments before, but Aurora could still hear every word.

"You have killed all of the intruders? And everyone who tried to escape?"

"All the ones who fought back, Your Majesty. We have a couple of others in custody. We thought we might interrogate them."

The king scoffed. "All you'll get from them is lies," he said. "Kill them and be done with it."

"Yes, Your Majesty."

Aurora flinched again. Tristan had run the other way, away from where the king now stood. Away from the ongoing fight. She turned to Finnegan for confirmation. "The way that boy took," she whispered. "Would it lead out of the dungeons?"

Finnegan nodded. "It wouldn't lead to the north wing, at least. He probably got out."

The footsteps stopped. Aurora strained to hear the words. "And the other prisoners?" the king said. "How many remain?"

"Most of them. We haven't done a full check, but it seems only those recently arrested for seditious activity were freed."

So Tristan had not been here to free all the innocents in the dungeons after all. He had only been trying to rescue his allies, his friends.

"We can't have this happen again," the king said. "Tell the guards to slit the prisoners' throats."

Aurora jerked forward, but Finnegan wrapped an arm around her chest, pulling her back.

The attendant hesitated. "A-all of them, Your Majesty?"

"All of them. Then bring the guards who were on duty tonight to me. I want to deal with them myself."

Aurora pulled away from Finnegan again, but he did not let go. "He can't do that," she said. She saw that old woman again, bent double in court, so certain that her king would protect her. The terror on her face as she was dragged away. "He can't kill them."

"He can, and he will. What do you think he'll do to you if he sees you here too?"

"He won't hurt me," she said. "He needs me."

"So much that he wouldn't take the chance to get rid of you?

Don't be stupid, Aurora. Think."

"I am not stupid." She wrenched her arm away and spun to face him. "He's going to kill them, Finnegan. Innocent people."

"He was going to kill them anyway, if they're locked down here." Finnegan's voice was low and steady. "You know he was." He shook his head. "Let's get out of here, before it gets any worse. If they see us . . ."

"We can't just leave."

"We have to. There is nothing you can do." He pulled her arm, dragging her farther into the shadows, until they stumbled against the stairs.

She shoved him backward, letting her anger, her disgust, snap through her arms. "Why did you bring me here?" she said. "Why, if there was nothing we could do?"

"Because I wanted you to know," Finnegan said. "I wanted you to see for yourself." He sighed and ran a hand through his hair, making the black waves stand on end. The movement made him look suddenly vulnerable. "I'm sorry," he said. "I didn't realize that was going to happen."

He sounded so genuine that Aurora paused. "It would have happened whether we saw it or not," she said. "But leaving without helping—"

Finnegan brushed a hand across her shoulder. "You can't help," he said. "Not now. We need to go before they find you missing, or things will get a lot worse."

As they climbed the stairs, Aurora imagined she could still

hear swords ringing in the distance. Hear the shouts of helpless prisoners as metal slashed across their throats.

Finnegan walked her back to her room. "Are you all right?" he asked as she reached for the doorknob. His hand lingered on her shoulder.

"No," she said. The word scratched her throat. "I don't think I should be."

Finnegan nodded. "I'm here for you," he said.

"You're here for my throne."

"No." His grip tightened. "I'm here for you." He leaned closer, and Aurora froze. He was going to kiss her. His lips brushed against her cheekbone. Her skin burned where he had touched. Aurora fought the urge to tilt her head, to slip her lips closer to his. She had already had one ill-advised kiss in the past few weeks, and she hated Finnegan. She hated him. Yet the hatred was a rush of warmth against the horror of what she had seen, and she did not want to move away.

Finnegan's nose trailed along hers, and then he stepped back, no trace of a smile on his face. "Remember what I said."

Aurora pushed the door open and stepped back into the room. He was too close, but suddenly, she did not want him to go. She did not want to be left alone.

"I'll lock the door behind you," Finnegan said. She nodded. The door closed, and she was alone.

Several floors below her, people were dying. They were dying, murdered in their cells, while she stood in her bedroom, safe, cold, a world away from it all. She could almost see the blood, red on stone, splattered on skin. But there was nothing she could do.

She strode across the room and poured herself a glass of water. Her wrist shook, water splashing over the edge of the glass. She stared at her hand. It seemed to belong to somebody else, too pale, moving of its own accord. And she remembered the queen, sitting in this room, her hand shaking around the same glass, because Aurora had disobeyed her, because she had put everything at risk.

Aurora slammed the glass down on the table. Her hand still shook.

Had Tristan made it out alive? He and his men had fled, leaving the slow and the innocent to face the king's fury. He had chosen this risk, not them. Maybe he deserved to face that failure with them too.

She could do nothing for those people now. But soon . . . soon she would be crown princess, next to be queen. Her place would be secure. Then they would see who she had the potential to be.

TWENTY-ONE

"ARE YOU FEELING ALL RIGHT, PRINCESS?" BETSY ASKED the following morning as she pinned up Aurora's hair. "You are looking pale."

"Yes," Aurora said. She had slept little, her mind too full of the king's orders, of people dying within the castle while she huddled in her room. Surely Betsy would know something about what had happened, even if it was distorted by lies. But Aurora could not tell her what she had seen. "I just—I heard some things, late last night. People running and shouting. I wasn't sure what was happening."

"Nothing happened last night, Princess, as far as I know. Maybe you were dreaming."

"Maybe." She glanced at Betsy's reflection. The maid's expression was steady, her hands sure. She did not look like she was hiding anything. "It sounded real."

"Everything was fine, Princess," Betsy said firmly. "And if it wasn't, you are safe here, with your guards."

Aurora nodded. Yet she had put Betsy at risk again, by leaving her room at night, ignoring all locks and warnings and running straight toward trouble. She felt a tug of guilt. "I am sorry, you know," she said softly. "For what happened before."

Betsy's hands stilled. "It's not your place to apologize to me, Princess."

"But it is." She stepped away, sliding her hair out of Betsy's reach and turning to look at the younger girl. "I ignored your warnings, and you got in trouble because of me. And I really am sorry."

Betsy nodded. She smiled. "There's no need to worry about the past, Princess," she said. "We've got your wedding to think on." She stepped up on tiptoe and pinned another curl away from Aurora's face. "And the banquet tomorrow. The queen's got a dress all picked out for you, but I was thinking about your hair. Perhaps some twists from the front, sweeping to a bunch of rosettes on the back of your head, and then loose curls . . . if that pleases you, of course."

"Yes," Aurora said. A smile crept across her lips despite herself. "That sounds lovely."

Betsy nodded and slid a pin into place. She opened her mouth to speak again, but the door opened, and Queen Iris swept into the room. She wore a tense, pinched expression, her hands clutched in front of her.

"Prince Finnegan wishes to see you," the queen said. She emphasized the *ns* in Finnegan's name so that it sounded like an insult.

Aurora turned. A lock of hair tumbled, brushing her shoulder. "Right now?"

"Yes, right now," the queen said. "Why else would I be here? Betsy, leave her hair. She will have to do as she is."

He must have news, some new information about the events of the previous night. Aurora removed the loose pin, trying to appear calm. "What does he wish to see me about?"

"Goodness knows, Aurora. If that prince has any logic in his head, he is loath to share it with me."

The queen led Aurora to a small lounge filled with comfortable-looking chairs on one of the castle's upper floors. Finnegan stood up when the door opened, offering her a casual smile. His expression did not give a single hint about the last time they had spoken.

"Ah, Princess Aurora," he said. "How lovely to see you again." He bent down and brushed his lips across the back of her hand. Her cheek tingled with the memory of his kiss, the anticipation that burned when she thought he would really kiss her, the thrill of uncertainty over whether she would shove him away. "Thank you for allowing us another meeting, my dear Iris. I appreciate it, as always."

The queen tilted her head in acknowledgment. "I am afraid I can only spare the princess for half an hour. We have many things to do in preparation for tomorrow's banquet."

"Yes, of course," Finnegan said. "I will savor the moments."

The queen nodded again, her hands held before her. "I will return to collect you, Aurora. My guards will wait outside the door if you need anything." Then she departed, her skirts flowing out behind her.

Aurora spoke as soon as the door clicked shut. "What is it?" she said. "Did you learn something about last night?"

"Nothing more than what you heard. The king is keeping it quiet. I doubt Iris even knows."

Aurora shook her head. "He can't keep it quiet for long," she said. "So many people are dead."

"People that nobody cares about," Finnegan said. "If we hear about it, it'll be about rebels storming in and killing the king's men. But they'll keep that quiet too, if they can. It wouldn't be good for the king to reveal flaws in his defenses, so close to the happy day."

"You heard about it," Aurora said. "You knew before it even started."

"I have my sources," he said.

"You have spies, you mean."

"Of course."

"Why didn't you stop it?" she said. "If you knew what was going to happen?"

He sat down on one of the comfortable chairs. "How would I stop it, Aurora? Please, enlighten me. How do I stop people I don't know from doing something they've already started, or stop the sovereign of another country from dealing with his own criminals? Should I swoop in with my dragons and threaten them all? Or maybe you were thinking something subtler. Charming them all into submission, perhaps?"

She frowned. "Don't mock me," she said. "Not now."

"It's strange how you always take the truth as mockery. Perhaps there is just something inherently mockable about you."

"Or perhaps there is just something inherently insufferable about you."

"Insufferable?" he said. "Harsh words, Aurora. But remember, I was the one who kept you informed last night. Without me, you'd be as ignorant as you were before."

"I guess that makes you my spy," she said. "Although not a very informative one."

"I live to serve. If not very well."

She still refused to sit down. She paced, the nervous energy of the night buzzing through her.

"Things could have been worse," Finnegan said, after a few moments of silence. "That friend of yours was lucky to escape."

"Friend?" She stopped. "What do you mean—?"

"I saw your face, when they were threatening that boy. You knew him."

She stared at him. There seemed little point in lying. "Yes," she said. The confession made her dizzy. "I did. Or I thought I did."

"Thinking of betraying Rodric, were you? And with someone other than me? I'm hurt, Aurora, truly I am." He spoke lightly, but something hard and intense gleamed in his eyes.

"If you want to give me that nonsense, now is not the time."

"Now seems exactly the time." He stood up, so that she had to crane her neck to look at him. He was at least six inches taller than she was. For once, his expression was sincere, without a hint of a grin. "You saw King John for who he really is last night. You can't stay here, not after that."

"I have to stay."

"No," he said. "You don't. And you'd be a fool to do so. There's no hope for you here. There's no hope for anyone."

"So you're trying to convince me to betray my country to save it? How noble of you."

"Well, my motives aren't entirely noble," he said. "But you summed it up rather well." He leaned closer, until his nose almost brushed hers. "Things are only going to get worse, Aurora. Last night was just a taste of what will happen if you stay."

"How can you know that?"

"Because I've seen these things before. This is only the beginning, Aurora. Which is why you should listen to me. Have you wondered why, even though we're small, your king and queen fear Vanhelm? It's because we're rich. Well organized. People are happy to ally with us."

She stepped backward, forcing more space between them. "It's because they're stupid enough to think someone like you could control the dragons. Not because you're actually powerful."

His smile grew at her assertion, as though he expected nothing less from her. "Ah, but I made them think I had that kind of power. Don't you think that shows some intelligence and initiative too? I'm sure you know plenty about letting people believe lies, with your wedding to your true love so close. The only difference is, my lie makes me look powerful. It gets me what I want. Your lie just puts you in the background. And you do look so stifled there."

"I will not be in the background for long," she said. "I will make a difference."

"Really? Is that what you think?"

She forced herself not to look away. "I woke up for a reason," she said. "I'll make sure of it."

"And who says that reason is Rodric? Who says the reason is staying here?"

She threw up her chin. Her hair tickled her neck. "The fact that he woke me up, and you didn't? Rodric will make a good king. And I will make a good queen."

"I don't doubt it," he said. "But let me tell you something. Rodric might make a good king someday, but not now. Not in this mess. What do you plan to do in the meantime?" She did not reply. "For someone so fierce, you seem surprisingly happy to be powerless. You don't have to stay here and go down with the rest of them. If you came with me, you could let some of that fire out. Be who you are actually meant to be."

Fire. The burns on her hands throbbed.

"I would have thought you have enough fire," she said. "What with that dragon problem of yours."

"The dragons are beautiful," he said. "But none is quite so lovely and terrifying as you. John and Iris don't even know what they have in you."

"And what is that?"

"Now, I'd be a fool to tell you, wouldn't I, if you aren't going to be on my side. But you should be careful, Princess. I doubt setting your dear Rodric on fire would fit in with your plans."

She drew in a breath, cold and sharp. "How did you—"

"So it is true," he said. "I thought so. Word of advice, Princess: don't ever assume that anyone knows as much as you do. You never know what you might end up giving away."

She pressed her lips together, hating him, hating herself for revealing too much. For falling under the spell of the argument, of the terrible possibilities he promised, and forgetting to guard herself. "You're despicable."

"No," he said. "I am honest. At least with you." He was standing too close to her, but she could not move away. "They will destroy you, you know," he said. "When they find out who you really are."

"I will not betray my kingdom."

"It would not have to be a betrayal, Aurora," he said. "Everyone else is playing the game. Why can't you?"

She stepped back, her heart pounding. "It isn't a game," she said. Finnegan was still too close, his presence filling the room. She moved toward the door, trying to hide the way her hands shook. "Thank you for your advice," she said. "But I will not change my mind."

"Of course not, Princess," he said. The name seemed taunting on his tongue. "But I'll be waiting if you do."

The queen called Aurora to her chambers again that afternoon for the final fitting of her wedding dress. It fell in streams of gossamer and ice, floating ethereal on the air and transforming her into a fairy that might have slipped, like a dewdrop, out of the mist. Two of the seamstresses gasped and exclaimed at her beauty, while the third, the tall, austere one, stood farther back and watched the scene with stern, approving eyes.

"What do you think of it, Aurora?" the queen asked as a seamstress placed a single lily behind the princess's ear. The queen clutched Aurora by the shoulders and spun her gently toward a full-length mirror, decorated with swirling silver and darted through with jewels.

"It's beautiful." And it was. Her hair fell down her

shoulders like a waterfall of golden silk, while the material of the dress shimmered with such delicacy that one touch might make it melt away into nothing. The bodice was tight, forcing in Aurora's stomach, but it also straightened her back, making her tall, elegant, regal. She reached out and touched the cold glass with the tip of her index finger. The skin still seemed to prickle from the point of a needle. *This is my destiny.* Her head began to spin.

After the dress had been pinned and tucked, and the seamstresses had scurried away, the queen met her eyes in the mirror. "I think you will do," she said. She ran a hand down the back of Aurora's hair. "If you follow my instructions, perhaps things will turn out well."

If she practiced her lies. If she remained as careful, as false, as Iris herself.

Aurora stared at their reflection. The queen's elegance was effortless, but beneath it, Aurora thought she seemed rather tired. "Tell me what it is like," Aurora said slowly. "To be queen."

The queen frowned, and for a moment, Aurora thought she was going to dismiss her. Then she spoke, her voice soft. "It is . . . hard," she said. "They are always watching you, Aurora. You have all the appearance of authority, but no actual power. And if you let that appearance slip, you lose even that."

"If you knew—if your husband were doing something terrible, would you stop him?"

"Aurora, my dear, I can as little control my husband as I can stop the rain. After many years, I have learned to cajole him. But my opinion stopped counting the moment I was sent here to marry him." She ran her fingers through the ends of Aurora's hair. "But you need not worry yourself about that. You have been given a good lot, for all your grief. Rodric is not that sort of boy."

For a moment, Aurora considered going to Rodric and telling him what she had seen. About sneaking into the dungeons, about Tristan, about his father's brutality. But she couldn't do it. Not if it meant losing Rodric's trust. He deserved more than her lies and fake smiles. He deserved the things she could not be.

Suddenly, she knew what she wanted to do. "I wish to see Rodric," she said. The words burst out in an ungainly tumble.

Iris frowned. "The banquet is tomorrow, Aurora, and we have much to do. I am sure it can wait."

"I wish to give him a favor," Aurora said, clutching her skirt with her hand. From what she had read, it was precisely the thing a young princess would request. "I wish . . . to settle things. Before we marry."

Perhaps it was her use of the word "marry," the admission and acceptance of her future, that made the queen pause. "What is it you wish to give him?" she said.

"A book."

The queen raised her eyebrows. "A book? That is hardly a traditional gift."

Aurora's fingers twisted in her skirt. She forced herself to look the queen in the eye. "No," she said, "but I am hardly a traditional bride."

She waited for Rodric in the queen's garden, sitting stiffly on the chilly wooden bench. The trees here were still bare, but a few brave daffodils had poked their heads free from the soil and burst into bloom, a spattering of sunshine against the shadows of the afternoon. The book lay heavy in Aurora's lap. She clutched it tightly and closed her eyes, trying to ignore the insistent footsteps of patrolling guards, trying to catch fragments of birdsong in the air.

"Princess?" Rodric stood in front of her, a concerned frown on his face. "Mother said you wanted to speak with me."

She nodded and began to stand.

"No, please," he said. "Let's sit. I do not want to walk with the guards trailing us like assassins may jump out of the bushes at any second."

"All right." She held out the book as he sat. The gold lettering glinted in the fading sunlight. "I wanted to give you this."

The Tale of Sleeping Beauty. Her thumb pressed over the golden spinning wheel engraved on the cover, right in the center. He did not move to take it.

"But . . . it's yours."

"No," she said. "No, it's not." When he still did not move, she placed it on his knee. It wobbled, lurching toward the ground, and Rodric caught it with the heel of his hand.

"Why are you giving this to me?"

"I wanted you to have it." It was all she could say. How could she explain? She wanted the story out of her room, the words and paintings mocking her every imperfection. How could she say that he deserved this dream version of her, that he deserved to hold the story in his hand, even if it could never materialize in her? This was the way things should be, the way things were fated to be, and maybe this was a denial that she could ever be the girl in the pages, but also a promise to him, that she would try her best. That their reality would not be this, but she was accepting, fully, finally, that it must be whatever they could make, together, or else everything would fall apart. That she was setting the story aside, so that she could try to put something like reality in its place.

He continued to stare at the cover of the book, running his hands along the leather binding. "It's a good book," she added.

He opened it. *Once upon a time, when wishes still came true, Alyssinia was ruled by a beloved king and his gentle wife.* The illustration was dreamlike and elegant, a bearded king and a woman with hair like sunlight. It had been less than a month since Aurora had seen her parents in person, but she already felt the memory slipping, replaced by the blurry ideal of the paintings. Did her father have wrinkles around his eyes? What did her mother's hair smell like when she hugged her close? The more she thought, the more she tried to snatch at the memories, the farther they seemed to float, laughing, from her grasp.

Rodric turned page after page, lingering over every word

as though reading them for the first time. Finally, he reached a painting of Aurora, or someone like her, staring at an old battered spinning wheel, her finger outstretched. Aurora pressed her fingertip against the image, trying to remember, fighting to piece together the conflicting scraps left in her thoughts. *Why did you do it?* he had asked. *There's always a choice.* And maybe she did choose. Maybe this was her fault after all.

"It was forbidden," she said, her voice shaking. It explained so much about her life if it was true. "That's why I did it. Because it was forbidden."

"You remember?"

She trailed her finger across the painting, tracing the outline of the spinning wheel. "No. I don't know. I remember—I remember music, pulling me from my room and into . . . I am not sure. I remember going upward, but that's impossible. There was no up from my tower."

"Celestine was powerful," Rodric said. "She could do it."

"Maybe." Aurora closed her eyes. "There was a light, a beautiful, bobbing light, like a fairy, or—I don't know. I followed it up, higher and higher—" And it was as though she could feel the creaking wooden stairs beneath her feet, hear the haunting melody, now replaced by Nettle's voice, filling the air around her. "There was a dusty, round little room, but—but it wasn't like the painting. An old woman sat spinning. I had never seen a spinning wheel before, but I had seen pictures, and I think—I think I knew what it was. It was the night before my eighteenth birthday, the very last day before the curse was broken, and it was like . . ."

A shiver ran through her, as if she were in the room once again, and suddenly she understood what people meant when they spoke of fate. It was a pull, an impossible lure, a sense deep in her stomach that this was the moment, the event she had been waiting for her whole life. "The woman looked up at me. I didn't ask why she was there. And she said, 'Would you like to try?'"

Aurora opened her eyes. Rodric was staring intently at her, his mouth slightly open, as though absorbing every breath she sent his way.

"And I knew, I knew, that I shouldn't. I knew. But I had spent my whole life running from this. And I thought . . . what would it be like? The wheel spun so smoothly, and the needle glinted, and . . . I wanted to know. I was tired of being afraid."

"You pricked your finger on purpose?"

"No," she said slowly. "No. But I sat at the stool, and the woman showed me how to turn the wheel, so that the thread came out smooth." She closed her eyes again, and reached out with her fingertips, as though the thread still ran across her skin. Maybe it had been a spell, maybe it had been her own exhaustion, but she thought she had felt the world fade as she sat there, guided by the strange old lady. She couldn't quite remember, but the sense of it lingered in the back of her mind, like a tale she had been told as a child and had since let slip away. It felt like truth.

"But I was clumsy," she continued. "I was clumsy, and my finger slipped. It landed on the point of the spindle, the tiniest of pinpricks against my fingertip. It was cold and sharp. . . ."

"And?"

She opened her eyes, staring out over the path. The daffodils bobbed in the breeze. "And that's it. The next thing I remember is waking up. And even that isn't clear anymore. It's like I've been here my whole life." Part of her yearned for a poetic end to the tale. A feeling of drifting off to sleep, a sense of finality, the thought, *Well, that is done*, something that would help connect this flutter of a memory with her present self. But sleep never worked like that. It happened all at once, and the final moments were as lost as if they had never been.

With a steady hand, Rodric turned the page. A princess slept in a grand four-poster bed, golden hair spread out over the pillow, a single red rose clutched to her chest.

"Did you dream?"

Aurora sighed. What difference would it make? She might have lived a whole other life in the century that had passed, lived and loved and died all inside her head. But no trace remained of it now. "I don't know," she said finally. It was, after all, the truth.

Rodric turned to the final page, the painting of a beautiful princess, dressed in white, standing under an arch beside a handsome prince, as crowds looked on and doves fluttered above. *And we will all live happily ever after.*

As Aurora stared at the picture, she felt a deep longing within her, not for the scene it portrayed, but for the *after* that it promised. She wanted to turn the page and see more words, more promises and guidelines for her trembling little life. Even if every syllable were a fantasy or a lie, there would be some comfort in being told *this is what you must do and this is how it will be*. Rebelling against an idea was better than having no idea at all.

"It's so soon," she whispered.

"Is this what you wanted?" Rodric asked. "When you sat down at that wheel. Were you looking for your happily ever after?"

The thought had never even occurred to her. "No," she said. "I don't know what I was looking for. I think—I just wanted to do something. I was sick of spending my life waiting."

He was quiet for a long moment. "Are you glad you did it?"

"I don't know." Doubt was beginning to creep into her stomach.

Rodric closed the book with a gentle thud. "Even if it weren't fate, I would choose you."

"Do you love me?" She had to ask, had to hear the words on the air.

He did not look at her. "You are wonderful, Aurora. And we will make things better together. I know that."

She nodded, all her suspicions confirmed. Yet the thought nagged at the corner of her mind, demanding to be voiced.

"But are you in love with me? Am I everything you would have dreamed of?"

"I do not think—"

She gripped his hand. "Tell me," she said. "I want to hear you say it."

"I care for you," he said quietly, "but no. I am not in love with you." His expression was one of genuine pain, as though terrified that his words might break her heart.

He was brave, she realized. He could say what she could not. He knew, unquestioningly, the right thing to do, and he did it without hesitation. He would make a good king. But that did not change the truth of her feelings.

"Me either," she said. "I do not love you."

"Maybe it will come," Rodric said. "But I believe—we will do good together. That must be more important than true love."

"Yes," Aurora said. "Yes, perhaps." She released his hand, letting her arm fall heavy against her side. "Please, keep the book." It promised so much that she could not give.

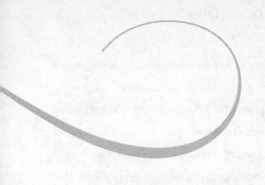

TWENTY-TWO

THE FOLLOWING EVENING, AURORA ENTERED THE banquet hall on Rodric's arm. She felt almost sick with nerves. An evening of smiling, of curtsying and saying precisely the right thing, awaited her.

Rodric's face looked pale, almost clammy, as though he too was nervous about the performance.

The ambassadors and courtiers paraded, one after the other, to greet their lost princess and give her their best wishes. She curtsied and bobbed her head so often that she felt slightly dizzy, as man after man clasped her hand, kissed it, and praised her beauty. "It is so wonderful to see you," they would say. "Never would I have imagined that, in my lifetime . . ." Aurora smiled at every one of them, playing the role of the demure, shy, loving princess for all that she was worth. It wasn't a difficult disguise to wear. The shyness, the reluctance to speak, were all too genuine, and she did not have enough energy to hold a large, bright smile, managing only an uptick at the corner of her lips that gentleman after gentleman described as elegant, mysterious, perfect. Yet she could not help wondering how many of them were performing, just as she was. As Finnegan had. What did they really think behind their spoken clichés?

Occasionally, very occasionally, someone would ask her a question, speak to her rather than at her beauty. One large man, wearing so many chains and jewels that Aurora imagined he must be dragged down into a permanent bow, asked her in a cheery voice how she was liking the new Alyssinia. "The innovations in the past hundred years," he said, gesturing around at the hall as if the very stones gleamed with technology. "Could you have imagined? Life is marvelous now, is it not?"

"I could not have dreamed it," Aurora said, despite the fact that the castle was mostly the same as before. The instruments, perhaps, the way the buildings hung over the streets and the lamps that lit the way around the outskirts of the castle—these things had taken her breath away, but they were outside, things she was not supposed to have seen.

Another man asked her why she clung to her old-fashioned dresses, instead of embracing the modern beauty that was being created in this very city (recommending, of course, his wife as a master of design), but the queen stepped in before Aurora could reply, speaking of comfort and adjustment and waving over the fact that the outfit had been made new, by the queen, to emphasize the sense of other. Aurora had never worn a dress quite like it in her whole life before.

As visitor after visitor came, offering names she could not remember, Aurora's own thoughts slipped away, melting into this rhythm of courtesies and smiles. But she could not stop herself looking over the crowd, searching for a trace of Celestine. She could not shake the feeling that the witch was watching her, waiting for her chance to make her presence known. She was, after all, famous for her theatrics.

There was no sign of her.

Prince Finnegan was the last to clutch and kiss her hand. His voice was all politeness. "It is an honor to see you again, Aurora," he said. "I hope I will be able to steal a dance from you later this evening?"

"Of course," the queen said, before Aurora could reply. "She would be delighted."

Aurora bowed her head in an echo of a curtsy.

"I am sure," he said. "She is, as ever, the very image of politeness." With a nod to Iris, he walked away.

"Enough of the formality," the king shouted from the head of the room. "Everyone must be hungry. I know I am! Let us eat!"

As Aurora approached the king, she wondered how he could maintain such a mask of cheerfulness. He had killed every person in his dungeons only two nights ago, but whenever he appeared in public, he always seemed jovial. Perhaps it wasn't a mask. Perhaps he truly believed that he was the best ruler Alyssinia could have, and did everything in his power to ensure its stability. Perhaps he took no pleasure in people's misery. Perhaps.

Aurora found herself sitting at the center of a long table at the head of the room, sandwiched between Rodric on one side and Isabelle on the other. The young girl wore a simple dress with jewels in her hair, and she stared across the crowded room with rapturous eyes, too awed to speak. Aurora squeezed her hand under the table. The king and queen sat on Rodric's other side, and beyond them sat Prince Finnegan and his escort. At least she would not have to smile at him during the meal, or sit next to the king, knowing what he had done.

The servants brought out course after course, meats soaked in rich sauces and birds stuffed with creatures and nuts that Aurora had never heard of, and every time the wine cups began to empty, Prince Finnegan called for another round, until everyone around her was red-faced and laughing. She picked at her food, kept her head bowed over her plate, and listened to the mindless chatter. Occasionally, someone would ask her to tell them how life had been in her time, but she only smiled and commented that it was "incomparable to this," and that was enough to spark another half hour of laughter and gossip that was increasingly nonsensical, endlessly bawdy, and completely substance-less. Throughout it all, only Rodric and the queen remained quiet. The queen sipped at her wine, but never had an empty cup, and Rodric did not touch his at all.

"Do you remember the time," John said with a booming laugh, "that Sir Merrick thought he had seen a dragon in the woods?"

"Man was so drunk he could barely stay on his horse."

"He galloped and stumbled for hours in the wrong direction, convinced it was going to eat him and steal his family's treasure."

"What happened to him?" Finnegan asked. Despite the fact that he kept calling for more drink, he seemed somewhat steadier than the others. Aurora was not sure she had seen him refill his cup once.

"Nothing, the fool. Just a fire in the woods, wasn't it? Started by a peasant, no doubt. Throw in the shadow of a baby deer, and he was trembling in terror."

"Could it really have been a dragon?" Aurora asked.

"No," Finnegan said. "Alyssinia is lucky. Dragons will not cross water, so they are my kingdom's treasure and menace alone. We had thousands of years without them, of course, but then they awoke and flooded the skies, as though the world had been waiting for them. Rather like you, now that I think about it."

Aurora blushed, but any reply was cut off by the king's laugh. "Oh, such a fearsome thing, our Aurora. One smile, and the whole world is on its knees." The nobles around them joined the laughter, and Finnegan gave her a gracious nod. *Of course,* it seemed to say. "But let us not talk about such dire things. We are supposed to be celebrating! My dear, when will the music begin?"

"Soon," Iris said. "The castle musicians became unfortunately ill this afternoon, so we had to seek a replacement. A somewhat unusual one, I must add, but—"

"I made the request myself," Finnegan said. "I heard tell that a traveling musician we enjoyed in the palace at Vanhelm was in Petrichor, and of course I could not pass up the chance to be enchanted by her once again. It is not traditional music, I grant you, but this is all about merging the old and the new, is it not? Joining together and heralding a new age."

"Indeed, indeed," the king said. "But I wish this singer would make an appearance. It is not a proper banquet without music to serenade us. And the young ones must have their dancing!"

"She had to be sought out in the city," Iris said. "I am sure it will begin soon."

Another course later, a group of guards walked toward the king, a tall figure hidden in their midst. Only the black hair on her head was visible.

"Presenting the performer for tonight's festivities, Your Majesty."

Nettle stepped out from among them, her black hair pinned into a twist at the back of her head. Aurora had not seen the singer since that evening outside the Dancing Unicorn, when they had sat in the rain. It felt jarring to see her here, gliding into Aurora's prison world as though she belonged there too.

Nettle slipped into a graceful curtsy, her skirts flowing around her feet, and held it as the king surveyed her. She did not glance at Aurora.

"Well, stand up, my dear," he said. "Tell me. What is your name?"

"They call me Nettle, Your Majesty."

"That's an unusual name," the queen said. "Where do you come from?"

"Eko," she said with another bobbing curtsy. "A long time ago."

"My darling Nettle," Finnegan said, getting to his feet. "I am delighted to see you again. Promise me you'll dazzle these skeptics with your modern music, won't you?"

She raised her head slightly, and when she saw Finnegan, her smile seemed genuine. "I promise I will try."

"Excellent!" King John said, clapping his hands together. "Then let us begin the dancing. Rodric, I am sure you'll want to take the first turn with your fiancée, am I right? I'm amazed we managed to keep the two of you apart for so long!"

Rodric danced as stiffly as he bowed, with one hand holding hers, and the other barely skimming her waist. He looked directly ahead, above Aurora, staring at nothing, and he steered her in a circle with clumsy steps. His forehead was screwed up in concentration.

"Are you all right?" she asked, after he stepped on her toe.

"Not really," he said. "Everyone is watching."

So she remained silent, letting him turn her around and around. She stared at a point over his shoulder, watching the colors on the walls spin together. Nettle's music swirled around them, a steady, waltzing beat, but wrong, somehow. Less honest and more restrained, like it too was stifled in the walls. Or perhaps Aurora was imagining it. She had heard this song before, but the notes sounded different now, too loud, too jarring against the rules and the formality of the dance. They were the sounds of mead and dust, lazy smiles and walks in the dark. Not of straight backs and awkward princes, rules and smiles that did not meet the eyes.

Over Rodric's shoulder, she glimpsed a servant carrying plates from the tables. Dark brown hair, rumpled in several directions. Tristan? Panic shot through her. Rodric spun her again, and she craned over her shoulder, trying to see, but the boy—if he had ever existed—was gone.

"Princess?" Rodric said. "Are you all right?"

"Yes." She settled back into his hold with a shake of her head. "I just—I thought I saw something."

They kept moving through song after song, neither of them willing to break apart until an explicit signal was given. Rodric's hand took a firmer hold on her waist, but his palm was sticky with nerves, and Aurora began to feel slightly sick as her sleepless head and nearly empty stomach twisted around and around.

"Getting dizzy yet?" Prince Finnegan appeared behind them. "You've been dancing for a long time."

Rodric released her hand, and she stumbled back slightly, forgetting, for a second, to hold herself up alone. "Yes," she said, staring at the intruder. "He's my fiancé."

"Of course, of course. Well, then I hate to interrupt, but I was hoping the princess would share her favor with me. Just for one dance."

Rodric gaped at him, frowning slightly. Then he bowed. "Of course, Finnegan." Dislike flickered in his voice, but if Finnegan noticed, he did not comment.

"Wonderful. My lady." He snatched up Aurora's hand and pulled her away.

He was a better dancer than Rodric, skillful even, and he whisked Aurora around at a fast pace, making her skirts whirl in the air. He held her back firmly in his palm, pressing her close to him, and Aurora could not stop her jolt of excitement as their stomachs pressed together. She leaned back, standing as stiffly as Rodric had only moments before.

"So, Aurora," he said in a low voice, under the fever of the music. "Have you had a chance to reconsider your decision?"

"I am not going to change my mind."

"Even after what you heard?"

"Especially after what I heard."

"You know it will not go as you plan," he murmured, his breath brushing against the curve of her ear. "You know you cannot stop him while sitting here, playing his game. You know it, and yet you continue to pretend that you don't."

"It is the best chance I have." The words vibrated in her chest.

They whirled faster and faster. The world behind his head blurred.

"So tell me, Aurora, what precisely is your plan? Keep pretending to be the person they all expect you to be? That's not the way to have power."

"Maybe I don't want power," she said. "Maybe you don't know anything about me."

"Maybe," he said. "But it seems unlikely. I know you." He dipped her backward, letting her hair sweep across the floor. A couple of bystanders applauded, and when Aurora stood upright again, she felt breathless and dizzy. "It's adventure for you, dragon girl. Just try to disagree."

Her face felt flushed, and the world spun slightly. "I am no dragon girl," she said.

"Again, she lies." His breath on her ear made her shiver. "How can you be who you were meant to be, when you cannot even be honest with yourself? You have power inside you, Aurora. Magic and fire. Use it."

He dropped her hand. With a sweeping bow, he vanished back into the crowd. The room swayed, and when Aurora took a step, the floor was farther than she expected. She stumbled. One of the dancers knocked into her side, and she jerked away. Rodric was nowhere to be seen. Back at the main table, she thought. Hiding from the dancing for as long as he could.

The walls seemed to press toward her, shuddering with color and light. The music stopped.

A guard placed a hand on her arm. "Another course is about to be served, Princess," he said. "If you would . . ."

"I wish to thank the singer," she said, slipping her arm out of his grasp. The air that filled her lungs felt hot and heavy, almost too thick to breathe. Nettle had been so kind, so wise before, and her songs . . . She picked her skirts up in her hands and hurried to the far end of the room, where Nettle was about to step out of the door. "I wish to speak to her," she said to the guard who hovered by the singer's shoulder. "Alone, if you please."

"Princess, dessert will soon be—"

"It can wait." She needed to get out of this stifling air. She needed to leave, just for a moment, and hear Nettle's soothing voice. She had made things seem so much plainer once before. Aurora could not miss the chance to speak to her again.

The guard nodded. "You heard the princess," he said to Nettle. "Do as she commands."

They stepped into a passage beyond the hall, not the bright corridor that Aurora had entered through but a narrow, dimly lit place. Servants scurried past, carrying plates.

"I did not mean to command you," Aurora said. A blush crept over her cheeks. "I just . . . wanted to talk to you."

"Do not apologize," Nettle said. "You did nothing wrong."

Aurora stared up at the singer. Her dress was more elegant

than usual, fine material clinging to her waist and pooling at her feet. Her instrument hung loosely from her fingertips, and she watched Aurora with her head tilted slightly to one side. "What did you wish to speak of?"

"Tristan," Aurora said quickly. "Is he—"

"He is alive, if that is what concerns you."

Relief rushed through her. "You've seen him?"

"Yes, I have seen him. I was supposed to perform at his inn tonight, before the guards forced me away."

"And he's all right?"

"He has more bitterness in him than before, and guilt, I believe, too. His efforts over the past few nights have not gone as he had hoped."

"His efforts?" Aurora echoed. "You know about what— about what happened?"

"I know about many things. It is my job to observe."

Aurora thought again of the servant with scruffy brown hair, walking to the higher tables. "Is he here tonight?" she asked.

"I do not believe so," Nettle said, "but he does not tell me all his secrets."

"I wish I had known what he was like," Aurora said softly. "Before—" Before she kissed him, before everything. "Just before."

"You should not," Nettle said. "Change one thing, and everything else may tumble apart." She ran her fingers across Aurora's elbow, the lightest of touches. "I believe he cares for you, in his own way."

"He cares for his revenge more."

"Perhaps," Nettle said. "Things are getting tense."

"Tense? With Tristan?"

"With everyone." Nettle's expression was almost sad as she looked down at her. "There is so much joy before your wedding, so much hope . . . it always turns to fear in the end. People think . . . what if it goes wrong? What if you are an impostor? They are nervous."

Aurora looked down at her feet. They were hidden under masses of skirt, so heavy and impractical compared to the fashions donned by the queen. "Then I will have to make sure I don't disappoint them," she said.

Nettle's smile was definitely sad now. "Impossible."

Aurora did not want to think about that. She hardly had a choice. "You performed for Prince Finnegan?" she asked instead. "In Vanhelm?"

"Yes." Nettle's expression closed off. "You should watch him. He is another who is more than he seems."

Aurora did not doubt that. "Did you ever see a dragon?"

"Once. I took a boat across the river from the city. Everyone was so afraid of them, and I was young. I saw a flash of fire in the sky, and a shadow that swept over me. . . ."

"Were you afraid?"

"Yes," she said. "And no. It was beautiful."

"I wish—" Aurora paused, not sure how to put her dreams

of fire and freedom into words. Before she could finish the thought, a guard appeared in the doorway.

"Princess, the queen requests that you return to the banquet hall immediately. Dessert has been served."

Nettle instantly sank into a curtsy. "Thank you for speaking with me, Princess."

Aurora nodded in response. She wanted to stay out here, away from the crowds and the expectations, but she did not dare ignore a direct order from the queen. Everyone was already seated inside the hall. They watched in silence as Aurora moved slowly across the room and took her place between Rodric and Isabelle.

"I am glad you have finally rejoined us," the queen said.

"I wished to speak to the singer."

"Still." The queen frowned. "It does not do to keep everyone waiting."

"Leave the poor girl alone, Iris," the king said. "Girls will be girls. We must all have our frivolities. But now, I say we eat."

A thick slice of cake waited on a plate in front of Aurora. It looked heavy and sickly, with cream lashed around the outside and piles of soft fruit gathered at the edge. Aurora did not want it. She wanted the night to be over.

"You have cherries," Isabelle said. She spoke quietly, her chin inches from Aurora's arm. "I love cherries."

"Do you not have any?" Aurora asked. Isabelle shook her head. "Here." Aurora plucked a cherry off her plate with her fork. Cream stuck to the red. "Have as many as you like."

"Don't you like them?"

"I'm not hungry. Go on." She held out the fork, and Isabelle bit it. She grinned.

"Good?" Aurora asked.

Isabelle nodded. "Thank you," she said. She picked up her own fork and skewered another cherry. Then she coughed. Her fork clattered onto the table.

"Isabelle? Are you okay?"

Isabelle nodded and coughed again. She gasped in a breath, but that only made her cough harder.

"Isabelle?" Rodric leaned forward and placed a hand on his sister's back. "What's wrong?"

"She just ate some fruit," Aurora said. "I don't know, is it stuck in her throat? Isabelle?"

Isabelle bent forward over the table, coughing and gasping.

Iris was behind her in an instant. "What happened?" she said. "What's wrong? Somebody help her!"

The realization that something was wrong rippled through the room. Several people were now on their feet, pushing toward the gasping Isabelle. Her skin had turned white.

Iris shoved Aurora out of the way and knelt in front of her daughter. She pressed one hand on either side of her face and leaned in close. "Isabelle, Isabelle, talk to me. It'll be all right. Take a deep breath."

Isabelle sucked in another breath, but that only made her cough and splutter worse than ever. Then she threw up. Red splattered on the edge of the queen's skirts, but Iris did not even glance down. Several onlookers scrambled away.

Someone grabbed Aurora by the arm, yanking her backward. She gasped and pulled away, but another firm hand held her in place. "Princess." It was one of the guards. "We need to get you out of here. King's orders."

"What?" she asked. "Why? What's happening?"

"It isn't safe," the guard said in a gruff voice. With a firm arm around her waist, he dragged her toward the door. "You have to come with me."

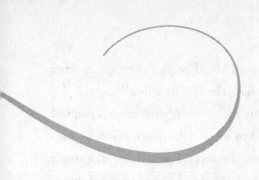

TWENTY-THREE

AURORA PACED HER ROOM. HER FEET ACHED. HER HEAD ached. Every time she tried to rest on her bed or sit in her chair, she sprang back up like it had burned her, the stillness too much to bear. Occasionally, footsteps hurried along the corridor, or loud, indistinct voices floated up from the courtyard below, but Aurora's guards stood in front of her door, refusing to let it open, refusing to answer any questions.

The sun was peeking over the horizon when the queen appeared. Her face was pale and pinched, and her elaborate hairstyle had begun to uncurl, hitting her shoulders in ropes. Dark circles surrounded her eyes, and her lips were tight and red, worried by her teeth until blood peeked through. Aurora hurried toward her. "What happened? Is Isabelle all right?"

Iris slapped Aurora with such force that Aurora stumbled backward. A muscle seemed to snap in the queen's face, a wildness leaping up and possessing her eyes. For a moment, a single moment, hatred filled her. Aurora pressed a hand over her cheek. Her skin stung under her fingers.

The queen sucked in a breath through clenched teeth, and her face settled back into the inscrutable mask she usually wore. "Isabelle is dead," she said.

"What?"

"Are you deaf, or just stupid? My daughter is dead." Aurora stared. The words didn't make sense, not together, not like that. She swayed on her feet. "She is dead, and you, you ungrateful brat . . ." She raised her hand as though preparing to slap Aurora again, but stopped at the last second, her fingers held so tightly that they quivered in the air.

It didn't make sense. "How?"

"Poison."

Aurora took an unsteady step backward, then another, until her knees collided with the arm of her chair. Uncertain questions burst onto her lips, but she held them back at the look of barely suppressed agony on the queen's face.

"It should have been you," the queen said. She spat out every word, like speaking was almost more effort than she could manage. "They meant it for you. If you had just eaten your fruit . . .

if you hadn't decided to feed it to my daughter . . ."

"I didn't know," she said. The words scraped against her throat. "Who—I mean . . ."

"Who do you think? The rebels have been trying to destroy us for years. Do you believe me now? Do you believe what lengths they will go to?"

She remembered the servant she had seen during the dance. A boy with scruffy brown hair, carrying plates to the higher tables. *No,* she thought. *He wouldn't.* But she could not know that.

"I will kill them all," the queen said, her face as still as ice. "I will tear them out of hiding and burn them until their very ashes scream. And you will watch. And you will smile and be grateful for all we have given you."

"What happens now?" Aurora said. Her throat felt raw. "I mean, the wedding . . ."

"Is in two days' time, as it always was. Do you think we will let them win?" The wildness flickered in Iris's eyes again, but she held it back. "If it were up to me, you would be thrown out to starve on the street with the dogs. If it were up to me, we would cancel this farce of a wedding and properly mourn for my daughter. But as you may have noticed, nothing is really up to me. You will marry Rodric. And you will smile and thank the world for all it has given you. And then you will come to my daughter's funeral and you will look at the body of the girl you killed. Do you understand?"

Aurora did not reply.

"You are cursed. I knew you would bring nothing but ruin to us all." She left so quickly that it was almost a run. The door hung open in her wake, and a guard moved to close it, shutting Aurora back up, alone.

Her legs buckled, and she sank to the floor. Her head scraped against the side of the chair, and she crashed it backward, savoring the way the thud rang through her. She did not know how long she sat there, staring at the door. The wind howled outside, sending spring rain splashing against the window. Aurora could not stop picturing the girl who had peered at her around doors and stared up with huge, curious eyes, doubling up over her stomach, spitting blood onto the table, shrieking and screaming in pain, or falling over sideways, dead without a sound. *It was meant for me*, she thought, over and over, and she shivered, guilt crawling under her skin. Guilt and filthy, sickening relief that she had not taken a bite herself, that she was not as dead as every law of the world demanded she must be.

At some point, she began to doze in fitful bursts. She woke with a jump, cold sweat sticking to her arms.

She leapt to her feet, ignoring the shudder that ran through her, the way her collapsed hair stuck to her neck and her cheek. She had never asked for any of this. People were suffering and dying and it was all her fault and she hadn't asked for any of it. They expected her to save them, but what could she do? She smiled and curtsied and played along, and now Isabelle was dead, and her mother did not even have the time to grieve. Who was to say that when Aurora became queen, she would have any more power than Iris had now? Alyssinia did not need change decades away. It did not want to wait through hunger and murder and fear, through the cruelty of the king and the spiteful retaliation of the rebels, with innocent people thrown to the wayside. If she sat and did nothing, it would only continue.

There's always a choice, Rodric had said.

He had had faith in her, through everything. Faith that her presence was a gift, that together they would make things better. And this was his reward. He had loved Isabelle, and now she was dead, and Aurora was alive, and nothing was as it should be.

She wanted to see him. She wanted to apologize to him, or comfort him, or do *something.* She did not want him to be alone.

She hurried across the room and pushed the door. It rattled against the lock. "Please," she said. "Open the door."

The lock clicked, and one of the guards pulled the door open. He glowered at her under heavy eyebrows, but his expression softened as he took in her appearance. "Princess?" he said. "What is it?"

"I wish to see Rodric," she said.

"You must remain here."

"Please," she said. She clutched the doorframe to keep herself upright. "I know the king and queen wish me to stay here, but—I need to see Rodric. Please."

The guard looked at her for a long moment. Something like

pity crossed his face. He nodded. "Of course, Princess," he said. "I can get you a few minutes with him."

Her relief, her gratitude, almost brought tears to her eyes. She exhaled slowly, trying to calm her pounding heart. "Thank you," she said.

The guard led Aurora to a wing of the castle that she did not recognize, far from her own rooms. He knocked once on a thick wooden door.

There was no answer.

"These are Rodric's rooms?" she asked.

"Yes, Princess."

She nodded. "Thank you for your help. I will only be a moment." The door creaked as she pulled it open and slipped inside. It closed behind her with a dull thud.

The room was large and neatly kept, with red fittings and little in the way of decorations or amusements. The only thing out of place was Rodric himself. He sat on the floor in the middle of the room, a book clutched in his hands. He was holding it so tightly that the pages bent.

"Rodric?"

"I was going to give her this," he said. "Before the wedding. But I can't now." His grief was so intense that Aurora could feel it in the air.

I did this, she thought. *I allowed this to happen.*

"I'm sorry, Rodric," she said. Tears stung her eyes. "I'm really sorry. Isabelle was—I can't believe—"

"She was here," he said. All the joy, the cautious optimism, had been sucked out of his voice, leaving a dull, resigned mono-tone in their place. "And now she's just gone. How can that be possible? It doesn't really make sense, does it?"

"None of this makes sense." She knelt beside him, their bodies inches apart. The gap felt huge, uncrossable. She rested a hand on his shoulder, but even that contact felt too distant, like he was in a place she could not reach. "Everything's gone wrong," she said, and her voice cracked. "I didn't mean for this to happen."

"Someone tried to poison you," he said. "It isn't your fault." But she knew it was. For ending up here in the first place, for offering Isabelle food off her own plate when she had been warned, over and over and over again, that people were willing to hurt her. They had all been right, and she had been so stu-pidly, blindly wrong.

"I should have—I don't know. I've done everything wrong."

Rodric shook his head. "It's not your fault," he said again. "I am sorry, Princess. We must carry on, I know. I am simply—I need a second to collect myself."

He sounded so confused, so guilty, that she had to take a moment to breathe, to steady herself, before she spoke. "You don't need to collect yourself," she said. "Why should you have to? Why should you pretend this is anything other than awful?"

He stared at the twisted book in his hands. "Because every-thing is awful," he said. "That's why you're here, isn't it? That's why all this is happening. To make things right. We can't stop now."

"We can," she said. "We can always stop. We can—"

"No," Rodric said, more forcefully than she'd ever heard him say anything before. "We can't. Why would we? If we don't marry now, what was the point of this? What was the point of any of this?"

She looked at the floor. Her hand slipped off his shoulder. *What if there isn't a point?* she thought, but she could not say it aloud. She could not bear to make Rodric look any more broken than he already did, to take his last bit of certainty away.

"If I stay," Aurora said, "if we marry now, what's to stop these things from happening again?" She grasped at her skirt, twisting the silk in her fist. "I don't know, Rodric. I don't know what to think."

He looked up at her, his eyes pleading. "Are you going to leave?"

Was she? It sounded so impossible. "I don't know," she said again. The thought filled her with terror, but every thought terrified her now, and she had sat still and allowed the world to make her decisions for too long. "I don't know."

He looked back down at the book. "I was happy, you know," he said. "I know I wasn't always the most eloquent person to be around, but I was happy. I finally felt . . . capable. This is the first time I've been of use to anyone."

"That's not true," she said. "I know you don't believe it,

but—you're wonderful. Isabelle loved you. And you've been a friend to me. You didn't have to be, but—you've always been kind."

"Kind?" He laughed bitterly. "What difference does that make?"

"It makes all the difference."

He shook his head, and she reached out, wrapping an arm around his neck. For a moment, they hung there, barely touching. Then Rodric clutched her side, pulling her toward him, until her face pressed into his chest, his arms squeezing her so tightly that she could barely breathe. He rested his cheek on the top of her head. She opened her mouth, hoping that the right words would appear if she began to speak, but before she could make a sound, someone knocked on the door.

"Princess?" It was the guard. "I must return you to your room. Their Majesties will not like it if we linger."

"You should go," Rodric said. "But—I was glad to see you."

"Yes," she said softly. "You too." She got slowly, achingly to her feet, and then sank into a curtsy, her skirts sweeping behind her. It seemed natural, somehow, in this moment when no words would do. Rodric stood up as well, and gave her a jerking little bow. Then he reached out and took her hand. He squeezed it, once.

"Do what you think is right, Aurora," he said. His voice broke. "I'll do the same."

She nodded. His hand fell from hers, and she walked slowly out of the room.

Another guard waited by Aurora's door when they returned. He bowed as they approached.

"I took the princess to see Prince Rodric," the first guard said, as though daring the newcomer to criticize him. "She wished to stretch her legs."

"Of course." He held out a roll of paper. "I only wished to give this to the princess. A letter of condolence."

She reached out and took it automatically. The paper felt rough under her fingertips—certainly not the high-quality stock used in the castle. Her throat tightened. "Thank you," she said. "I trust you are busy with your duties."

Her dismissal was clear. He bowed again, and she watched him until he had walked completely out of sight.

When she was back in her room and the lock had clicked behind her, she opened the note. It was written in the rough, unsteady hand of someone unaccustomed to writing.

I heard what happened. The king is keeping it quiet, but I heard. And I know how it looks, but I had to tell you, it wasn't me. It had nothing to do with any of us.
You are not safe in the castle. Come to the inn tonight.
Trust me. —T

She read the note over again, then again.

She wanted to believe him. He had been her friend, the fire when everything else felt cold and dead. But he had warned her that he could not protect her. He had broken into the castle and then fled when danger approached. He might have cared for her, but he cared for his cause more. If he had to sacrifice her in order to take down the king . . . he might be willing to do it.

And Tristan did not know everything about those around him. He might believe that they were innocent, but that did not make it true.

It did not change the fact that Isabelle was dead because of people like him.

She tossed the note into the fire and watched as it burned.

TWENTY-FOUR

AURORA MUST HAVE SLEPT THAT NIGHT, ALTHOUGH she did not recall closing her eyes. She awoke to the sound of fists hammering against the door. The sun had not yet fully risen, casting a chilly red glow over her room.

"Who's there?" she said. The door shook under the force of the knocks. "I am not yet dressed."

"The king has summoned you, Princess," a voice said. "Please prepare yourself. We must return to the throne room with you at once."

"The king?" Why would the king wish to speak to her, so early in the morning? She felt a stab of dread.

"Yes, Princess," the voice said. "Come along, or we shall have to enter your room, permission or not. He was very insistent."

"My maid is not here," she said. "I will have to wait for her."

"Not this morning, Princess. It has to be now."

"All right," she said, and she was proud that her voice remained steady. "I will only be a moment." She quickly changed into a simple dress, yanking her fingers through her collapsed curls to release some of the knots.

A crowd of guards waited outside her door. They pressed around her as she stepped into the corridor, until she was surrounded by their glittering mail.

"King's orders," said the guard who had spoken before when he noticed her looking around at them. "For your protection."

"Of course," she said. She doubted that was true.

The king and queen waited in the throne room. Rodric stood to the side, a few feet from their thrones. His face was still pale, and his hair stuck up at the back at an angle that would have been funny if he did not look so tragic. The queen, too, looked pale and drawn, but the mask of regality was back, her emotions hidden behind powder and pins. The king's face was red and stern.

"Ah, Aurora," he said. "Thank you for joining us." He glanced at the guards who had accompanied her. "Sir Stefan, please watch the door from the outside. The rest of you may leave."

The guards bowed and walked out of the room, leaving only the king's personal escort, lined up behind the throne, to witness what might happen next.

"Aurora," the king said, and his voice was almost cheerful. "Come closer so I can see you."

He was not smiling. His voice boomed out like the jolly figure presiding over the feast, but his eyes were hard and cold, like two wet stones glinting in the moonlight. As though pulled by the words, Aurora began her slow walk across the room. Only the echoes of her footsteps broke the silence. She stopped a few paces from him, her hands loose at her sides, trying to keep her chin high, her face confident.

"I assume you know why you're here."

"No, Your Majesty," she said. She refused to curtsy to him, not until she understood what this charade was about. "The guards did not explain."

"I did not think you would need an explanation," he said. "I am sure you recall the unfortunate incident at your banquet. I am sure you recall the suspicious circumstances of my daughter's death."

"Yes," she said. Her voice cracked on the word. "Of course I remember."

"Not the best omen for your wedding, I am sure you'll agree. I would say we should carry on regardless, but—well, with circumstances being as they are, I cannot leave things uninvestigated."

"Are you saying you want to postpone the wedding?"

"I am saying, Aurora, that I want an explanation for that night. You must see how it looks. Your being out of the room, talking to a singer who just happened to be called in at the last minute, when dessert is brought in. My daughter eating poison off your own fork."

"You think that—" She broke off, swallowed, fighting to steady herself. "I wouldn't hurt her," she said. "I would never—"

"You fed her the poison yourself," he said. "You can hardly claim that you were uninvolved."

"If I'd known it was poisoned, I would never have let her near it." Panic filled her voice, but the king seemed unmoved. "Why would I hurt her? Why, when she was so good to me?"

"I do not know," he said. "I wonder about many things you do. And it is quite a surprising coincidence."

"Somebody tried to kill me," she said. "I didn't do anything."

"Come now," the king said. "Who would want a lovely thing like you dead?"

The question was so filled with venom, so false, that Aurora started. He might, she realized. He was the one who would benefit most from her death. It would hardly bring the rebellion popular support. But if she died, and the rebellion was blamed . . . the king would get rid of two problems in one move. Any potential sympathy for the opposition would vanish in a moment, and he would lose a burden that he might be unable to control in the bargain.

But surely he would not do something so risky. Surely, if he had been responsible for the poison, he would be more distraught over his daughter's death.

"Her involvement seems unlikely, dear," the queen said. "The princess does not strike me as vicious, whatever her flaws."

"If I wanted your opinion, Iris, I would have asked for it." The queen blinked, her expression unchanging. "As it is, you have had far too much contact with the girl. It is time I was in charge of her."

"I was not involved, Your Majesty," Aurora said. Her voice shook. "You must see that."

"I am the king, Aurora. There is nothing I *must* do. Meanwhile, you must see how suspicious this all looks. You have never seemed fully grateful for all my family has done for you. You have never seemed quite like the girl who was promised to us. And if your involvement were to be proved, you would not only be a murderer but also a traitor. Do you know what we do to traitors, Aurora? We burn them."

She bit the inside of her cheek, so hard that she could taste blood.

Rodric was staring at his father, his face pale, mouth open, but he did not move to defend her. For all his nobility and sweetness, she was entirely on her own.

"I am not a traitor," she said.

"Ah," he said. "But how do I know that?"

She pressed her hands against her sides, fighting the urge to bunch them into fists, trying to hide the way they shook. "I have never lied to you," she said steadily. "I have always been what I claim."

"That may be true," the king said. "And I am inclined to believe your pleas. It would be a shame to delay the wedding on such charges. But I must take precautions, you understand. To be sure that you are not an imposter, not a traitor, plotting to use your marriage against us all. You will have to be watched closely, kept under even tighter guard. If you are who you claim, we will see that in you, in your behavior, and we will know we can trust you. Until then, you must be under my supervision."

So it came back to this. Whether or not the king was responsible for Isabelle's death, he was certainly willing to use it to his advantage. A few well-placed words, a smile of a threat, and Aurora would be his puppet for as long as he needed. "How long?" Aurora asked softly. "How long will I be watched?"

"As long as it takes to be certain of you," he said. "And certain of others. If you are innocent, surely you could not object. If someone did try to poison you, you will also benefit from the extra protection. I hope you realize the severity of this," he added. "If I hear so much as a word of protest, it will be proof of your lack of loyalty. Do not think that your fame will protect you. If you are found responsible, you will burn for what you did to my daughter."

She had been so naïve to believe that she could make a difference here. That it would end with anything other than this. At best, the king intended to cow her into obedience, to make sure every second of her future was his. And at worst . . . he could kill her and use her death to his advantage.

She looked at the queen. Uncertainty passed across Iris's face, something that might have been sympathy, but she did not speak again.

Rodric had not moved at all.

There was nothing more Aurora could say in her own defense. She had left it all too late. "Yes, Your Majesty," she said. "I understand."

"Good," he said. "Good. I am glad we see eye to eye. I will not detain you longer—you will want to rest before your wedding tomorrow, I have no doubt. Sir Lanford, Sir Richard." Two of his personal guard stepped forward. "Escort the princess back to her tower. It seems like the safest place. And lock the door to her room. We cannot risk trouble finding her again."

TWENTY-FIVE

THE ROOM WAS NOT AS AURORA REMEMBERED. EVEN in the short month that she had been away, details had blurred. The room was smaller than she recalled, and the windows and fireplace jutted out in an odd way that invited drafts into the room.

She paced back and forth across the carpet, looking at the remnants of her life before. She would spend her whole life trapped in these walls, staring out of the window, waiting for her escape. Or waiting for the king to kill her, as he may have killed Isabelle, as he had killed so many people.

An empty water pitcher stood on the table beside her bed.

She snatched it up and threw it. It landed with a satisfying thud. Then she threw a book, that precious story of Alysse, all its traitorous promises crumpling as it smacked into the wall. She followed it with a plate, then the remains of a candle. Her hands shook, and she turned, looking around her room, searching for more things to destroy.

Her eyes fell on the fireplace. It was a tall, wide thing, large enough for a girl to walk through with ease. The old ashes clung to the stone. She paused, breathing hard. She remembered the music, the flickering of light . . . with a jolt in her stomach, Aurora hurried over, kneeling down in the ash and pushing at the wall beyond. *Please,* she thought, over and over as she pressed her fingers against the solid stone. *Take me back.*

Her hair tumbled down over her eyes, and she clenched her teeth, desperation crashing within her. *I don't want this,* she thought. *I don't want any of this. Please. Let me back.*

The stone burned, sharp like red-hot iron. She snatched back her hands.

The wall was gone. Behind the ancient ash, impossible stairs reached out of sight.

Aurora stretched out her hand. It slipped through the air where the wall had been, and she pressed her stinging finger-tips into the wood of the first step. It was rough, solid, almost prickly. Familiar. Definitely real.

Knees aching, shoulders shaking, Aurora stood up and began to climb.

The stairs were steep, and they curved around, hugging the wall of Aurora's room like vines. The darkness swallowed her, until she was nothing more than the thud of her heart, the brush of stone against her sleeve, the creak of wood beneath her feet.

Above her, light glowed.

The stairs ended in a round attic room. Narrow beams of light peeked through the rafters. Rain pattered on the roof. And in the center, a spinning wheel sat, rocking in a ghostly breeze. The spindle gleamed.

Aurora stepped forward, arm outstretched. The floor whined in protest, as though it were about to collapse, but she pressed her foot into the wood, daring it to hurt her. The wheel was smooth in her hand. She spun it, her fingers flicking over the spokes.

Such a simple, harmless thing.

She sank onto the three-legged stool and closed her eyes. Was she imagining that spark of memory, the tingling across her skin that said yes, she had been here before, and yes, she must be here again?

So much power in one little finger prick.

The spindle did not even look sharp.

She ran her index finger down the length of it, avoiding the tip. The metal was cold. What would happen if she pricked her finger again? Would she blink and wake up in the past, her family around her? Would she sleep for another century, or two, or four, until Alyssinia was smoke and ash, and nobody remembered she had ever existed? Would she die?

She ran her finger down the length again. The wheel spun, as though pushed by a phantom hand, filling the attic with a gentle click, click, click.

What would it feel like?

At least it would be a choice.

Slowly, deliberately, she pricked her finger on the tip of the spindle.

The wheel continued to click. Rain tapped on the roof. Her fingertip burned cold where the metal broke her skin.

Nothing.

She pulled her finger back. The spindle tugged as it slipped out of her flesh. Red blood bubbled in its wake.

She pricked her finger again, digging harder against the spindle, fighting the urge to flinch.

Still nothing.

She could not even do this.

The staircase creaked. She stood up, turning to look. No one was there. But a message was burned into the wall above, black charred letters that flowed and looped, so precise and so deep that they could only be magic.

She is mine.

As she watched, fresh letters scorched the stone, written by an invisible, curling hand: *You cannot stop it now.*

Celestine.

Prickles ran up and down her skin. She spun on her feet, but the attic was empty. The rain pounded.

"I'm not yours!" she shouted. "I don't belong to anyone!"

Another lie.

"You can't control me!"

It was as if the stones were pressing tighter and tighter around her, into her skin, into her ribs, squeezing her lungs until she could barely catch her breath. Shocks ran down her spine, her legs, into her feet, which were running, pounding down the stairs.

She crashed into her bedroom and ran to the window, pressing her palms flat against the sill, staring out at the city as she had done on that first day, when it had seemed possible that this was all a mistake.

She had been wrong, she realized, as she took a steadying breath, watching the bustle of the day. She was not back where she'd begun. So much had changed. She might not be able to reverse time with a prick of her finger, but she was no longer willing to smile and sit pretty and let the world move her where it desired. If she married Rodric, nothing would change. She did not want to hurt him, or see him blamed for a failure he could not control, but she could not stay and let things continue to unravel around her. People did not deserve to have their hopes dashed and their lives torn apart.

She could not sit here any longer, waiting for things to happen. Hoping that the future would be better than all sense suggested. She had to go. Away from the castle, away from this place. She needed to learn more about the strange powers that burst out of her and led her up those stairs to that cursed place, back to the first choice she had made, all those years ago.

She thought again of the king, of Celestine, of Tristan, all manipulating her, all assuming that she would go along with their plans, that she would bow to whatever they told her to do, and punishing her, hating her, when she dared to have a thought of her own. Defiance filled her. She would not vanish quietly now. She would not slip away into the shadows, and let them believe what they would. She would not let the king twist it all against her, against everything she believed.

She would give the king his wedding. She would walk to that altar, smiling and beautiful, and then she would show them all just how traitorous she could be.

TWENTY-SIX

DEAR FINNEGAN, SHE WROTE. THANK YOU FOR ALL YOUR kind words to me. I would be delighted if you would visit me sometime before my wedding tomorrow, to solidify the good relations between us. . . .

She scanned the letter, checking that she had written nothing objectionable, nothing that could be used against her. The stubborn part of her flinched away from involving Finnegan, but she knew that she could not humiliate the king and escape without a little outside help. If she was going to do this, she needed him.

Leaving the note unsealed, so anyone could see how innocent it was, she hurried to the locked door. "Excuse me," she said in her sweetest, most harmlessly regal voice. "Sir Lanford, Sir Richard?"

"They are no longer here," a voice said. "Is there anything we can do to help?"

"I have a message for Prince Finnegan."

There was an uncertain pause. "Princess, we cannot unlock this door. You are to stay here until tomorrow."

"I know," she said. "I do not wish to go anywhere. But Finnegan requested a meeting with me today, before the wedding, and I would hate to disappoint him. So would the king and queen, I am sure. I simply want to inform him that I am willing to meet with him whenever he is available. If you could take a note to him from me, I would greatly appreciate it."

Another pause. "Slide your note under the door," the guard said eventually. "I will see that he receives it."

For a moment, she considered it. Then she stopped. "No," she said. Finnegan had once told her that important people could do as they liked. It was time to test how important they considered her. "I am the princess, not some prisoner passing secret messages through gaps in the wall. You will open this door, and you will take this message to Finnegan, and if he requests it, you will escort him back here yourself. Do you understand me?"

He did not reply for a long time. Then the locks clicked. "As you wish, Princess."

"Thank you." She passed the paper through the narrow gap

in the door. "Please tell Finnegan that I look forward to seeing him soon."

The guard bowed. "Of course, Princess," he said. Then the door closed with a dull thud. She remained close to it, listening to the sound of his footsteps fading down the stairs.

She did not wait long. Barely any time seemed to have passed before the door swung open again, and Finnegan stepped into the room.

"What a pleasure to see you again," he said as the door closed behind him. "I haven't been in this room for . . . oh, three years at least. Have you finally decided my kiss was what you'd been dreaming of all these years?"

"Yes," she said sharply. "That is exactly why I sent for you on the day before my wedding. To declare my secret love for you."

"I am glad to hear it," he said. "Sadly, I must decline your advances. Politics, you know." He looked around the room. "Strange choice," he added. "Stairs in a fireplace. I don't recall seeing them before."

"You must not have looked closely enough."

"Perhaps not," he said. "There were far more interesting things to hold my attention." He gave her the same searching look he had given her so many times before, casual yet discerning, like he already knew everything she could possibly think or say or do. "So to what do I owe the pleasure of this meeting?" he finally said. "It cost me a fair few silvers to get here, you know, despite your reckless invitation. I hope it will be worth my while."

"I hope so too." She grabbed his arm and led him farther away from the door, away from any listening ears. "I have a proposition for you."

"A proposition?" He raised an eyebrow. "Sounds intriguing."

"I want you to help disrupt my wedding."

He stared at her for a long moment. "Does that mean you are accepting my offer of an alliance?" he said. "What a team we'll make."

"No," she said. "It doesn't. This would be a temporary arrangement."

"Then what, may I ask, would be in this scheme for me?"

"I will be in your debt," she said. "And you'll get to humiliate King John. But the benefit to you should be irrelevant. Either you're my ally or you're not."

"I am, of course. What precisely are you thinking?"

"A distraction," she said. "I need you to provide a distraction as the wedding starts. Something to attract the attention of the guards."

"Attract attention away from you? Impossible."

"Perhaps," she said. "I'm not planning to be subtle. I'll walk up in front of the crowd, say what I mean to say, have all eyes on me . . . and then I need you to take their eyes off me. For as long as you're able."

"Anything more specific?"

"You're smart," she said. "You'll think of something."

"Why, Aurora," he said. "You flatter me. And what will you do with this distraction? Kill the king? Burn the castle to the ground?"

A tiny part of her, hot and terrifying, stirred at the idea. She could make the king suffer, like she had suffered, like the prisoners, like Isabelle. But she couldn't. She couldn't. "No," she said. "I'll run."

"That doesn't sound very dramatic."

"I don't want to be dramatic," she said. "I want to leave."

He chuckled. "Then why wait until the wedding to run? If you want to leave, I could probably get you out tonight. Just say the word. It'll be so much easier, so much less risky."

She did not reply.

"See?" he said. "You're not as sweet as you pretend. But don't worry. I'll help. I have a few ideas. Just give the sign tomorrow, and help will be there. But tell me. How, exactly, do you plan to leave the city after you run?"

"I'll figure it out."

He smiled. "Of course you will. But in case that doesn't work out for you, I have a suggestion. Western edge of the city, beyond the slums, there's an old drainage tunnel through the walls. Just past the main tower, near the drunken fairy. Small, but you're not exactly large yourself. It should get you where you need to go. And I will leave you some supplies nearby, if you like. Help you on your way."

She could hardly refuse him. "Thank you," she said.

"Of course. You're full of surprises, Aurora. I look forward to seeing what else you might do." He gave her a sweeping bow. "Until the morning then."

"Wait," she said as he turned away. She remembered the last time she had stood in front of the crowd, the blood and the screaming filled her mind. "No one can get hurt."

"You truly are an innocent, aren't you?"

He left before she could reply.

She stared at the door for a long time after he had gone. She knew she should try to sleep, grab whatever extra energy she could, but she felt too fidgety, too alert, to stay still for long. She began pacing again, running through every possible scenario in her head. Trying to ignore Finnegan's chilling last words.

She would not turn back now.

Resting her hands against the windowsill, she stared down at the city where a forest had once stood and tried to imagine what might await her in the world beyond.

TWENTY-SEVEN

THE DOOR DID NOT OPEN AGAIN UNTIL DAWN PEEKED in through the window. The king strode in, surrounded by guards.

"Aurora," he said with a smile, as though they were meeting for a casual breakfast and a chat. "I trust you slept well. Big day today!" He clapped a friendly hand on her shoulder, his thumb digging into her neck. "Are you ready for your wedding?"

"Yes, Your Majesty," she said. Her voice barely shook.

"Excellent," he said. "Excellent. Well, we had better get you cleaned up, if you are to look beautiful for the crowd. Guards, take her to my own chambers. We can't have all the dust in this tower ruining her dress, and we wouldn't want anyone to get the chance to interrupt our happy day before it has begun, now, would we?"

She sank into a curtsy, trying to breathe through her clenched teeth. Pretending was easier, now that she was resolved, now that she knew what she wanted and needed and planned to do. One guard took either arm, the others walking so close that she almost tumbled over her own feet to keep pace with them as they climbed down the winding staircase, through empty corridors, and toward the king's private rooms.

Guards blocked the door, inside and out. They stood by the screen as a girl—another stranger—bathed her and changed her into her wedding dress. They hovered by her shoulder as the maids arranged her hair. *Keep smiling,* she told herself. *Keep pretending. Wait for the right moment.*

Someone knocked sharply on the door, and a guard wrenched it open. Prince Finnegan entered. Aurora struggled to keep her expression neutral, but her throat tightened in panic. Had something gone wrong with their plan? Or was he already planning to betray her?

"I wish to give my regards to the princess," he said to the guard who hovered by her shoulder. "Wish her luck on this most joyous of days." The guard nodded—he could hardly refuse— and Finnegan swept forward to take Aurora's hand. "You are a vision, Aurora."

The guards were watching them closely. She sank into a

curtsy, letting her curls fall over her eyes.

"I bought you a gift," he said. A necklace looped through the fingers of his free hand. A small silver dragon hung from the chain, wings unfurled, head thrown back in a silent roar. Light reflected off the delicate, fearsome detail in its neck, creating the illusion that it was shifting, rippling like water. Its eyes gleamed red. "A small trinket from my kingdom," he said. "It will tell anyone who sees it that you are a true friend of Vanhelm, and of mine." He spoke kindly, casually, but his intent hovered beneath, sharp and sure. *Wear this*, he said, *and I will know you. Seal our deal with this.* "May I?"

She nodded, too tense to speak. He slipped behind her, brushing her hair aside, allowing his hands to linger at the nape of her neck as he fastened the clasp. The dragon was surprisingly warm against her skin. It settled above her heart.

"It suits you."

She gave him another curtsy. "Thank you for your kindness," she said. "It—it is beautiful."

"Ah, but not as beautiful as you." He raised her hand to his lips and brushed a kiss against her skin. His fingers curled along the inside of her palm, and something small and rough fell into the curve of her knuckles. His grin was decidedly mischievous as he stepped back. "Enjoy your day," he said. "I will count the moments until we meet again."

"It will be a pleasure," Aurora murmured. She clutched whatever he had placed in her hand—parchment, it felt like. *I need him*, she thought, as he bowed and turned to leave. He was loathsome where Rodric was sweet, but maybe to do the right thing, she would have to be loathsome too. She slipped the piece of parchment underneath the thick, pearly ribbon around her waist.

The queen appeared a few minutes later. She too was closely trailed by a guard. She stared at Aurora with her clear brown eyes, her face wan with grief, a pinch in her lips.

"You look beautiful, dear," she said, running a hand through Aurora's curls. She sounded almost sad. "You will make a lovely bride."

Aurora stared at her own reflection. She looked pale, pained, white skin hidden behind gleaming golden curls. The perfect tragic princess. Not exactly a happy ending, she thought. But perhaps people would not notice. Or perhaps they would not care. As long as they got one story or another.

One of the guards put a firm hand on her arm. "Time to go, Princess," he said. She nodded, and her suffocating escort led her out into the corridors again. She kept her head down, letting her curls hide her face. Her heartbeat quaked. The world felt sharp, each second distinct and new, but the guards left her no room to breathe, forcing her along at a stumbling pace. In the time it took to blink, she was standing in the entrance hall of the castle, and the king had his arm around the curve of her waist, his fingers digging into her stomach. She struggled to stop herself from flinching away.

"Come along then, my dear," he said with the same hungry smile as before. "Let's make you one of the family."

Disgust rose in her throat, and she bit the inside of her lip, trying to catch the feeling, build it into something she could use. Not helpless. Angry. Blood rushed through her ears, drowning out the comments of the guards and the roar of the crowd and the music floating in through the doors.

She felt herself moving forward, through the doors and out into the sunlight. Spots burst before her eyes. A huge crowd had gathered in the square, climbing on rooftops, spilling out into the streets beyond, but they were much farther back than the last time Aurora had stood here, separated from the royal family and the rows of honored, noble guests by a wall of guards. She looked over the crowd, and saw a boy who might have been Tristan, but he was too far away for her to be certain. She tore her eyes away from him. He was not part of this now.

Rodric stood at the top of the steps, underneath an archway of roses that looked as though it had fallen out of an illustration in her book. He did not turn to look at her as she approached.

She reached for his hand, slipping her fingers between his own. She felt a rush of something in her chest—of gratitude, of friendship, of remorse for what she was about to do. She could not tell him now. She could not apologize. But at least she could give him something like good-bye.

She let go.

"I have something to say," she said. She spoke so quietly that she doubted many people heard her, but Rodric stared down at her, and the king stepped closer, his hand curling under her lowest rib.

"Now, now, my dear," he said. "There'll be time for speeches later."

"No." She stepped away from him, her voice louder. Out of the corner of her eye, she could see the queen, watching her with a steady expression on her face. "I need to say it now."

"Aurora," the king said, reaching for her again, but she slipped away, turning to address the crowd. Everyone was staring at her, and the attention made her stomach constrict, but she pushed back the feeling. She had to do this. She had to.

"I—I am honored that you all came here today," she said. "And that you have put so much faith in me. Things here—they're very different from what I remember. And what I've been hearing—all I've been hearing—is that people want change. No more hunger. No more rebellions. No more wars. And everyone seems to think that I'm the one to change all that." She could hear every word that she spoke, sharp and clear, ringing out over the crowd, like some other girl was speaking them, some girl who was confident and honest and unafraid. "I don't know how to change things," she said. "I don't know what the right thing to do will be. But I want to help. I want to make things better. And I don't think—this isn't the right way." She glanced at Rodric. He was staring at her, his face pale. "Rodric is wonderful," she said, "but marrying him . . . it won't make things better. It won't change anything. It will only keep things exactly as they have been." She wanted to speak out against the king, but she swallowed the words. She would be dignified and assured. She would not say anything that he could turn against her. "So I'm leaving," she said, "until things become clear. Please believe me when I say that I am not abandoning you. But I need to go. I need to find out what the right thing to do will be."

Silence. Then the king laughed, the sound a little too loud. "Dear Aurora," he said. "Our bride has cold feet." He turned to the crowd. "We all must show her our support, help her get over her nerves!"

The crowd did not respond. The king grabbed her arm, squeezing her wrist painfully tight. "You will do as you are told," he said in a low, threatening voice. "And then you will pay for this little show."

"No," she said softly, steadily. "I won't." She tugged her arm away, but he did not loosen his grip. "Let me go." When he squeezed tighter, she said it again, louder, so that everyone could hear. "Let go!" The bones in her wrist seemed to crack under his palm. *He killed Isabelle*, she thought. *He killed her.* She would not give in to him.

Magic burst out of her, hot and desperate, shattering an ornate fountain deep in the crowd. It showered everyone with dust and smoke. Flames licked the base of the statue, dancing over the surface of the water. Aurora felt another burn, over her heart, as the dragon pendant flared against her skin. Several people screamed, and then the crowd was moving, shoving and scrambling away from the destruction Aurora had caused.

"Now!" The shout came from one of the guards. Steel glistened. More screaming, louder this time, as half of the guards turned their swords on the others, running blades through throats and eyes. Blood spread onto the stone, followed by clashing metal.

Aurora darted backward, too horrified to think, but the king still held her by the arm, and he yanked her toward him. Cold metal rested against her throat.

"Not so fast, girl," he said. "You think you can get away with this? You're going to be sorry you ever opened your mouth by the time I'm done with you."

Aurora heard a crack, the sound of a boot meeting bone. The king's dagger clattered to the floor. Rodric—wild-eyed, white-faced Rodric—took several steps back from his father. For no more than a millisecond, their eyes met, and he jerked his head in an almost imperceptible nod. The king fell to the ground, clutching the back of his leg, still shouting. Iris was screaming, while the crowd wailed and metal clashed and the tangy stench of blood hit the air, and Aurora could only think one thing. *Run.*

In one fluid movement, she snatched the dagger from the ground and sped across the steps, skirts streaming out behind her.

"Stop her!" the king gasped, but the guards were fighting one another, and the nobles were too busy scrambling out of the way to listen. One man lurched toward her, but when Aurora glanced at him, pressure seemed to burst from her chest, and he flew backward, leaving her a clear path into the crowd. Stunned by her own magic, she slipped in a pool of blood, already slightly sticky, but managed to keep her feet, shoving people out of the way with her spare hand and her panic, not able to take in a single thing except that she was moving, she was running, and she could not stop, not for a moment, not for anything.

Several men were sweeping through the streets beyond the square, shoving people back in, trying to contain the violence, but the panicked crowd was trampling them out of the way, pushing and screaming.

She ran. She ran, and she ran, blind and terrified through the streets. Her beautiful dress, glowing white and spattered with red, screamed her name to everyone she passed. Once she was several turns away, she darted into a narrow alley, pressing herself flat against the wall behind some crates, struggling to catch her breath, to understand what she had seen.

Her escape route was somewhere on the western edge of the city, but she had no clue which way was north or south, or how many streets she had come down, or what Finnegan's "drunken fairy" could possibly be. She was utterly lost. But she could not go back.

"Ah, there you are, girl." A guard, so wide-shouldered that he filled the whole alley, walked slowly toward her, sword raised. His face glistened with sweat, and the blade was stained red. "Come with me, now," he said. "There'll be a valuable reward for me when you're safe back home."

She raised the dagger. It shook in her hand, and he chuckled. "Come on, now," he said. "We'll have none of that." Aurora stepped backward, but she had nowhere to go. "Now drop it. Drop it!"

They stared at each other. Then the guard gasped, just once, eyes bulging. His face turned red. His hair began to smoke. And then his skin cracked and crumbled, contorting into dust.

The sword rang as it hit the cobbles, and Celestine stepped into the alley, her face thin and pallid like a skull. Her lips bled. Clumps of blonde hair fell onto her shoulders and around her feet, but her eyes burned like shards of ice.

"What . . . Did you do that?" *It can't have been me,* Aurora thought, taking another stumbling step backward. *Please don't let it have been me.*

"Stupid girl," Celestine said. Her voice cracked. "Are you ready to come with me now? I can help you, you know."

"I don't want your help."

"It seemed to me that you needed it a moment ago." Celestine coughed, a hacking, rasping sound. "Give me a little of your magic then. I saved your life. Give me a little, and this debt shall be settled, at least." Celestine grabbed Aurora's wrist with bony fingers. The other hand tugged at her hair, tangling in the flowers and knots. "You're burning with it," she said. "Every inch of you, burning up. I never imagined you would have such strength." She ran her thumbnail down Aurora's cheek. "Just a taste of it. I saved your life, and now I'll let you go." She leaned close, her breath hot on Aurora's skin. She smelled like rot and ashes. "Just give me this. I saved you."

Aurora flinched away. The energy welled up inside her again, the hate. It slammed out of her, and fire scorched the air. Celestine jerked aside. Her fingers were still caught in Aurora's hair, so Aurora's head jerked forward as well. The muscles in the back of her neck snapped.

Celestine's grip tightened. She shoved her face in front of Aurora's. Their noses almost touched.

"Don't try me, girl," she said. "I may be weak, but I could still make you burn in an instant if I wanted. Right now, you are nothing without me. So don't underestimate me, like your dear mother did. It won't end well for either of us."

Aurora did not dare to move. "You knew my mother?"

"Yes." Celestine smiled, ever so slightly. "I did. She was so like you. So willful, and so unwilling to accept when she was beaten." That did not sound like the mother Aurora had known at all. She continued to stare at Celestine, not saying a word. "Give me a little of your magic," Celestine said. "Repay me for saving your life, and I will tell you how I know her. There is so much I could tell you."

Aurora swallowed. "And if I do," she said, "you will leave me alone?"

"For now," Celestine said. "If you wish."

She had to know. Even if Celestine lied to her . . . she had to know. "All right," Aurora said. "Do it."

Celestine's fingers curled like talons. She slashed her nails across Aurora's cheek, slicing into her skin. Before Aurora could react, Celestine pressed her fingers over the scratches, her nails digging into the wounds. Heat spread along the lines, building and building, a hand reaching through Aurora's veins, snatching and squeezing at her chest. A jolt ran through Aurora, and she retched.

"There." Celestine released her, and already her voice sounded warmer. "Thank you."

Aurora continued to gag, her arm against the wall to hold herself steady. "I did what you asked," she said. "Tell me how you knew my mother."

"Why, she came to me. Like you will come to me one day. Crying and desperate. Begging me for help. For who is more hated than a foreign queen who cannot have a child?"

Aurora swayed with the effort to keep upright. "You're lying."

"Do you still wish to believe that?" Celestine said. "I never lie. She came to me. She pleaded for my magic. She wanted the only thing that could save her, the only thing that would make people support her again. She tried to betray me, of course, as I knew she would. She had the choice to follow our agreement. But she did not. And so we have you."

"You cursed me to punish my mother?"

"I cursed you because I need you," she said. "Because of what you are. You chose to prick your finger, as your mother chose to betray me. You chose to bring yourself here. And so I know that you will join me, in the end." She turned to look down the alley. "Listen to those screams, Aurora. The city is burning. People are dying, because of you. If you had left with me when I offered, they would still be alive."

Aurora shook her head. "That's not true," she said. But it was.

"It is a familiar story, Aurora. Fleeing the city, fleeing their control, determined to be so very good. They will beat it out of you in the end. They will wear you down until all that is left is bitterness. Until you are just like me."

"No," she said. "I could never be like you."

"You are exactly like me. That is your curse, you see. Not true love, not sleeping the years away. Those were all just threads to bring you here, to this moment. If you fail to help these people, they will destroy you. And if you show them how powerful you really are . . . they will destroy you for that too. Your curse is that you cannot help but choose me. The only question is how much you burn along the way."

"I would rather burn everything than work with you."

Celestine's fingers brushed Aurora's neck, leaving spots of blood. "That is a pretty necklace you're wearing," she said. "A gift from the prince of Vanhelm, perhaps?" She ran one finger along the chain. "I can understand the allure. I also have a fascination with dragons." She slid back, smiling. "We will see each other soon, I know. Tomorrow, or next week, or a year from now, when everything is crumbling around you . . . you will wish you had accepted my offer. Until then—good luck, my dear."

Her footsteps faded away. Aurora stood still, barely daring to breathe. Celestine did not return.

She could hear panic in the streets, people shouting and screaming, weapons clashing together. She could not stay here, but her legs shuddered under her weight, and her head felt hot and clammy, like she had been struck with a sudden bout of the flu. Her mother had made a deal with the witch.

But Celestine could not be trusted. She was only trying to trick Aurora, to bewitch her. Nothing she said could be believed.

Footsteps passed the entrance of the alley. She flattened herself against the wall, but the person did not stop.

She had to leave. Now.

She stared at the pile of crates. Tristan had said it was possible to get halfway around the city on the roofs. High up out of sight. Could she get out that way as well? The crates looked rotten, unstable, but if she was careful . . . Her heart pounding in the back of her throat, dagger tight in her left fist, she hoisted herself up. Her skirt caught on a splinter, and she ripped it free. The wood creaked and buckled beneath her feet, but it did not break. And then she was on the roof.

People below were running, jostling, fighting. Guards hurried in every direction. Swords clashed. In the sky, she could see the sun, creeping toward noon. Turning her back to it, she hurried west. She would have to trust Finnegan's word one more time.

TWENTY-EIGHT

AURORA CLIMBED DOWN FROM THE ROOFS NEAR THE western edge of the city. The buildings were sparser here, with beaten earth for roads. The whole place felt deserted. Everyone, it seemed, had gone to the wedding.

The wall loomed ahead. Aurora looked up, her eyes roving over every building nearby. Most of them were rundown huts, houses thrown up too quickly or old stone things that no one had bothered to care for except the birds. She tilted her head back toward the sky, following the path of lazy clouds, seeing the ragged ends of the wall, the high tower Finnegan had mentioned, and the few tall buildings in this part of town, crooked and twisted so much that they seemed to be held up by hope alone. A stylized fairy perched on top of one, balanced on tip-toe, her wand held out pointing north. She had taken quite a battering, and she was half toppled over, as though about to fall to her death.

The drunken fairy.

Aurora hurried over to the building, following the curve of the wall. The tower looked even more decrepit up close. Shadows hung from the windows, and a rough ditch wove through the ground in front, reaching toward the wall. The ditch ended in a patch of brambles. She scrambled forward and pulled the branches aside, revealing a carved hole in the base of the wall, just large enough for a small person to wriggle through. And beside it, hidden among the brambles, a brown satchel. She pulled it open. A flask sat on top, and she gulped down the liquid without stopping to check what it was, too thirsty and worn to care. Then she threw the satchel over her shoulder and crawled forward into the gap, pushing the brambles out of the way with one hand while keeping her balance with the other. Her knees scraped on the hard ground, and her skirts caught around her shoes and in the branches that crashed back behind her, but she kept crawling, until she was forcing herself through a tiny space in the stone. Her shoulders banged the wall, and she pictured herself stuck for the rest of forever, but then she wriggled free, her head plunging forward into the fresh air.

The forest grew right up to the edge of the city, with the

highest branches brushing against the top of the wall. Light filtered through the evergreens, dappling the grassy floor, while buds, in pinks and whites and greens, were sprinkled over the branches of the otherwise naked, stooping trees. The smell of pine tickled Aurora's nose, and she could hear the birds, hurrying about in a twittering, fluttering chorus.

It smelled like home. Aurora pressed her hand against the nearest oak. The gnarled knots on the trunk seemed to whisper a story under her fingertips, running round and round, deeper and deeper and older and older into the tree.

Every princess part of her, everything that connected her to the past, everything that had brought her solace in this past month had been discarded or burned or torn from her, leaving nothing but empty space. She was a mixture of guilt and fear and selfishness, yet for the first time in weeks, in her life perhaps, she was free of the panic that clutched her chest, of the restriction that weighed her down. She was breathing open air, and for this moment, even if it only lasted this very moment, she was free to be whoever she pleased. And no one, not the king, not Iris, not Tristan, not Celestine, could take that away.

She set off through the trees.

Light broke through the branches in dappled patches, and the birds were chirping above her, waiting for the spring. After a while of hurrying through the undergrowth, her knees shook with exhaustion, so she sat down against the trunk of a tree, pulling the satchel onto her lap. A woolen dress lay inside, of the modern style but cheaply made. Perfect for blending in. She tugged it on, stuffing the bloodstained wedding dress in the bag in its place. Blood clung to her fingers as well, although she had no memory of how it got there. It could have been anyone's.

People were dead because of her. They had died, and she had not even looked over her shoulder as she'd run from them. But death had been inevitable, no matter what she chose. She had only had impossible choices, ever since she awoke.

She dropped her head against the tree trunk, hard, and the chain around her neck rattled.

Finnegan's gift. A silver dragon, and a note pressed into her palm.

She slipped her fingers underneath the waistband of her wedding dress. The paper was still there. She pulled it free and unfolded and unrolled it, until she revealed a piece of parchment slightly bigger than her hand.

A map. Tiny but detailed, showing a city, with buildings all crammed together, surrounded by water on all sides. Vanhelm. A star lay in the very center, marking a large building labeled as the palace. Beyond the river on the left side, the cartographer had drawn a dragon, similar to the one she now wore.

Underneath, someone had scrawled a message in black ink. It had been slightly blurred in the rolling, but Aurora could still make out the words.

Burn them all, little dragon.

She almost balled it up but stopped herself, and instead placed it carefully inside her bag. He had helped her, after all. He had told her things she did not want to hear, but things that seemed truer with every day. And he had warned her that her escape would not come without cost. She could not trust him, not yet, but one day . . . one day he might prove useful.

When she set off again, she walked more slowly, allowing her hands to stretch out and wander across the trunk of every tree that she passed. *I am not a dragon*, she thought. *I don't know what I am.*

The ground sloped upward, and she began to climb, using roots for leverage under her feet. She had never been this far into the forest before. She took a deep breath, trying to calm her trembling heart once again. The breath caught in her chest as she peered over the edge of the hill.

The ground dropped away sharply in a smooth, treeless slope, cradling a large lake at the bottom of the valley. It reflected the afternoon sun, but the surface was far from smooth, broken by drinking deer and the splash of birds. Beyond it, trees stretched out into the distance, an endless blanket of brown and green.

For a moment, she stared. Then she set off at a run, her skirts flying behind her. The bag crashed against her side, jingling with coins that would be her salvation. *I know nothing*, she thought as her feet pounded the ground, tumbling, down, down, down toward the lake. Not who she was, not where she was going, not what she should do. She was going to get her answers . . . but where that would lead her, she did not know. She had no path to follow, except instinct and desire and the sense that something awaited her, out in the world, beyond the edge of the trees. Duty would catch up with her, and she would play the part she was meant to play, but not yet.

She felt invisible, impossible. Infinite. *I am nothing*, she thought. *Nothing but myself.*

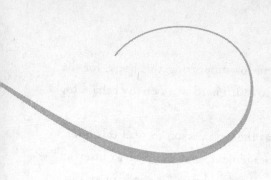

ACKNOWLEDGMENTS

I'M SO LUCKY TO BE SURROUNDED BY MANY AMAZING, wonderful, supportive people who make writing possible. Endless thanks are due to:

My agent, Kristin Nelson, who believed in me and my book from the beginning. I'd be lost without her.

Sarah Landis, whose insight and enthusiasm helped take a book called *After* and guide it into the far superior *A Wicked Thing*.

Catherine Wallace, who rescued this book from the editor-less abyss and immediately threw herself into giving it the best chance possible.

Everyone at HarperTeen, for supporting this book, for the gorgeous cover design, for so much hard work on my behalf, for everything!

Phoebe Cattle, who was the first person to read this book, the first to give me encouragement, and the first to utter an oft-repeated, vital piece of editing advice: "It needs more Finnegan." Our weekly hot chocolate sessions (and brief adventure as booksellers together) kept me sane(ish) as I wrote, and I don't know what I'd do without her.

Alexandra Ashmore, who became my first fangirl, asked all the hard questions and gave me the best Christmas present I've ever received—little paintings of scenes from the book. We're in this thing together, and I couldn't ask for a better writing partner or friend.

All the people who read early incarnations of this book and gave their opinions while I revised: the world's best roomies Meg Lee and Anna Li; fellow nerds, board-game mentors, and fantastic friends Matthew Goodyear and Rachel Thompson; and wonderful Colonialites Brendan Carroll, Maria Chevtsova, William Nguyen, and Andrew Weintraub.

And finally, my parents, Brian and Gaynor Thomas, who gave me a love of fantasy and made the whole writer dream possible. They've put up with every one of my crazy schemes—"I'm going to move to America!"; "I'm not going to grad school! I'm going to be an author!"—without looking too scared, and they've always believed in me. I'll let you read the book now, Mum!

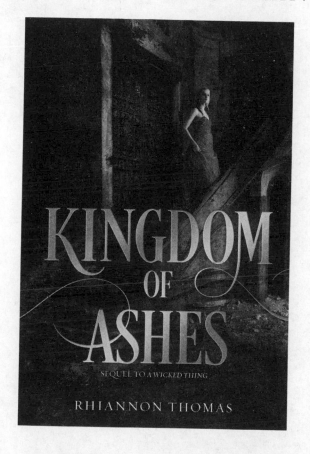

ONE

Wanted: Alive, for treason and crimes against the realm.

For a thousand gold coins, even Aurora could believe that the smiling girl in the picture was a murderer.

Aurora tore down the poster and crumpled it into a ball. She had been on the run for a week now, but she had not run far enough. Even this small jumble of houses by the forest edge knew to expect her.

She had been so naïve, to think she could do this. Dirt itched under her fingernails. Her hair had matted around her shoulders, and blood had congealed around the blisters on her feet. She did not know where to go. She did not know how to build shelters or catch food. She didn't even know how people outside the capital spoke, so she stood out wherever she went. And now the kingdom was covered with wanted posters, promising riches to whoever might capture her. The king's guards could not be far behind.

But Aurora had to go into the village. She had never felt so hungry before. She had never had to hope that she would come across a forest stream, or figure out whether a berry was edible, or spend her day worrying about whether she would eat. She had never once considered where her food came from or doubted that it would appear, had left so much uneaten to be tossed away. . . . She needed more food, or she wouldn't make it much farther, and the king's guards would catch her either way.

Besides, who would think she was the princess, if they looked at her now?

The village was quiet in the early dawn. A few people walked along the street, but they were mostly half-asleep, or so absorbed in their errands that they barely glanced at Aurora as they passed.

Aurora could smell baking bread. She followed it to a shop with a sign above the door showing a single ear of wheat. Aurora closed her eyes and breathed in, savoring even the *smell* of food. Her stomach ached in response.

She looked around. No guards or soldiers in sight. She would have to take the risk.

A little bell rang as she opened the door. A middle-aged

woman worked behind the counter, arranging steaming hot loaves onto trays. "Welcome, welcome," she said, without looking up. "Pardon our appearance, it's been one of those mornings. What can I get you?"

"Uh . . ." Aurora stepped closer. The woman glanced at her, and then paused, a bun held inches above the tray.

Aurora tensed. She glanced at the door, ready to run.

"My goodness, girl," the woman said. "You look a fright. What *have* you been up to?'

"Oh," Aurora said. "I've been traveling." She struggled not to cringe at the words, the way she spoke so *crisply*, in her old-fashioned accent.

The woman tutted. "So many traveling these days. Not enough food, is there, not enough work, so everyone thinks they have to move. It's not safe for young things like you to be out there. Not safe at all."

Aurora stepped closer. The fresh bread smelled too delicious to resist. "I wanted to buy some bread."

"Oh yes, yes, of course. I would give you some for free for your troubles, honest I would, but things are tight for us here, too. I really can't spare it."

"That's all right," Aurora said. "Thank you. I have money." She reached into her satchel and pulled out the purse that Finnegan had given her. The woman's eyes widened as the coins clinked together. Aurora made sure to tilt it toward herself as she opened it, concealing the flash of silver and gold. She picked out a few copper coins and pulled the drawstring closed.

The woman recommended the local specialty, so Aurora ordered two loaves. "If you want somewhere to stay," the woman added, as she placed the loaves in a paper bag, "you should try the Red Lion down the street. Good people there. Discreet, you know."

Aurora tightened her grip on the bag. "I have nothing to hide," she said. "But thank you for the advice."

The bell rang again. A younger girl ran in, her braid bouncing behind her. "Mum!" she said. "Mum! There are soldiers here."

Soldiers. Aurora turned so quickly that her hip slammed against the counter. Had the guards been following her? Or had someone spotted her in the five minutes she had been here?

The woman glanced at Aurora. "How do you know, Suzie? What did you see?"

"They're coming out of the forest. I was delivering the bread to Mistress Jones, like you told me to, and the soldiers marched into the street and started ordering everyone out of their houses."

The baker paused for a moment. "That's no reason to stop your deliveries, is it, Suzie? People'll need their bread, whatever happens. Quick, take the next lot to the Masons. Don't worry about the soldiers."

"But—"

"Do it!"

The girl gaped at her mother. She shot Aurora a curious look, and then nodded.

"All right," she said. "I'm going. I just thought you'd want to know." With another glance at Aurora, she sped back out of the door.

"Thank you for the bread," Aurora said, trying to keep her voice from shaking. "I'll look at the inn, like you said."

"Nonsense, child." The baker strode around the counter. "Better get you away quickly, hadn't we, if they're looking for you."

"Looking for me?" Aurora tried to frown, pushing her panic away. That was the right look, wasn't it, for innocent confusion? But the baker would have none of it. She grabbed Aurora's wrist and pushed her toward the door behind the counter.

"At least go out of the back door, then. No point in dealing with soldiers if you don't have to, if you ask me. It's a quieter street back there, and not too far from the edge of the village."

She ushered Aurora into a cramped storeroom, with sacks of flour resting against one wall and a huge counter covered in trays of rising dough against the other. The low ceiling was held up by two beams, and the baker swerved around them as she headed for the back door. "This way, this way," the baker said. "No point in hiding you, they'll only look, and then how will you get away? This door here now."

Someone knocked on the back door. "Open up!" a man shouted. "King's orders. We need to inspect the property."

The baker jerked back, her hand tightening on Aurora's wrist. She turned toward the shop front again, but the bell above the front door rang. Two soldiers marched into the bakery. They stopped when they saw Aurora, eyes widening. They might have known she was in this area, but they had not known she was in here. She should have hidden as soon as she heard they were looking for her.

The soldiers pulled out their swords, one shouting to the others outside. Aurora wrenched her wrist free of the baker and ran for the back door. A soldier kicked it open, and three men advanced into the storeroom, swords raised. Aurora scrambled back. She grabbed the dagger in her bag.

She had been foolish to think entering a shop would be safe. Now they would catch her, they would drag her back to the capital, back to King John's booming laugh and his stony eyes and his threat of the pyre.

The nearest soldier grabbed for her arm. She dodged, panic and defiance swelling inside her, and fire shot across the storeroom floor. The soldier's cloak caught, and he tore it away, yelling. The burlap bags burned too, and the wooden pillars in the center of the room. The baker screamed, and Aurora jumped around her, around the shouting soldiers, running for the door.

Her whole body seemed to blaze. She dodged, and she ran, out of the storeroom and onto the street.

More soldiers hurried toward the commotion at the

bakery. Aurora spun on the spot. There had to be somewhere she could run.

"Stop!" one of them yelled. He held a crossbow. "Stop, or I'll shoot."

But he couldn't kill her. The king wanted her brought back alive.

Smoke billowed from the bakery. Aurora swerved around the side of the building, twisting as a crossbow bolt flew toward her. Flames danced in the window. The baker was screaming.

Aurora ran onto another street, and then another, but the village was not that big. There was nowhere she could hide. She tore toward the edge of the forest, but her feet were aching and blistered, and she stumbled.

A soldier grabbed her arm. She shoved him away, fire crackling again. The man shouted in pain and let go.

The air stank of smoke. And the soldiers still ran after her, still shouted. Her head rang with the sound of their voices. They were going to catch her. There was nowhere to hide here, and they were going to *catch* her; they'd catch her, and the king would burn her, torture her, make her into nothing again.

She could not let that happen.

She sent flames across the ground, burning a line between her and the soldiers, reaching higher than the buildings around them, fed by nothing but Aurora's fear.

A house on the edge of the village caught fire. More people screamed, and the flames swelled again. They were too hot, too strong. *Stop*, she thought, but the flames swelled, as though driven by her panic.

She dove into the forest. As she ran, she dodged brambles and tree roots, racing for the stream. She leapt over the mud by the bank, the water splashing as she landed, and *ran*. Steam rose around her.

A tree with low-hanging branches stood ahead. Aurora scrambled up, the bark digging into her palms. She climbed and climbed, until the branches shuddered under her weight.

In the distance, smoke rose into the air.

The whole village was burning.

The baker had helped her, tried to protect her, and she had burned her shop to the ground.

She should keep running. Follow the flow of the stream as far as she could, before the guards caught her. But she could not move. She stared at the flames, so fierce now that they reached above the trees. She could not look away.

It had come from her. She had not decided to use magic. She had not wanted to set things alight. But the panic had taken over, and now . . .

She had done this. She did not know what else she was capable of, if she did not get her magic under control.

She stared, and she stared, as the fire burned itself out, and the sun rose and fell in the sky.

She had to go back. She *had* to. Even with the guards, she had caused this. The fire was hers. She had to help.

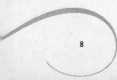

But it was dark before her legs agreed to climb down from the tree. She followed the stream back, each step cautious, certain the guards would snatch her at any moment.

She saw no one.

The stench of smoke and burned wood got stronger the farther she walked. And then the end of the forest was in sight. The world beyond was black, hidden by the lingering smoke that formed a blanket across the night sky.

She crept to the edge of the trees. There were no soldiers waiting. There was no one.

The village was nothing but ashes.

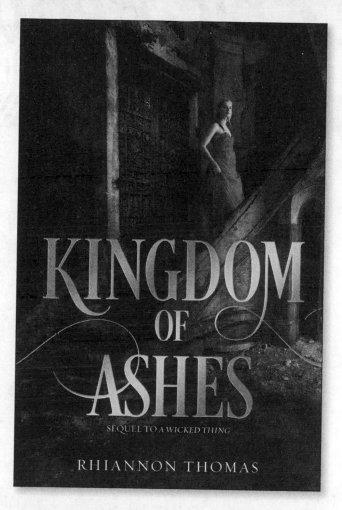

JOIN THE

Epic Reads
COMMUNITY

THE ULTIMATE YA DESTINATION

◄ **DISCOVER** ►
your next favorite read

◄ **MEET** ►
new authors to love

◄ **WIN** ►
free books

◄ **SHARE** ►
infographics, playlists, quizzes, and more

◄ **WATCH** ►
the latest videos

◄ **TUNE IN** ►
to Tea Time with Team Epic Reads